THE BLACK
SPECTACLES

THE BLACK SPECTACLES

JOHN DICKSON CARR

With an Introduction by
Martin Edwards

Published by Poisoned Pen Press, an imprint of Sourcebooks, in association with the
British Library
P.O. Box 4410, Naperville, Illinois 60567-4410
(630) 961-3900
sourcebooks.com

The Black Spectacles was first published in 1939 by Hamish Hamilton, London.

Cataloging-in-Publication Data is on file with the Library of Congress.

Printed and bound in the United States of America.
VP 10 9 8 7 6 5 4 3 2 1

CONTENTS

INTRODUCTION

The Black Spectacles is among the most popular of the Gideon Fell novels written by John Dickson Carr, who is widely recognised as the king of the locked room mystery. Intriguingly, though, this story *isn't* a locked room mystery, and Fell doesn't become involved in the investigation until half-way through the book. What is more, the sub-title, "Being the Psychologists' Murder Case," is hardly characteristic of Carr, a mystery author who specialised in dazzling feats of legerdemain rather than the exploration of the criminal psyche. Yet the story brims with classic tropes, above all the ingenious use of illusion to disguise what is *really* going on. No wonder the late Bob Adey, author of the indispensable reference book *Locked Room Murders*, regarded this as one of Carr's best books.

In essence, *The Black Spectacles* is essentially a classic English village mystery, but this tale of the unexpected opens in Pompeii, of all places, with "the silence of the Street of Tombs broken by English voices." In this evocative setting, a man (not identified until the end of the chapter) witnesses a curious scene involving a group of British tourists. He is immediately attracted to a young woman, Marjorie, who is accompanied by her Uncle Marcus, a young man called George Harding whose "shipboard flirtation" with Marjorie has become serious, a doctor called Joe who is brother to Marcus, and Marcus's employee Wilbur Emmet.

George is told a bizarre story about a recent case of poisonings in Sodbury Cross, the home of his companions. Three children and an eighteen-year-old girl were poisoned with strychnine as a result of eating chocolate creams sold by a shopkeeper called Mrs Terry. One of the children—of whom Marjorie was especially fond—died. Alarmingly, "everyone who could have had access to the chocolates, everyone who could have done this at certain established times, is a person well known in Sodbury Cross." In other words, the case is a "closed circle mystery" with a defined pool of suspects, although as ever with Golden Age detective fiction, readers who hope to solve the puzzle will be well advised to take nothing for granted.

In the second chapter, the scene shifts to Sodbury Cross. Carr's regular Scotland Yard detective, Superintendent Hadley, despatches young Inspector Elliot—who "did very well on a cold trail in that Crooked Hinge business"—to the village with a view to trying to solve the puzzle of the poisoned children. Almost immediately, however, a further murder is committed. This time the scene of the crime is Bellegarde, Marcus Chesney's country home, and in the finest Carr tradition, the circumstances of the killing (another poisoning, this time by means of a green capsule) are both strange and melodramatic.

Among the striking features of the story is the attention Carr pays to real-life murder mysteries. The initial poisonings recall the case of Christiana Edmunds, who "was mad, if you like, but she had as sound a motive as most murderers. This young lady, in the Brighton of 1871, fell violently in love with a married doctor who gave her no encouragement. She first attempted unsuccessfully to poison the doctor's wife with strychnine... To show that she was innocent... she conceived the idea of doctoring the chocolate creams in a sweet-shop and killing people wholesale." The fictional use that Carr makes of this factual precedent is extremely clever.

Baffled by the mystery, Scotland Yard's Inspector Elliot consults Dr Gideon Fell. The local constabulary has already tried to interest him in the original crimes, but with no luck: "Wasn't sensational enough for him... No hermetically sealed rooms. No supernatural elements. No funny business at the Royal Scarlet Hotel." But the weird events at Bellegarde are a different matter, and Fell throws himself into the mystery with his inimitable verve.

Towards the end of the book, Fell gives a fascinating mini-lecture on real-life poisoners and their activities. Not for him the cliché that "poison is a woman's weapon." He talks about male poisoners who "are usually men of some imagination, education, and even culture. Their professions indicate as much. Palmer, Pritchard, Lamson, Buchanan, and Cream were doctors. Richeson was a clergyman, Wainewright an artist, Armstrong a solicitor, Hoch a chemist, Waite a dental surgeon, Vaquier an inventor, Carlyle Harris a medical student."

The psychological elements of the story are well done, and focus on the unreliability of witness testimony, an ingredient of high-calibre crime fiction from the days of Wilkie Collins right up to the present. Any lawyer who has interviewed a number of witnesses to an incident (as I have done many times) will confirm that each person sees things differently and from their own perspective. Sometimes the discrepancies are trivial, sometimes they are astonishingly significant. This phenomenon is fundamental to the storyline, and Carr describes it with his customary gusto:

"All witnesses, metaphorically, wear black spectacles. They can neither see clearly, nor interpret what they see in the proper colours. They do not know what goes on on the stage, still less what goes on in the audience... Show them a black-and-white record of it afterwards, and they will believe you; but even then, they will be unable to interpret what they see."

The Black Spectacles was Carr's preferred choice of title for the novel, but his American publishers were unconvinced of its commercial merits and prevailed upon him to accept their preferred but less sophisticated title, *The Problem of the Green Capsule*. Carr's British publisher was happy to call the book *The Black Spectacles*, as did Carr's biographer Douglas G. Greene; the British Library also, I'm glad to say, considers that Carr's original choice was the most suitable one.

Carr published this novel in 1939, and there is a passing negative reference to life in Nazi Germany at that time. The previous September, Carr and his wife had taken a cruise around the Mediterranean, from which came the background for his description of Pompeii.

The novel's dedication, "to the memory of Powys Mathers," deserves comment. Edward "Bill" Powys Mathers died not long before the book's publication, at the age of forty-six.

He was a noted translator, and some of his work was set to music by Aaron Copland, but he owes his lasting fame to his alter ego of "Torquemada," who set fiendish crossword puzzles for the *Observer*, for which newspaper he was also an astute reviewer of detective fiction. His work included a play, *Cold Blood*, staged in London in 1932, and the curious and convoluted mystery *Cain's Jawbone*, which originally appeared in *The Torquemada Puzzle Book* and has recently been reissued in a new edition. Marie Mayhew, who has researched Mathers's life and work, points out that he made a great impression on Carr, who wrote an introduction to Torquemada's posthumous *112 Best Crossword Puzzles* as well as dedicating this novel to him.

As Douglas Greene's biography points out, Mathers described Carr as one of "the Big Five" of writers of the classic mystery living in England at that time. The others included Agatha Christie and Dorothy L. Sayers; Carr must have been gratified to find himself in such company. On the strength of books such as *The Black Spectacles*, many readers will agree that the accolade was well deserved.

Martin Edwards
www.martinedwardsbooks.com

were originally published with the inclusion of minor edits made for consistency of style and sense, and with pejorative terms of an extremely offensive nature partly obscured. We welcome feedback from our readers.

To the memory of
POWYS MATHERS

I

First View Through the Spectacles

'How shall I sleep to-night?'

**CHRISTIANA EDMUNDS,
BRIGHTON, 1871**

I

IT BEGAN, AS A CERTAIN MAN REMEMBERED IT, AT A house in Pompeii. He never forgot the hot, quiet afternoon; the silence of the Street of Tombs broken by English voices; the red oleanders in the ruined garden, and the girl in white standing in the midst of a group in sun-glasses, as though in the midst of a group in masks.

This man who saw it had been in Naples for a week on business. His business there does not concern this narrative. But it took up all his time, and it was not until the afternoon of Monday, September 19th, that he found himself free. He was leaving that evening for Rome, and thence back by way of Paris to London. For that afternoon he was in the mood for a little idle sight-seeing, and the past had always fascinated him as much as the present. That was how, in the quietest part of the day, under the quiet of a blazing sun, he found himself in the Street of Tombs.

The Street of Tombs lies outside the walls of Pompeii. It leads from the Herculaneum Gate, descending a shallow hill like a broad trough of paving-blocks between a footway on either side. Cypresses stand up over it, and make this street of the dead seem alive. Here are the burial-vaults of the patricians, the squat altars hardly yet blackened to ruin. When this man heard his own footsteps there, he felt merely that he had got into a neglected suburb. The hot, hard light shone on paving-stones worn to ruts by cartwheels; on grass sprouting in cracks, and tiny brown lizards that darted before him like an illusion of moving shadow in the grass. Ahead of him Vesuvius rose beyond the mausoleums, dull blue in a heat-haze, but no less large in the mind because it was half a dozen miles away.

He was warm and half drowsy. These long streets of gutted shops, these glimpses of painted and pillared courts, were having a disturbing effect on his imagination. He had been wandering for over an hour; and since he entered the town he had seen not a living soul except one mysterious party, with a guide, which had suddenly appeared at the end of the Street of Fortune and then vanished in ghostly fashion amid a rattle of small stones.

The Street of Tombs brought him to the end of the town. He was debating whether to call it a day, or to turn back for more exploring, when he saw the house among the tombs. It was a large house, evidently a patrician's villa which in the heyday of Pompeii had stood at a soothing distance out into the suburbs. He climbed the stairs and went in.

The atrium was gloomy and damp-smelling, less well kept than the re-touched town houses he had already seen. But beyond it lay the garden of the peristyle, closed in by pillars, with the sun pouring down into it. The garden was overgrown, full of red-flowering oleanders and with Asiatic pines round a ruined fountain. He heard a swishing in the long grass, and he heard English voices.

By the fountain, a girl in white stood looking in his direction. And he saw not only beauty, but intelligence. Her dark brown hair was parted and drawn back behind the ears into small curls at the nape of the neck. She had an oval face with small, full lips, and wide-set eyes that expressed good-humour despite the gravity of her expression. They were grey eyes, rather heavy-lidded and thoughtful. Her pose was easy; she smoothed the white frock idly. But she was nervous; you saw it even in the arch of the eyebrows.

Facing her stood a dark-haired young man in a grey flannel suit, who was holding up a small ciné-camera with his eye pressed to the view-finder. The ciné-camera began to hum and click. With his cheek against the side of it, the young man spoke out of a corner of his mouth.

'Well, do something!' he urged. 'Smile or bow or light a cigarette or anything, but do something! If you just stand there, it might as well be a photograph.'

'But, George, what on earth can I do?'

'I've told you. Smile or bow or—'

The girl was evidently afflicted by that self-consciousness which people feel when they know any movement they make will be recorded. After looking preternaturally solemn, she managed a guilty smile. She lifted her white handbag and waggled it in the air. Then she looked round for an opportunity to get away, and concluded by laughing in the face of the camera.

'We're using up film,' howled the young man, rather like a studio-executive.

To the observer in the doorway, only a dozen feet away from that group, there came a sudden conviction. He knew that this girl was in a dangerously nervous state of mind; that her healthy complexion was a sham; and that the insistence of the clicking little camera was beginning to affect her like the nightmare of an eye.

'Well, what *can* I do?'

'Walk about, or something. Move over there to the right; I want to get those columns in behind you.'

Another member of the group, who had been watching this with his fists on his hips, uttered a kind of snort. This was a brisk little man whose dark glasses partly masked the fact that he was much older than his holiday attire indicated. You saw the withered skin along the side of his jaw, and the edge of his whitish hair under the brim of a down-turned Panama hat.

'Trippers!' he said with withering scorn. 'That's what you are: trippers. You want to get the columns in behind her, eh? You don't want a picture of Marjorie. You don't even want a picture of a Pompeian house. What you want is a picture of Marjorie in a Pompeian house, to show you've been there. I call it disgusting.'

'What's wrong with it?' inquired a thunderous voice. This proceeded from a taller and burlier man with a short ginger beard, who stood at the other side of the offending couple.

'Trippers,' said the man in the Panama hat.

'I disagree with you entirely,' said the burly man. 'And I do not understand your attitude, Marcus. Every time we go to a place where there are some sights to see, you want to stay away from them (if I understand you) solely because they *are* the sights. May I inquire what in the hell'—he made the word thunder through the garden—'is the good of going to a place unless you do see the sights? You object that thousands of people go to see them. Does it ever occur to you that, if thousands of people go to see a place for thousands of years, it may just possibly be because there is something worth seeing?'

'Behave yourself,' said the man in the Panama hat. 'And stop yelling. You don't understand; you never will. What have you seen, for instance? Where are we now?'

'It's easy enough to find out,' said the other. 'What about it, young fellow?'

He turned round to the dark-haired young man with the camera. The latter had reluctantly stopped taking pictures of the girl, who was laughing now. Replacing the camera in a case slung round his shoulder, he took a guide-book from his pocket and conscientiously turned over the pages.

Then he cleared his throat.

'*Number thirty-four, two stars. Villa of Arrius Diomedes,*' he read, with conscious impressiveness. '*Though so-called only because*—'

'Nonsense,' said the burly man. 'We saw that one ten minutes ago. Where they found all the skeletons.'

'What skeletons?' protested the girl. 'We didn't see any skeletons, Doctor Joe.'

Behind his own dark glasses, the face of the burly man grew more fiery. 'I didn't say we saw any skeletons,' he returned, settling his tweed cap more firmly on his head. 'I said it was the place where they found all the skeletons. Just down the road: don't you remember? The hot ashes trapped the slaves there, and they found 'em there later; right bang all over the floor, like a set of skittles. It was the house with the pillars painted green.'

The little, brisk old man in the Panama hat folded his arms and cradled them. There was a faintly malicious look on his face.

'It may interest you to know, Joe, that they weren't.'

'Weren't what?' demanded Doctor Joe.

'Painted green. Over and over again I've proved my contention,' the little man resumed, 'that the average person, you—or you, or you—is absolutely incapable of reporting accurately what he sees or hears. You don't observe. You can't observe. Eh, professor?'

He turned and glanced over his shoulder. There were two other persons who completed the group, and these two men stood in shadow just inside the columns of the peristyle. The watcher was hardly conscious of them; he did not see them in the same way he saw the four others in sunlight. He noticed only that one was middle aged, the other young. With the aid of a magnifying-glass they were examining a piece of stone or lava which they seemed to have picked up from the balustrade of the peristyle. Both wore dark glasses.

'Never mind the villa of Arrius Diomedes,' said a voice from beyond the balustrade. 'Whose house is this?'

'I've got it now,' volunteered the young man with the camera and the guide-book. 'I was on the wrong page before. This is number thirty-nine, isn't it? Right. Here we are. *Number thirty-nine, three stars. House of Aulus Lepidus the poisoner.*'

There was a silence.

Up to this time they had seemed an ordinary family-or-friendly group, with the tempers of the elder members a little upset by heat or the wear of travel. By a certain family resemblance, no less than their tendency to snap at each other, it might be deduced that Doctor Joe and the little man in the Panama hat (addressed as Marcus) were brothers. The girl called Marjorie, too, was some relation to them. All as usual.

But, at the reading of the words out of the guide-book, there was a change of atmosphere as palpable as a chilling or darkening of the courtyard. Only the young man with the book seemed unconscious of it. Everyone else half turned round; and then remained very still. Four pairs of sun-glasses were turned towards the girl, as though she stood inside a ring of masks. Sunlight gleamed on the glasses, making them as opaque and sinister as masks.

Doctor Joe said uneasily: 'The what?'

'The poisoner,' said the young man. '*By the design of sword and stripped willow tree ("lepidus" = "stripped of bark," "polished," hence "witty" or "agreeable") set into the mosaic pavement at the entrance to the atrium, Mommsen has identified this villa as belonging to—*'

'Yes, but what did he do?'

'*—who, according to Varro, killed five members of his family by means of poisoned mushroom sauce,*' continued the young man. He looked round with an air of refreshed interest, as though he half expected to see the corpses still there.

'Here, this isn't bad!' he added. 'I suppose it was easy to get away with wholesale poisoning in those days.'

And then suddenly he knew that there was something wrong; the bristly hair seemed to rise on the back of his neck. He shut up the book and spoke quietly.

'Look here,' he blurted out. 'Look here, have I said some-thing I shouldn't?'

'Of course not,' replied Marjorie with the greatest com-posure. 'Besides, Uncle Marcus's hobby is the study of crime. Isn't it?'

'It is,' agreed Uncle Marcus. He turned to the young man. 'Tell me, Mr.—I keep forgetting your name?'

'You know perfectly well what it is,' cried Marjorie.

But by the exaggerated respect the young man paid to Marcus, it was clear that Marcus was not only Marjorie's uncle: he was her acting parent.

'Harding, sir. George Harding,' he answered.

'Ah, yes. Well, Mr. Harding, tell me: did you ever hear of a place called Sodbury Cross, near Bath?'

'No, sir. Why?'

'We come from there,' said Marcus.

He walked over briskly and sat down on the rim of the fountain settling himself as though he were preparing to harangue them. Taking off both his hat and his sun-glasses, he balanced them on his knee. This removal of the mask showed that he had wiry greyish hair standing up in humps and angles which sixty years' combing had been unable to subdue. His blue eyes were bright and intelligent and malicious. From time to time he would rub the shrivelled skin at the side of his jaw.

'Now Mr. Harding,' he went on, 'let's face facts. I'm assum-ing that this affair between you and Marjorie isn't just a kind of shipboard flirtation. I assume you are both serious, or think you are.'

Another change had passed over the group. It also affected the two men inside the balustrade of the peristyle. One of these (the watcher noticed) was a cheerful-looking middle-aged man with a felt hat pushed back on his bald head. His eyes were masked, but he had a round face coloured with good-living. He cleared his throat.

'I think,' he said, 'if you'll excuse me, I'll just run down and—'

His companion, a tall young man of remarkable ugliness, turned round and began to study the interior of the house with elaborate forgetfulness.

Marcus looked at them.

'Rubbish,' he said crisply. 'You may not be members of the family, either of you. But you know what we know; so stay where you are. And stop this infernal delicacy.'

The girl spoke quietly. 'Do you think, Uncle Marcus,' she said, 'that this is the place to have this out?'

'I do, my dear.'

'Quite right,' agreed Doctor Joe with violence. He had assumed a stern, stuffed, momentous look. 'For once in your life, Marcus—quite right.'

George Harding himself had assumed a stern, stuffed, heroic look.

'I can only assure you, sir—' he began in heroic tones.

'Yes, yes, I know all that,' said Marcus. 'And oblige me by looking less embarrassed. It is nothing unusual; most people get married, and know what to do when they get married, as I trust you both do. Now, this question of marriage is entirely subject to my approval—'

'And mine,' said Doctor Joe sternly.

'*If* you please,' said Marcus annoyed. 'And my brother's, of course. We've known you for a month or so, under conditions of travelling. As soon as you began going about with my niece, I cabled my solicitors to find out all about you. Well, you seem to be all right. Your record is good; and I've got no complaint. You have no family and no money—'

George Harding started to explain something, but Marcus cut him off.

'Yes, yes. I know all about your chemical process, which may make a fortune and all that. *I* wouldn't put a penny into it, if both your lives depended on it. I take not the slightest interest in "new processes"; I detest new processes, particularly chemical ones; they exalt the brains of fools and they bore me green. But you will probably make a good thing of it. If you go soberly and steadily, you already have enough to live on, and you'll have perhaps a bit more from Marjorie. Is all that understood?'

Again George started to explain something; this time it was Marjorie who interposed. Her face was slightly pink, but her eyes were candid and she showed great composure.

'Just say, "Yes",' she advised. 'It's all you will be allowed to say.'

The bald-headed man in the felt hat, who had been leaning on his elbows on the balustrade and watching them with a slight frown, now waved his hand as though to attract attention in a classroom.

'One moment, Marcus,' he interrupted. 'You have asked both Wilbur and me to be present at this thing, though we're not members of the family. So let me say a word. Is it necessary to cross-examine the boy as though he were—'

Marcus looked at him.

'I wish,' he said, 'certain people would get out of their heads the curious notion that any form of questioning is always a "cross-examination." Every novelist seems to be under this impression. Even you, professor, are addicted to it. It annoys me intensely. I am *examining* Mr. Harding. Is that clear?'

'Yes,' said George.

'Oh, go soak your head,' said the professor amiably.

Marcus settled back as far as was possible without tumbling into the fountain. His expression had grown even more bland.

'Since all this is understood,' he went on, in a slightly different voice, 'you ought to know something about us. Has Marjorie told you anything about it? I thought not. If you think we are members of the strolling idle rich, who are accustomed to take a three months' holiday at this time of year, get it out of your head. It is true that I am rich: but I am not idle and I very seldom stroll. Neither do the others: I see to that. I work; and, though I consider myself more of a scholar than a business man, I am none the worse a man of business for that. My brother Joseph is a general practitioner in Sodbury Cross; *he* works, in spite of his constitutional laziness; I see to that too. He is not a good doctor, but people like him.'

Doctor Joe's face went fiery behind the dark glasses.

'Please be quiet,' said Marcus coolly. 'Now, Wilbur—Wilbur Emmet there—is the manager of my business.'

He nodded towards the tall and spectacularly ugly young man who stood inside the balustrade of the peristyle. Wilbur Emmet kept a wooden countenance. Towards Marcus he showed a respect as great as George Harding's, but it was a stiffer and more dignified respect, as though he were always ready to take notes.

'Since I employ him,' continued Marcus, 'I can assure you he works too. Professor Ingram there, that fat fellow with the bald head, is just a friend of the family. He doesn't work, but he would if I had any say in the matter. Now, Mr. Harding, I want you to understand this from the start, and I want you to understand me. I'm the head of this family; make no mistake about that. I'm not a tyrant. I'm not ungenerous and I'm not unreasonable: anybody will tell you that.' He stuck out his neck. 'But I'm an interfering, strong-minded old busybody who wants to find out the truth of things. I want my own way and I generally get it. Is that clear?'

'Yes,' said George.

'Good,' commented Marcus, smiling. 'Now, then. Everything else being so, you may wonder why we did take this three months' holiday. I'll tell you. It was because in the village of Sodbury Cross there is a criminal lunatic who enjoys poisoning people wholesale.'

Again there was a silence. Marcus put on his spectacles, and again the ring of dark glasses was complete.

'Has the cat got your tongue?' inquired Marcus. 'I did not say the village contained a drinking-fountain or a market-cross. I said it contained a criminal lunatic who enjoys poisoning people wholesale. Purely to afford pleasure to this person, three children and an eighteen-year-old girl were poisoned with strychnine. One of the children died. It was a child of whom Marjorie had been particularly fond.'

George Harding opened his mouth to say something, and stopped again. He looked at the guide-book in his hand, and hastily thrust it into his pocket.

'I'm sorry—' he began.

'No; listen to me. Marjorie was ill for several weeks with nervous shock. Because of this, and certain other— atmospheres,' Marcus adjusted his glasses, 'we decided to come for this trip.'

'Never been robust,' muttered Doctor Joe, staring at the ground.

Marcus silenced him.

'On Wednesday, Mr. Harding, we go home by the *Hakozaki Maru* from Naples. So you had better know a little about what happened in Sodbury Cross on last June 17th. There is a woman named Mrs. Terry who keeps a tobacconist's and sweet-shop in the High Street. The children were poisoned by doses of strychnine in chocolate creams sold by Mrs. Terry. She does not (you may gather) sell poisoned chocolates as a regular thing. The police believed that poisoned sweets were substituted for harmless ones—in a certain way.' He hesitated. 'The point is that everyone who could have had access to the chocolates, everyone who could have done this at certain established times, is a person well known in Sodbury Cross. Do I make myself clear?'

Here the dark glasses looked very hard at Marcus's listener.

'I think so, sir.'

'Speaking for myself,' continued Marcus, '*I* am anxious to get back home—'

'Good Lord, yes!' exploded Doctor Joe, with powerful relief. 'Decent cigarettes. Decent tea. Decent—'

From the shadows of the peristyle, the stern-faced and exceptionally ugly-faced young man spoke for the first time. He had a deep voice, which gave his somewhat mysterious words the effect of a Sybilline prophecy. His hands were dug into the pocket of a blue blazer.

'Sir,' said Wilbur Emmet, 'we should not have been away in July and August. I do not trust the Early Silver to McCracken.'

'Please understand me, Mr. Harding,' said Marcus sharply. 'We are not a band of pariahs. We do as we please. We take a holiday when we please, and come home when we please: at least, I do. I am particularly anxious to get back home, because I think I can solve the problem that has been tormenting them. I knew a part of the answer months ago. But there are certain—' Again, hesitating, he lifted his hand in the air, shook it, and brought it down on his knee. 'If you come to Sodbury Cross, you will find certain innuendoes. Certain atmospheres. Certain whispers. Are you prepared for them?'

'Yes,' said George.

To the man who was watching them from the doorway of the atrium, there always remained a picture of that group in the garden, framed in ancient pillars and strangely symbolic of what was to happen. But his thoughts were not metaphysical now. He did not go farther into the house of Aulus Lepidus the poisoner. Instead he turned round and went out into the Street of Tombs, where he walked a little way up towards the Herculaneum Gate. A tiny blur of white smoke coiled and crawled round the cone of Vesuvius. Detective-Inspector Andrew MacAndrew Elliot, Criminal Investigation Department, sat down on the high footway, lighted a cigarette, and stared thoughtfully at the brown lizard that darted out into the road.

II

ON THE NIGHT THAT MURDER WAS DONE AT BELLEGARDE, Marcus Chesney's country house, Inspector Elliot left London in his car—of which he was inordinately proud—and arrived in Sodbury Cross at half-past eleven. It was a fine though very dark night after a day of brilliant sunshine, and warm for the third of October.

There had been, he thought gloomily, a kind of fatality about it. When Superintendent Hadley told him to take over, he did not say what was in his mind. Haunting him was not only a Pompeian scene, but a certain ugly business at a chemist's shop.

'As usual,' Hadley had complained bitterly, 'we've been called in when the trail is as cold as last year's flat-iron. Nearly four months ago! You did very well on a cold trail in that Crooked Hinge business, so you may be able to do something. But don't be too optimistic. Do you know anything about it?'

'I—read something about it at the time, sir?'

'Well, it's being stirred up again. Devil of a row, it appears, since the Chesney family got back from a trip abroad.

Anonymous letters, scrawls on the wall, that sort of thing. It's a dirty business, my lad: poisoning kids.'

Elliot hesitated. There was a dull anger in him. 'Do they think it was one of the Chesney family, sir?'

'I don't know. Major Crow—that's the Chief Constable—has his own ideas. Crow is inclined to be more excitable than you'd think to look at him. When he gets an idea, he freezes to it. All the same, he'll give you the facts. He's a good man, and you ought to work well under him. Oh, and if you need any help, Fell is close at hand. He's at Bath, taking the cure. You might ring him up and see that he does some work for a change.'

Andrew MacAndrew Elliot, young, serious-minded, and very Scottish of soul, was considerably heartened at the knowledge of the vast doctor's presence. He might even, he thought, tell Dr. Fell what was in his mind, for Dr. Fell was that sort of person.

At half-past eleven, then, he arrived in Sodbury Cross and pulled up at the police-station. Sodbury Cross in status hovers between a town and a village. But it is a market-town, and close to the London Road, so that it carries a volume of traffic. At that time of night it was sealed up in sleep. The lights of Elliot's car picked up blank rows of windows; the only other light was in an illuminated clock over the Diamond Jubilee drinking-fountain.

Major Crow and Superintendent Bostwick were waiting for him in the Superintendent's office at the police-station.

'Sorry to be so late, sir,' Elliot told the former. 'But I picked up a flat tyre on the other side of Calne, and—'

'Oh, that's all right,' said the Chief Constable. 'We're night-hawks ourselves. Where are you putting up?'

'The Superintendent suggested The Blue Lion.'

'Couldn't do better. Would you like to go over and knock 'em up and turn in now, or hear something about the case first?'

'I'd like to hear something about it, sir, if it's not too late for you.'

For a time it was silent in the office, except for the ticking of a noisy clock; and the gaslight flared nervously. Major Crow held out a box of cigarettes. He was a shortish, mild-mannered, mild-voiced man, with a close-shaven grey moustache: one of that type of ex-Army man whose success always surprises you until you come in contact with its absolute efficiency. The Chief Constable lit a cigarette and hesitated, his eye on the floor.

'I'm the one,' he said, 'who ought to apologise to you, Inspector. We ought to have called in the Yard long ago, if we were going to call you in at all. But there's been rather a stir in the past few days, since Chesney and his crowd got home again. People will think enormous strides are being made'— his smile was without offence—'just because Scotland Yard is on the job. Now, a lot of them want us to arrest a girl named Miss Wills, Marjorie Wills. And there isn't enough evidence.'

Elliot, though tempted, did not comment.

'You'll understand the difficulty,' pursued Major Crow, 'if you just get a mental picture of Mrs. Terry's shop. You've seen hundreds like it. It's a very small place, narrow but deep. On the left-hand side there's a counter for tobacco and cigarettes; on the right-hand side there's a counter for sweets. An aisle barely wide enough to turn round in runs between them to the back of the shop, where there's a small circulating library. You know?'

Elliot nodded.

'There are only three tobacco-and-sweet shops in Sodbury Cross; and Mrs. Terry's is (or was) by far the best patronised. Everybody went there. She's a cheerful soul, and absolutely efficient. Husband died and left her with five children: you know?'

Again Elliot nodded.

'But you also know how the sale of sweets is managed in those places. Some of the stuff is under a flattish glass show-case. But a lot of it is simply spread out anyhow, in glass jars or in open boxes on the counter. Now, on top of this show-case there were five open boxes, slightly tilted up to show the contents. Three boxes contained chocolate creams, one box contained solid chocolates, and one box caramels.

'Now, suppose you wanted to introduce poisoned choco-lates among them. Nothing easier! You buy some chocolate creams elsewhere—they're a common type you can find everywhere. You take a hypodermic needle, fill it with strych-nine in an alcohol solution, and inject a grain or two into (say) half a dozen chocolates. A tiny puncture like that won't show.

'You then walk into Mrs. Terry's shop (or any other shop) with the chocolates hidden in the palm of your hand. You ask for cigarettes, and Mrs. Terry goes behind the cigarette counter. Say you ask for fifty or a hundred Players; so that she not only has to turn round, but has to reach or climb up to a higher shelf for the box of a hundred. While her back is turned, you simply reach behind you and drop the prepared chocolates into the open box. A hundred people go through that shop in a day; and who's to know or prove it was you?'

He had risen, a slight flush on his face.

'Is that how it was done, sir?' inquired Elliot.

'Wait! You can see the devilish ease with which a person who merely wants the pleasure of killing, and doesn't care who he kills, can get away with it. You see our difficulty.

'First, I'd better tell you about Marcus Chesney, his family and cronies. Chesney lives in a big house about a quarter of a mile from here; you may have seen it. Fine, spick-and-span place, everything up to date and of the best. It's called Bellegarde; named after a peach.'

'A what, sir?'

'A peach,' replied the Chief Constable. 'Ever heard of Chesney's famous greenhouses? No? He's got half an acre of 'em. His father and his grandfather before him grew what were supposed to be the finest luxury peaches in the world. Marcus has carried on. They're those big peaches you buy at West End hotels at fantastic prices. He grows them out of season; he says sun or climate has nothing to do with peach-growing; he says the trick is his secret, which is worth tens of thousands. He grows the Bellegarde, the Early Silver, and (his own speciality) the Royal Ripener. And it's certainly profitable: I hear his yearly income runs into six figures.'

Here Major Crow hesitated, looking keenly at his guest.

'As for Chesney himself,' he went on, 'he's not exactly popular in the district. He's shrewd, and tough as nails. People either dislike him intensely, or give him a half-tolerant respect. You know the sort of thing in pubs: "Ah, he's a one, old Chesney is!" and a shake of the head, and a half-chuckle, and down goes the tankard on the counter. Then there's popularly supposed to be something queer about the family, though nobody can tell what it is.

'Marjorie Wills is his niece; daughter of his sister, deceased. She seems to be quite a nice girl, for all anybody knows. But she's got a temper. For all her sweetly innocent looks, I hear she sometimes uses language that would startle a sergeant-major.

'Then there's Joe Chesney, the doctor. He redeems the family; everybody likes him. He goes about like a roaring bull, and I wouldn't trust his professional skill too far, but lots of people swear by him. He doesn't live with Marcus—Marcus won't have Bellegarde messed up with a surgery. He lives a little way along the road. Then there's a retired professor named Ingram, very quiet and pleasant, a great crony of Marcus's. He has a cottage in the same road, and he's well thought of hereabouts. Finally, the manager or foreman of Chesney's "nurseries" is a chap named Emmet, about whom nobody knows or cares much.

'Well! June 17th was a Thursday, market day, and there were quite a number of people in town. I think we can take as established that there were no poisoned chocolates in Mrs. Terry's stock until that day. Reason: she has five children, as I told you, and one of them had a birthday on the 16th. Mrs. Terry gave him a small birthday party in the evening. For the party, she took (among other sweets) a handful out of each of the boxes on top of the counter. Nobody suffered any ill-effects from eating any of it.

'For the Thursday, we've got a list of all the people—all of them—who were in the shop on that day. That's not as difficult as it sounds, because most of them took library books, and Mrs. Terry keeps a record. There were no strangers in the shop that day: this we can take as established. Marcus Chesney himself was there, by the way. So was Dr. Joe Chesney. But neither Professor Ingram nor young Emmet went in.'

Elliot had taken out his notebook and was studying the curious designs he had made there.

'What about Miss Wills?' he inquired—and again became conscious of the warm night, the singing gaslight, and the Chief Constable's worried eyes.

'I'm coming to that,' Major Crow went on. 'Miss Wills wasn't actually in the shop at all. This is what happened. At round about four o'clock in the afternoon, just after school was out, she drove in to Sodbury Cross in her uncle's car. She went to Packers', the butcher's, to make a small complaint about something. When she was coming out of the butcher's, she met little Frankie Dale, eight years old. She always has been very fond of Frankie, according to most people. She said to him—overheard by a witness—"Oh, Frankie, run down to Mrs. Terry's and get me three-pennyworth of chocolate creams, will you?" and she handed the child a sixpence.

'Mrs. Terry's is about fifty yards away from the butcher's. Frankie did as he was told. As I've mentioned, there were three boxes of chocolate creams on top of the glass case. Frankie, like most kids, didn't specify. He simply pointed firmly to the middle box, and said, "I want three-pennyworth of those."'

'Just a moment, sir,' interposed Elliot. 'Had anybody else bought chocolate creams up to that time?'

'No. There had been a fairly brisk trade in liquorice, chocolate-bars, and bull's-eyes, but no chocolate creams had been sold that day.'

'Go on, please.'

'Mrs. Terry weighed it out for him. Those chocolates are sixpence a quarter-pound; he got two ounces, which came to six chocolates. Then Frankie ran back to Miss Wills, with the chocolates in a little paper bag. Now, it had been raining that day; and Miss Wills was wearing a raincoat with deep pockets. She put the bag into her pocket. Then, as though changing her mind, she pulled it out again. At least, she pulled out *a* paper bag. You know?'

'Yes.'

'She opened the bag, looked inside, and said, "Frankie, you've got me the small ones with the white filling. I wanted the larger ones with the pink filling. Run back and ask Mrs. Terry to change them, will you?" Mrs. Terry, of course, obligingly changed them. She poured the chocolates into the middle box, and refilled the bag with others from the right-hand box. Frankie gave them to Miss Wills, who said he could keep the change from the sixpence.

'The rest of the business,' said Major Crow, drawing a deep breath and turning a grim eye on his listener, 'is told soon enough. Frankie didn't spend his threepence then; he went home to tea. But after tea he came back again. Whether or not he had already got his mind set on chocolate creams, from buying some before, I don't know. But he spent twopence on them—the small ones with the white filling—and a penny on liquorice. About a quarter past six, a maidservant named Lois Curtain (she works for Mr. and Mrs. Anderson) came in with the two Anderson children, and bought half a pound of mixed creams out of all three boxes.

'All those who tasted a chocolate from the middle box complained of their violently bitter taste. Frankie, poor little devil, wasn't going to be put off by this, because he'd spent his twopence. He wolfed down the lot. The pains came on about an hour later, and he died in terrible pain at eleven o'clock that night. The Anderson kids, and Lois Curtain, were more fortunate. Little Dorothy Anderson took a bite out of a chocolate; she cried out about it, and said it was too bitter—"nasty" was the word she used—to eat. Lois Curtain, curious, also took a bite out of it. Tommy Anderson set up such a clamour that *he* had to have a bite as well. Lois then bit into another chocolate, and that was bitter too. She decided that the chocolates were bad, and put 'em away in her handbag until she could go back and complain to Mrs. Terry. None of the three died, but it was touch and go with Lois that night. Strychnine poisoning, of course.'

Major Crow stopped. He had been speaking quietly, but Elliot did not like the look of his eyes. Extinguishing his cigarette, he sat down again.

He added:

'I've been twelve years in this part of the country, but I've never seen such an uproar as the one that followed that little bit of business. The first report, of course, was that Mrs. Terry had been selling poisoned chocolates, and all the blame fell on her. I think some people had a vague idea you could get tainted chocolates in the same way you can get tainted meat. Mrs. Terry was hysterical: you know? Screaming and crying, with her apron over her face. They smashed her windows; and Frankie Dale's father went half out of his mind.

'But in a day or two they grew saner, and started to ask questions. Joe Chesney frankly said in the bar of The Blue Lion that it was deliberate poisoning. He had attended

Frankie. Frankie had eaten three chocolates, and swallowed six and a quarter grains of strychnine. One sixteenth of a grain, you know, has proved a fatal dose. The other three victims had divided over two grains among them. The remaining chocolates from the middle box were analysed. Two more of them contained (each chocolate) over two grains of strychnine formate in an alcohol solution, and so did two more in the bag bought by Lois Curtain, in addition to the two she and the children had shared. In other words, ten chocolates altogether had been poisoned; and there was much more than a fatal dose in every one of them. Somebody had been out to kill, and kill with as great agony to the victim as possible.

'Now—pretty plainly—there were three possible solutions.

'One. Mrs. Terry had deliberately poisoned the chocolates. Which nobody believed, after the first uproar.

'Two. Someone who went into the shop during the day had added a handful of poisoned stuff to the middle box while Mrs. Terry's back was turned. Just as I indicated to you a while ago.

'Three. Marjorie Wills did it. When Frankie brought her the bag of harmless creams, she had in the pocket of her raincoat a duplicate bag of prepared poisoned ones. She put the harmless bag into her pocket, drew out the poisoned one, and asked Frankie to take it back and change it. So the poisoned stuff was emptied into the middle box. You follow that?'

Elliot frowned.

'Yes, sir, I see that. But—'

'Exactly!' interrupted the Major, with a hypnotic eye on his guest. 'I know what you're going to say. That was the snag.

She bought *six* chocolates. But there were, altogether, *ten* poisoned ones in the middle box. If she returned a duplicate bag of six, what about the extra four? And if the duplicate bag had contained ten chocolates instead of six, wouldn't Mrs. Terry have noticed it in emptying it into the box?'

Superintendent Bostwick of the local police had hitherto not said a word. A great lump of a man, he had been sitting with his arms folded and his eye on the calendar. Now he cleared his throat.

'Some people,' he said, 'thinks she wouldn't have. Not if she was rushed.'

Clearing his throat again, he added:

'Scotland Yard or no Scotland Yard, we'll get that damned murdering devil if it's the last thing we ever do.'

The heat of that outburst quivered in the warm room. Major Crow looked at Elliot.

'Bostwick,' he said, 'is trained to be fair-minded. But if that's what he thinks, what do you imagine the others think?'

'I see,' said Elliot, and inwardly he shivered a little. 'Is it generally believed that Miss Wills—?'

'That you'll have to find out for yourself. People in general aren't in a mood to argue niceties, as we have to. That's the trouble. First it was the completely meaningless nature of the thing, the pure crooked-mindedness of it, which stunned everybody. And then—well, it isn't helped by the fact (though fortunately most of the crowd at The Blue Lion don't know this) that the circumstances are almost exactly the same as in a famous poisoning case at Brighton over sixty years ago. You've heard of the case of Christiana Edmunds in 1871? She worked the poisoned-chocolates dodge, getting a child to take them back to the shop and exchange them, in exactly the same way. Carried a duplicate bag in—I think—her muff; and palmed it off on the child like a conjuror.'

Elliot considered. 'Christiana Edmunds, if I remember,' he said, 'was mad. She died in Broadmoor.'

'Yes,' agreed the Major bluntly; 'and some people think this girl will too.'

After a pause he went on with an air of reasonableness.

'But look at the case against her! Or, rather, the lack of a case. Won't wash: simply won't wash. First, no poison can be traced to her; it can't be proved that she bought, borrowed, found, or stole a millionth of a grain. The local answer to that is simple. She's a great favourite of Dr. Chesney; and Joe Chesney, they say, is the sort of careless person who would leave strychnine lying loose about the place like tobacco. It's true that he has strychnine in his surgery, but he's accounted to us for all of it.

'Second, Mrs. Terry herself swears that only six chocolates were returned in the bag Frankie Dale brought back.

'Third, if Marjorie Wills did that, she went about it in an incredibly asinine way. She didn't even take the precautions of mad Christiana Edmunds. After all, Brighton is a big place; and a woman who chose a child who didn't know her to make the exchange would run a reasonable chance of not being identified afterwards. But this girl!—smack in the middle of a small place like this, speaking to a boy who knew her, and in the presence of witnesses? Hang it, she went out of her way to call attention to herself! If she wanted to poison the chocolates, she could have done it completely unsuspected in the other way I've told you about.

'No, Inspector. There's not a point in the case against her that a good counsel wouldn't shoot to pieces in twenty minutes; and we can't afford to make an arrest just to satisfy Uncle Tom Cobleigh and all. Besides, I hope it's not true. She's a pretty little thing, and nothing has ever been known against her except that the Chesneys in general are queer.'

'Did this popular excitement against her start before the Chesneys went away on their trip?'

'Well, it was simmering a bit. It only came fully to the surface when they did go. And, now that they're back, it's worse. The Superintendent here has been in a stew for fear some hotheads will go up and try to smash up Marcus's greenhouses. I don't anticipate that, though. The local lad talks a lot, but he's almost heavily patient. He expects authority to act for him, and won't cut up rough unless it doesn't. Gad, *I'm* willing to do anything possible!' said the Major, with sudden plaintiveness. 'I've got children of my own, and I don't like this business any better than the rest of them. Besides, Marcus Chesney's attitude hasn't helped any. He came back from the Continent roaring for blood, and saying he was going to solve our problem for us after we had failed. In fact, I understand he was in here only the day before yesterday with some nonsense, asking questions—'

Elliot pricked up his ears.

'Was he?' Elliot demanded. 'About what, sir?'

The Chief Constable glanced inquiringly at Superintendent Bostwick. Speech struggled up massively in the latter.

'Gentleman wanted to know,' said Superintendent Bostwick, with sarcasm, 'the exact size of the chocolate-boxes on Mrs. Terry's counter. I asked him why he wanted to know. He flew off into a temper, and said it was none of my business. I said he'd better ask Mrs. Terry, then. He said'—the Superintendent chuckled with spectral enjoyment—'he said he had another question to ask me; but, since I was such a bleeding fool, he wouldn't ask it and I could take the consequences. He said he always knew I lacked the power of observation, but now he knew I hadn't any brains.'

'It seems rather an *idée fixe* of his,' explained the Major, 'that most people are incapable of describing accurately what they see or hear—'

'I know,' said Elliot.

'You know?'

Elliot did not have time to answer this, for at that moment the telephone rang. Major Crow glanced rather impatiently at the clock, whose noisy ticking filled the room, and whose hands pointed to twenty minutes past twelve. Bostwick lumbered over and picked up the phone, while both Elliot and the Chief Constable were sunk in an obscure but uncomfortable dream. The Major was tired and depressed; Elliot, at the very least, was depressed. It was Bostwick's voice which roused them—perhaps the very slight shrillness with which he repeated, 'Sir?' Major Crow swung round suddenly, knocking his chair with a bump against the desk.

'It's Doctor Joe,' said the Superintendent heavily. 'You'd better talk to him, sir.'

There was a glitter of sweat on his forehead, though the expression of his eyes told little. He held out the telephone.

Major Crow took it, and listened quietly for perhaps a minute. In the silence Elliot could hear the telephone jabbering, though he could make out no coherent word. Then the Chief Constable hung up the receiver with some care.

'That was Joe Chesney,' he repeated, rather superfluously. 'Marcus is dead. The doctor believes he was poisoned with cyanide.'

Again the ticking of the clock filled the room, and Major Crow cleared his throat.

'It would also appear,' he went on, 'that Marcus proved his pet theory with his last breath. If I understand what the doctor said, every single one of them saw him poisoned under their eyes; and yet not one single person can tell what happened.'

III

BELLEGARDE WAS A HOUSE ABOUT WHICH IT COULD BE said that there was no nonsense. Though very large, it was not an ancestral mansion, nor did it pretend to be one. It was solidly built of yellow Dutch bricks, with gable-facings in blue, now somewhat begrimed; its gables were set at the end of a long, low frontage with a steep-pitched roof.

But, at the moment, Inspector Elliot made out details with difficulty. The sky was thick and overcast. Not a light showed at the front of the house. But from the side, the side out of sight round to their left as they entered the drive, poured such a blaze that they had seen it from the main road. Elliot stopped his car in the drive, and Major Crow and Bostwick climbed out of the rear seat.

'Just a moment, sir,' Elliot said respectfully. 'Before we go in, there's something we had better straighten out. What is my status here? I was sent here over that sweet-shop case, but this—'

In the dark he felt that Major Crow was regarding him with a grim smile.

'You do like to have things in order, don't you?' the Chief Constable inquired. 'Well, well, that's all to the good,' he added hastily. 'It's your case, my lad. You handle it: under Bostwick's supervision, of course. When I've heard what has happened, I'm going home to bed. Now carry on.'

Instead of knocking at the front door, Elliot made straight for the side of the house and looked round the corner. Bellegarde, he saw, was not deep. This side consisted of three rooms set in a line. Each room had two French windows opening out on a narrowish strip of lawn with a line of chestnut trees running parallel to the line of windows. The first room—towards the front of the house—was dark. It was from the French windows of the other two that the light streamed, particularly the third room. It gave the smooth grass a theatrical green; it illuminated every yellow leaf on the chestnut trees, throwing theatrical shadows under them.

Elliot glanced into the first of the two lighted rooms. It was empty. Both French windows, backed with heavy velvet curtains, stood open. It was what used to be called a Music Room, of the elaborate variety, with a piano and a radiogramophone; the chairs now looked disarranged. Folding doors (closed) communicated with the farthest room of the three. The silence itself was thick enough to suggest unpleasant possibilities.

'Hello!' Elliot called out.

Nobody answered. He moved on to look in at the windows of the other lighted room, with which the folding doors communicated. And he stopped short.

In the narrow green aisle between the house and the chestnut trees, just outside the windows of the far room, lay as odd an assortment of articles as Elliot had ever seen. The first thing he noticed was a top-hat, a tall and shiny top-hat of the old-fashioned sort, its nap badly rubbed. Beside it had been flung down a long old-fashioned raincoat with deep pockets, also much worn. Near this lay a brown wool muffler—and a pair of dark sun-glasses. Finally, there stood amid this heap of cast-off clothing a black leather bag, rather larger than a doctor's bag but not so large as a suitcase. On the black bag had been painted the words, *R. H. Nemo, M.D.*

'It looks,' observed Major Crow coolly, 'as though somebody has been undressing.'

Elliot did not reply. For he had just looked into the room; and it was not a pleasant sight.

Both windows of this room were also ajar. It had been fitted up as an office or study. In the centre stood a broad table with blotter and pen-tray, and a desk-chair behind it on Elliot's left. A person sitting in this chair would be facing the double-doors to the other room. A bronze lamp on this table held an electric bulb of such intense, blinding brilliancy that Elliot knew it for a Photoflood bulb, the sort with which indoor photographs are taken; the shade of the lamp was tilted so that its full glare would fall on the face and body of anyone sitting in that desk-chair. And there was someone sitting in the desk-chair now.

Marcus Chesney sat sideways, his shoulders hunched together and his hands gripping the arm of the chair as though he were trying to push himself to his feet. But it was only the illusion of being alive. His feet trailed out, and his weight rested against the back of the chair. His face was cyanosed, the forehead-veins standing out dark blue and swollen. Against this the grey-white of his hair appeared in startling contrast. The congested eyelids were shut, and there was still a slight froth on the lips.

All this the Photoflood lamp, tilted and focused on him, brought out with a merciless clarity of white light. In the wall behind Marcus Chesney's back there was a mantelpiece of polished wood; and on this mantelpiece stood a white-faced clock whose busy little pendulum switched back and forth with loud ticking. Its hands pointed to twenty-five minutes past twelve.

'Yes, he's gone,' said Major Crow, in what he tried to make a brisk tone. 'But—look here—'

His voice trailed off in protest. The ticking of the clock was inordinately loud. Even from the window they could smell the bitter-almonds odour.

'Yes, sir?' said Elliot, memorising details.

'He looks as though he pegged out hard. Pain, I mean.'

'He did.'

'Joe Chesney said it was cyanide. And then there's that odour: I can't say I've ever smelled it before, but everybody knows about it. But isn't cyanide the stuff that strikes like lightning and kills instantaneously; no pain at all?'

'No, sir. There's no poison that does that. It's very rapid, but only rapid in the sense that it takes minutes instead of—'

Here, this wouldn't do; he had to get on with it. But, as Elliot stood in the window, his imagination took the ugly exhibits in that room and fitted them together in a picture of remarkable vividness. Here was the dead man sitting behind a table that faced the double-doors across the room, with a strong light set to shine on him. It was like a stage—with illuminations. If those folding doors were open, and people were sitting beyond them to look in here, this room would be like a stage. The folding doors would be curtains, Marcus Chesney would be the actor. And outside the window lay those curious stage-properties, a top-hat, a raincoat, a brown muffler, a pair of sun-glasses, and a black bag painted with the name of a phantom doctor.

Well, that could wait.

Elliot noted the time by his watch, which agreed to the second with the clock on the mantelpiece, and entered it in his notebook. Then he went into the room.

The bitter-almonds odour was very strong round Marcus's mouth. He had been dead only a very short time; his hands were still clenched in a final spasm round the arm of the chair. He wore a dinner-jacket whose shirt-front bulged up out of the waistcoat, and behind the handkerchief in his breast-pocket there stuck out the edge of a folded piece of paper.

If he had taken poison, Elliot could find no container or receptacle from which he had taken it. The table, with its neat desk-blotter and pen-tray, was brushed clean. There were only two other objects on the table. One was a lead-pencil, flattish rather than round or hexagonal, and dark blue in colour; it lay not in the pen-tray, but on the blotter. The other object on the desk was a two-pound box of cheap chocolates. It was unopened; the glazed cardboard was ornamented with a flowered design like blue wall-paper, and bore the words *Henrys' Peppermint Creams* in gilt letters on the lid.

'Hullo!' bellowed a voice from the other room.

The carpets were thick, and they heard no footsteps. Also, it was so dark beyond the core of light that they could see little even when someone fumbled at the folding doors and pulled them open. But Dr. Joseph Chesney hurried into the room, and stopped short.

'Oh,' said Doctor Joe. He was breathing hard. 'It's you, Major. And Bostwick. Thank God.'

The Major greeted him curtly.

'We were wondering where you'd got to,' he said. 'This is Inspector Elliot, who has come down from Scotland Yard to give us a hand. Suppose you tell him what happened here.'

Doctor Joe looked at Elliot with searching curiosity. The air was disturbed at his passing, as by a wind; he brought an atmosphere of brandy to mingle with the bitter-almonds. His short ginger beard and moustache were puffed out by the pursing of his lips and the breaths he drew. Seen here at home, rather than in Italy, he seemed less aggressive and perhaps even less burly in spite of his heavy tweed suit. He had scrubby ginger hair and scrubby red eyebrows over fiercely genial eyes, with moving wrinkles under them as though the whole lower part of his face were on a hinge. But the fat face was not genial now.

'*I* don't know what happened,' he retorted rather querulously. 'I wasn't here. And I can't be everywhere at once. I've just been upstairs attending to another patient.'

'Another patient? Who?'

'Wilbur Emmet.'

'Wilbur Emmet!' said the Major. 'He's not—?'

'Oh, no, he's not dead. Got a nasty crack on the back of the head, though. Concussion,' explained Doctor Joe, clasping his hands and rubbing them together with a washing motion. 'Look here, what about going into the other room? It's not that I mind being here with that,' he pointed to his brother, 'but those Photoflood lamps don't last for ever. If you keep that thing burning you'll burn it out, and then you ruddy well will be in the dark when you do the whatisit,' he washed his hands again, 'search for the clues and so on. Eh?'

At a nod from the Chief Constable, Elliot wound a hand-kerchief over his fingers and switched off the light. Joseph Chesney stamped rather quickly into the other room. In the Music Room he faced them with what Elliot realised was the aggressiveness of nervousness.

Major Crow half closed the double-doors.

'Now, then,' he said briskly. 'If they don't mind your using the phone, Superintendent, you might ring up the doctor and ask him—'

'What do you want a doctor for? *I'm* a doctor. I can tell you he's dead.'

'It's a matter of form, Chesney. You know that.'

'If you've got anything to say against me professionally—'

'Nonsense, my lad. Now Inspector.'

Doctor Joe turned to Elliot. 'So you're from Scotland Yard, eh?' he demanded, and then seemed to reflect. 'Stop a bit! How did you get down here so quickly?' He reflected again. 'You couldn't have.'

'I came down about another matter, Doctor. Poisoning the children.'

'Oh,' said Doctor Joe, and changed colour. 'Well, you've got a job on your hands.'

'I appreciate that,' admitted Elliot. 'Now, Doctor, if you could just give me an idea of what happened here to-night?'

'Tomfoolery is what happened here,' roared the other instantly. 'Tomfoolery. Marcus wanted to give 'em a show. And, by thunder, he did!'

'A show?'

'I can't tell you what they did,' Doctor Joe pointed out, 'because I wasn't here. But I can tell you what they were going to do, because they were arguing about it all through dinner. It was the old argument, only it never took such concrete shape before. Marcus said that ninety-nine people out of a hundred, as witnesses, are just plain lousy. He said they can't tell you what goes on under their eyes; and if there's a fire, a street-accident, a riot, or anything like that, the police get such wildly conflicting testimony that it's worthless as evidence.' He peered at Elliot with sudden curiosity. 'Is that true, by the way?'

'Very often, yes. But what about it?'

'Well, all of 'em disagreed with Marcus; each on different grounds, but all of 'em said you couldn't fool *them*. I said so myself,' Doctor Joe told him defensively. 'I still think it's so, in my case. But finally Marcus said he would just like to put it to a little test. He offered to try out on them a psychological test that had been used at some university or other. He said he'd put on a little show for 'em. At the end of it they were to answer a list of questions about what they'd seen. And he wanted to bet that sixty per cent of the answers would be wrong.'

Doctor Joe appealed to Major Crow.

'You know, Marcus. I've always said he was like What's-his-name—you know, that writer we had to read at school—the one who would walk twenty miles to get the right description of a flower that didn't matter a curse anyway. And, the minute Marcus got an idea, he had to go and do it smack-bang right off the reel. So they played this little game. Right in the middle of it—well, somebody came in and killed Marcus. If I've understood 'em properly, *every one of 'em saw the murderer and followed every move he made.* And yet they can't agree on anything that happened.'

Doctor Joe stopped. His voice had acquired a kind of thunderous hoarseness; his face was fiery; and by the expression of his eyes Elliot was afraid for a moment that he was going to break down and weep. The sight would have been grotesque if he had not seemed so absolutely sincere.

Major Crow intervened.

'But couldn't they give a description of the murderer?'

'No. The fellow was all bundled up like the Invisible Man.'

'Like the what?'

'You know. Long coat, collar turned up; muffler wrapped round his head and face; dark glasses; hat pulled down. Pretty ugly sight, they said, but they thought it was a part of the show. God, it's frightful! This—this goblin walks in—'

'But—'

'Excuse me, sir,' interposed Inspector Elliot. He wanted to get the facts in their proper order, for he had a dim feeling that this case was going to be a sizzler. He turned to the doctor. 'You say "they" saw this. Who was it?'

'Professor Ingram, and Marjorie, and young George What's-his-name.'

'Anyone else?'

'No, not that I know of. Marcus wanted me to sit in. But, as I keep telling you, I had a round of calls to make. Marcus said he wasn't going to start the show until late anyway, and he would wait for me if I promised to be back before midnight. Of course I couldn't promise anything like that. I said I would make it if I could, but if I wasn't back by a quarter to twelve to go on without me.'

After sniffing once or twice, Doctor Joe had himself under control. He sat down. He raised his big hands and forearms, like the claws of a bear, and let them fall on his knees.

'What time did the show begin, then?' Elliot went on.

'On the stroke of twelve, they tell me. That's the only ruddy point where they all agree.'

'About the actual murder, Doctor: you can't tell us anything from personal knowledge?'

'*No!* At twelve o'clock I was just getting away from a case on the other side of town. Difficult case: confinement. I thought I'd drive over here and see whether I might be in time for the party. But I wasn't. I got here about ten minutes past twelve, in time to find the poor old boy too far gone for me or anyone else to do anything about it.' Here some new reflection seemed to strike him, and brighten in his mind. He lifted a red-rimmed eye. 'And I'll tell you something else,' he went on, in a voice of honey. 'There's just one good thing that's come of this business. And will I cram it down their throats? Will I?

'Look here, Inspector. You say you've come down here to look into that poisoning business at Mrs. Terry's shop, so you probably know what I'm going to tell you, but I'm going to tell you anyhow. For over three months, nearer four, people have been going about saying my niece is a murderess. That's what they've said: they've said she poisons people to watch 'em squirm. They haven't said it to me. You bet they haven't!

But they've said it; and will I cram it down their throats now? Because one thing is proved: whoever killed my brother, it wasn't Marjorie. And whoever the poisoner is, it can't be Marjorie. And even if Marcus had to snuff out to prove that, it's worth it. D'ye hear me? It's worth it.'

He jumped, rather guiltily, and lowered his fist. A door across the room, evidently leading to a passage, had opened; and Marjorie Wills came in.

The Music Room had a crystal chandelier, all of whose electric candles were lighted. Marjorie's eyes blinked a little as she opened the door. She moved over quickly, soundless on the carpet in her small black slippers, and put her hand on Doctor Joe's shoulder.

'Please come upstairs,' she urged. 'I don't like the way Wilbur is breathing.'

Then she looked up, startled, and saw the others. First the grey eyes were blank; then, as they saw Elliot, they seemed to catch at something, and narrowed. It was like a fierce concentration, which was there and gone as she straightened up.

She said:

'Aren't you—that is, haven't we met before?'

IV

Whereupon Elliot made another slip. He spoke, for a certain reason of his own, with such barking sharpness that the Chief Constable stared at him.

'I think not, Miss Wills,' he said. 'Will you sit down, please?'

She was looking at him in that same puzzled way; how vividly his own memory returned he did not mention. Never had he met a person of whose presence he was so intensely *aware*, like a physical touch. He seemed to know what she would do, how her head would turn, how she would raise her hand to her forehead.

'You're hysterical, Marjorie,' said Doctor Joe, patting her hand. 'This fellow's an Inspector from Scotland Yard. He—'

'Scotland Yard,' said the girl. 'As bad as that, is it?'

And she began to laugh.

She checked herself immediately, but even such humour as it was had not reached her eyes. Elliot had forgotten no detail: the glossy dark-brown hair, parted and drawn behind her ears to small curls at the nape of the neck; the broad forehead, arched brows, and meditative grey eyes; the mouth that seemed to be always in repose. He saw now that she was not beautiful, but he hardly noticed this.

'I'm sorry,' she said, rousing herself again from the puzzled look she was directing at him. 'I'm afraid I didn't hear you. What did you say?'

'Will you sit down, please, Miss Wills? If you feel up to it, we should like to hear what you can tell us about your uncle's death.'

She gave a quick glance at the folding doors to the dark room beyond. After looking at the floor for a moment, and clenching her hands once or twice, she threw back her head with at least surface calm. But such humour and intelligence as he ascribed to her may not be proof against four months' whispering attack of tongues.

'That bulb can't have burned out, can it?' she said, and rubbed her forehead vigorously with the back of her hand. '*Have* you come down to arrest me?'

'No.'

'Then—well, what do you want to ask me?'

'Just tell me about it in your own way, Miss Wills. Dr. Chesney, if you would like to go to your patient?'

Elliot's sober-minded, quiet Scots courtesy was having its effect. She looked at him speculatively, and her breathing became less rapid. Taking the chair he set out for her, she sat down and crossed her knees. She was wearing a plain black dinner-dress, without rings or ornaments: not even an engagement-ring.

'Inspector, must we stay here? In this room, I mean?'

'Yes.'

'My uncle had a theory,' she said. 'Whenever he had a theory, he had to test it. And this is the result.' She told him about the theory.

'I understand, Miss Wills, that this all began with an argument at the dinner-table?'

'Yes.'

'Who started the argument? Introduced the subject, I mean?'

'Uncle Marcus,' answered the girl, as though surprised.

'And you disagreed with him?'

'Yes.'

'Why, Miss Wills? On what grounds?'

'Oh, does it matter?' cried Marjorie, opening her eyes a little and making a gesture of impatience. But she saw the tenacity of Elliot's jaw; and, puzzled and excited, she went on. 'Why? Just for something to do, I suppose. It's been rather beastly since we've been back home, even with George here. Especially with George here. George is my *fiancé*: I—I met him on a trip we took abroad. And then Uncle Marcus was so *sure* of himself. Besides, I've always really believed what I told him.'

'About what?'

'All men are unobservant,' said Marjorie quietly. 'That's why you make such bad witnesses. You don't pay attention. You're too wrapped up all the time in your own concerns, looking inwards, always concentrated on your business or your troubles. So you don't observe. Shall I prove it? You're always joking about a woman knowing what another woman is wearing, down to the last detail of a belt or a bracelet. Well, do you think a woman doesn't notice what a man is wearing as well? And can't describe it? It isn't a question of watching other women; it's a question of plain observation. But do you ever notice what other people are wearing? Another man, for instance? No. Provided his suit or his tie isn't offensive, you pay no more attention. Do you ever notice details? His shoes; or his hands?'

She paused, glancing over her shoulder at the double-doors.

'I'm telling you this because I swore to Uncle Marcus that no intelligent woman would ever be much mistaken about what she saw. I told him that if he gave his demonstration I shouldn't be. And I'm not mistaken.'

Marjorie bent forward with fierce earnestness.

'You see,' she went on, 'someone came in—'

'Just a moment, Miss Wills. Who else disagreed with this proposition of your uncle's?'

'Uncle Joe did, just on general principles. And Professor Ingram disagreed very strongly. You see, he's a professor of psychology. He said that the proposition in general was sound, but that *he* couldn't possibly make mistakes. He said he was a trained observer, and knew all the traps. He offered to bet Uncle Marcus fifty pounds on it.'

She glanced over towards Doctor Joe's chair, but Doctor Joe had gone: a remarkable feat to be done unobserved. Superintendent Bostwick had come back into the room, and Major Crow was leaning forward with his folded arms on top of the grand piano.

'What about your—*fiancé*?'

'George? Oh, he disagreed too. But he insisted on being allowed to film the whole thing with a little ciné-camera, so that there couldn't be any dispute afterwards.'

Elliot sat up.

'You mean you've got a film of what happened here?'

'Yes, of course. That's the reason for the Photoflood lamp.'

'I see,' said Elliot, with a deep breath of relief. 'Now, who were to be the witnesses to this demonstration?'

'Just Professor Ingram, and George, and myself. Uncle Joe had some calls to make.'

'But what about this other man who seems to have got knocked over the head somehow? This Mr. Emmet? Wasn't he there?'

'No, no. He was to have been Uncle Marcus's assistant, don't you see? He was to have been the other actor in the show.

'Here was how it happened, though we didn't know this until afterwards,' she explained. 'After dinner Uncle Marcus and Wilbur Emmet got together and decided on the performance they were to put on for our benefit, like people arranging charades. The stage was to be Uncle Marcus's office—there—and we were to sit here and watch it. Wilbur was to come in dressed up in some outlandish collection of clothes, the more outlandish the better, so that we should have to describe them afterwards. He and Uncle Marcus were to go through some rigmarole, which we should also have to describe without errors. Uncle Marcus had a list of questions prepared for us. Well, at close on midnight Uncle Marcus called us all in here, and gave us our instructions—'

Elliot interposed.

'Just a moment, please. You say at "close on midnight." Wasn't that rather late to begin?'

A tinge of what he felt was angry uncertainty came into her face.

'Yes, it was. Professor Ingram was rather annoyed about it, because he wanted to go home. You see, dinner was over by a quarter past nine. George and I sat in the library and played endless games of Rummy, wondering what was up. But Uncle Marcus insisted.'

'Did he give any explanation?'

'He said he was waiting to see whether Uncle Joe got home, so that Uncle Joe could join in. But, when Uncle Joe wasn't back by a quarter to twelve, he decided to get on with it.'

'One other thing, Miss Wills. You didn't know at this time that Mr. Emmet was to be in this—that is, that he was to help your uncle as an actor in the performance?'

'Oh, no! We didn't see Wilbur at all, after dinner. All we knew was that Uncle Marcus was shut up in these two rooms, making his preparations.'

'Go on, please.'

'Well, Uncle Marcus called us in here,' she continued 'and gave us our instructions. The curtains were drawn across the windows,'—she pointed—'and those folding doors were closed so that we couldn't see into the office. He stood in here and gave us a little lecture.'

'Could you possibly remember exactly what he said?'

She nodded.

'I think so. He said, *"First, you are to sit in absolute darkness during the performance."* George objected, and asked how he could be expected to take a ciné-film of the thing. Uncle Marcus explained that he had borrowed my Photoflood bulb, one I had bought for him that morning, and rigged it up in the office so that its light would shine directly on the theatre of observations. We would have every excuse for concentrating on it.'

Here Elliot felt a wave of uncertainty in his direction, as palpably as though the girl wore perfume.

'And yet I thought that there was a trick in it somehow,' she added.

'Why?'

'It was the way Uncle Marcus looked,' she cried. 'You can't live with a person for as long as I have—And then it was what he said. He said, *"Second, you are not to speak or interfere no matter what you see. Is that clear?"* Finally, just before he went into the other room, he said, *"Be careful. There may be traps."* With that he went into the office, and closed the folding doors. I turned out the lights, and in a few seconds the performance began.

'It began when Uncle Marcus opened the folding doors to their full width. I felt excited and nervous; I don't know why.

'He was alone. I could see nearly all the office. After he opened the doors, he walked back slowly and sat down behind that table in the middle, facing us. The Photoflood bulb was in a lamp with a bronze-metal shade, placed at the front of the table and a little to the right, so that it lit up everything without obscuring our view of Uncle Marcus. There was a dead white glare on the wall behind him, and a big shadow of him. You could see the white face of the clock on the mantelpiece behind him, with the pendulum shining and switching back and forth. The time was midnight.

'Uncle Marcus sat there facing us. On the table there was a chocolate-box; also a pencil and a pen. He picked up first the pencil, then the pen, and pretended to write with each. Then he looked round. One of the French windows in the office opened, and in from the lawn stepped that horrible-looking thing in the top-hat and the sun-glasses.'

Marjorie paused, only half succeeding in clearing her throat.

But she went on:

'It was about six feet tall, not even counting the top-hat with the curly brim. It wore a long dirty raincoat that had the collar turned up. There was something brown twisted around its face, and it had black glasses on. It was wearing shiny gloves, and carrying a kind of black satchel. We didn't know who it was, of course; but I didn't like the look of it even then. It looked more like an insect than human. Tall and thin, you know, with the big black glasses on. George, who was taking the film, said out loud, "Shh! The Invisible Man!"—and it turned round and looked at us.

'It put down this doctor's satchel on the table, and stood with its back to us, and moved to the other side of the table. Uncle Marcus said something to it. But it never spoke once: Uncle Marcus did all the talking. There wasn't any other noise except the clock ticking on the mantelpiece, and George's ciné-camera rattling away. I think what Uncle Marcus said was, *"You have done now what you did before; what else will you do?"* This time (as I say) it was on the right-hand side of the table. Working very fast, it took a little cardboard box out of the pocket of its raincoat, and shook out of that a fat green capsule like the castor-oil capsules we used to have to take when we were children. It leaned over as quick as *that*, and tipped back Uncle Marcus's head, and forced the capsule down his throat.'

Marjorie Wills stopped.

Her voice was shaking; she lifted her hand to her own throat, clearing it once or twice. She had such difficulty in keeping her eyes off those (now dark) double-doors that she finally pulled her chair round to face them. Elliot followed her.

'Yes?' he prompted.

'I couldn't help it,' she said. 'I gave a jump or a cry or something of the kind. I shouldn't have done it, because Uncle Marcus had warned us not to be surprised at anything we saw. Besides, there didn't seem to be anything wrong; Uncle Marcus swallowed the capsule, though he didn't seem to like doing it—he glared up once at the swathed face.

'As soon as this was done, the thing in the top-hat gathered up the satchel, made a kind of ducking motion, and went out by the French window. Uncle Marcus sat at the table for a few seconds more, swallowing a bit, and pushed that chocolate-box to another position. Then without any warning he flopped forward on his face.

'No, no!' cried Marjorie, as there was a stir through the group. 'That was only pretence: that was only a part of the show: it signified the end of the performance. For immediately after that Uncle Marcus got up smiling, and came over and closed the double-doors on us. That was the fall of the curtain.

'We put the lights on in this room. Professor Ingram knocked on the double-doors, and asked Uncle Marcus to come out and take a curtain-call. Uncle Marcus pulled the doors open. He looked—glittering, you know, pleased with himself; but rather annoyed with something all the same. He had a folded paper stuck into the breast-pocket of his jacket, and he tapped it. He said, "Now, my friends, get pencils and paper, and prepare to answer some questions." Professor Ingram said, "By the way, who was your hideous-looking colleague?" Uncle Marcus said, "Oh, that was only Wilbur; he helped me plan the whole thing." And then he shouted out, *"All right, Wilbur. You can come in now."*

'But there wasn't any answer.

'Uncle Marcus shouted again; and there still wasn't any answer.

'Finally he got annoyed and went to the window. One of the windows in this room—you see?—had been left open, because it was such a warm night. The lights were on in both rooms now, and we could see out into that strip of grass between the house and the trees. All of this goblin's trappings were lying there on the ground, top-hat and sun-glasses and bag with that doctor's name painted on it; but we couldn't see Wilbur at first.

'We found him in the shadow at the other side of a tree. He was lying on his face, unconscious. Blood had come out of his mouth and nose into the grass, and the back of his skull felt soft. The poker he had been hit with was lying near him. He had been unconscious for quite some time.'

She explained, her face screwing up in spite of herself:

'You see, the man in the top-hat and sun-glasses hadn't been Wilbur at all.'

V

'Hadn't been Wilbur at all?' Elliot repeated.

He knew quite well what she meant. That curious figure in the ancient top-hat was beginning to move and stir in his imagination.

'I haven't finished, you see,' Marjorie told him, quietly but wretchedly. 'I haven't told you what happened to Uncle Marcus.

'It was just after we found Wilbur lying there. How long the symptoms had been coming on I don't know. But they were lifting Wilbur up, and I looked round, and I saw there was something wrong with Uncle Marcus.

'Honestly, I felt physically sick. I know this has seemed all intuitions and inspirations of mine; but I can't help it. I knew what it was at that minute. He was leaning against the side of a tree, half doubled up, and trying to get his breath. The light from the house was shining through the leaves behind him. I couldn't see him very well, but the light was on the side of his face, and the skin looked roughish and lead-coloured. I said, "Uncle Marcus, what's wrong? Is anything wrong?" And I must have screamed it. He only shook his head violently, and made a gesture as though he were trying to push me away. Then he began to stamp on the ground with one foot; you could hear him breathe in a kind of whine and moan together. I ran to him, and so did Professor Ingram. But he struck Professor Ingram's hand away, and—'

She could not go on. She slapped her own hands against her face, covering the eyes, and slapped again.

Major Crow came forward from the piano.

'Steady,' he said gruffly.

Superintendent Bostwick said nothing; he had folded his arms, and was looking at her curiously.

'He began to *run*,' said Marjorie wildly. 'That's what I'll always remember: he began to *run*. Back and forth, up and down, but only a few steps each way, because he couldn't stand the pain. George and the professor tried to grab him and hold him down, but he broke away and ran through the window into his office. He collapsed by the desk. We lifted him up into the chair, but he never spoke at any time. I went out to phone for Uncle Joe. I knew where to find him; Mrs. Emsworth is expecting a baby. Uncle Joe walked in on us while I was still ringing up, but it was too late. You could smell that bitter-almonds stuff all over the room by this time. I still thought there might be some hope. But George said, "Come away; the old boy's a goner; I know what that is." And it was.'

'Bad luck,' growled Major Crow. It was inadequate, but it was sincere.

Superintendent Bostwick said nothing.

'Miss Wills,' said Elliot, 'I don't want to press you too much at this time—'

'I'm all right. I really am.'

'But you think your uncle was given poison in that green capsule?'

'Of course. Uncle Joe said it acted on the respiratory nerves, and that's why he couldn't speak, from the first second he felt it come on.'

'He didn't swallow anything else at any time?'

'No.'

'Can you give me a description of this capsule?'

'Well, as I say, it looked like the castor-oil ones we used to take when we were children. They're about the size of a grape, and made of thick gelatine. You think they'll never go down your throat, but they do: easily. Lots of people hereabouts still use them.' Checking herself, she looked at him very quickly, and colour came into her face.

Elliot ignored this.

'Then this is the position. You think that just before the performance someone knocked out Mr. Emmet—'

'I do.'

'Someone wrapped himself in those outlandish clothes so that even Mr. Marcus Chesney wouldn't recognise him. Then someone played Mr. Emmet's part in the show. But in place of a harmless capsule, which Mr. Chesney was supposed to swallow as a part of the show, this person substituted a poisoned capsule?'

'Oh, I don't *know*! Yes, I think so.'

'Thank you, Miss Wills. I won't bother you any more for the moment.' Elliot got up. 'Where are Professor Ingram and Mr. Harding; do you know?'

'Upstairs with Wilbur—they were.'

'Just ask them if they will come down here, will you? Oh, one other thing!'

She had risen, though she fidgeted, and seemed in no hurry to go. She looked at him inquiringly.

'I shall want you, before long, to make a very detailed statement of everything you saw during the performance,' Elliot went on. 'But there's one thing we might settle now. You described a part of the man's costume, raincoat, and so on. But what about his trousers and shoes?'

Her expression grew fixed. 'His—?'

'Yes. You said a while ago,' said Elliot, feeling a faint roaring in his ears, 'that you always noticed shoes. What about this man's shoes and trousers?'

'That light,' answered Marjorie, after a slight pause, 'was placed on the desk to shine straight across; so that things near the floor were pretty dark. But I think I can tell you. Yes, I'm sure of it.' The startled glitter in her eyes became even more fixed. 'He was wearing ordinary dress trousers—black, with a darker stripe down the side—and patent-leather evening shoes.'

'Were all the men here to-night wearing dinner-jackets, Miss Wills?'

'Yes. That is, all except Uncle Joe. He had calls to make; and he says the psychological effect is bad if a doctor goes to see a patient in evening clothes. He says it makes the patient think the doctor's mind isn't on business. But you don't think—?'

Elliot smiled, though he felt it turn into a mask of hypocrisy.

'How many people hereabouts are accustomed to dress for dinner?'

'Nobody that I know of,' said Marjorie. She was evidently growing even more flurried. 'We don't ourselves, ordinarily. But to-night Uncle Marcus asked us to, for some reason.'

'For the first time?'

'Well, for the first time since we've had a lot of guests, anyway. But Professor Ingram hardly counts as a guest, and neither does George.'

'Thank you, Miss Wills. Unless Major Crow or the Superintendent have some questions?'

Both the others shook their heads, though Bostwick looked highly sinister. Marjorie remained looking speculatively at Elliot for a moment; then she went out and closed the door with great softness, but he thought he saw her shudder. There was a silence in the bright room.

'H'm,' said Major Crow.

'You know,' he added, and a sharp little eye fixed on Elliot, 'I don't like that girl's testimony.'

'No more do I,' said Bostwick, and unfolded his arms with deliberation.

'On the surface it's a clear case,' growled Major Crow, speaking down his nose. 'Somebody overheard and saw Chesney and Wilbur Emmet making their preparations, and knew what the show was to be. He knocked out Emmet, played his part, and substituted a poisoned capsule for the harmless one. The gelatine would take a minute or two to dissolve. So Chesney wouldn't notice anything wrong when he took the capsule. That is, he wouldn't shout out immediately that he'd been poisoned, or try to stop the murderer. The murderer could fade away, leaving the disguise outside. When the gelatine melted, the poison would kill in a couple of minutes. All very clear. Yes. Apparently. *But—*'

'Ah!' grunted Bostwick, as the Chief Constable pounced on the word. 'Why hit Mr. Emmet out? Eh, sir?'

Elliot was suddenly conscious of a far greater shrewdness than he had expected emanating from the bulk in the corner. Bostwick was his superior officer, of course, but still he had not expected it. The Superintendent had been rocking back and forth, bumping his posterior at measured intervals against the wall; and now he looked at Elliot with such a broad and fishy expression that it was as though a searchlight had been turned on.

'That's exactly it, Inspector,' agreed Major Crow. 'As Bostwick says, why hit Mr. Emmet out? Why not let *Emmet* give Chesney the poisoned capsule in the ordinary course of the show? If the murderer knows what they're going to do, all he needs to do is change over the capsules. Why run the risk of knocking out Emmet, dressing up in the clothes and possibly being spotted straightaway, and walking in here exposed to everybody's eyes?—why let himself in for all those terrific risks when all he had to do was substitute one capsule for another, and let somebody else do the dirty work?'

'I think,' Elliot said thoughtfully, 'that that's the whole point of the crime.'

'The whole point of the crime?'

'Yes, sir. In the performance as it was rehearsed, Mr. Chesney never intended to *swallow* any capsule at all.'

'H'm,' said Major Crow, after a pause.

'He was only going to pretend to swallow it. You see, this whole performance was to be a series of traps for the observation. You've probably had similar tricks played on you in a course in psychology at college.'

'Not me,' said Major Crow.

'Nor me,' grunted Superintendent Bostwick.

All Elliot's stubbornness rose up fiercely in him; not only at this, but at the slight air of hostility which had come into the room. He wondered if he sounded as though he were swanking. Then he decided, with the tips of his ears tingling, that he did not give a curse.

'The instructor,' he went on, 'takes a bottle of some liquid, puts his tongue to it, makes a wry face, and comments on the bitter taste of the stuff. Then he passes the bottle to you. All it contains is coloured water. But, if you're not careful, you'll swear the stuff is bitter just from having it impressed on you. Or else it really is bitter, and he only pretends to taste it— telling you to do as he did. Unless you note carefully what he did, you'll take a swig of it.

'That's what happened here, very probably. Mr. Chesney warned them to look out for traps. You remember, Miss Wills said he looked surprised and annoyed when the capsule was shoved into his mouth. It's likely that his instructions to Emmet were to pretend to give him the pill, and he would pretend to swallow it. But the real murderer pushed it down his throat, that's all. To avoid breaking up the show. Mr. Chesney didn't make any audible protest.' Elliot shook his head. 'And I'll be very much surprised if in that list of questions he prepared we don't find some such question as—"How long did it take me to swallow the capsule?" or the like.'

Major Crow was impressed.

'By Jove, that's reasonable enough!' he admitted, with a gleam of relief. Then exasperation and bewilderment flooded out everything else. 'But look here, Inspector—even so—to do that—my God, are we dealing with a lunatic?'

'Looks like it, sir.'

'Let's face it,' said Major Crow. 'A lunatic, or whatever fancy name we want to call it, from this house.'

'Ah,' murmured Bostwick. 'Go on!'

The Chief Constable spoke mildly. 'To begin with, how would an outsider know they were going to arrange an observation test here to-night? They didn't know it themselves until dinner; and it's unlikely that an outsider would have been hanging about these windows so conveniently afterwards to overhear what Chesney and Emmet were arranging. It's even more unlikely that an outsider in dress trousers and evening shoes would be hanging about on the one particular night when they were going to dress for dinner. I admit none of this is conclusive; it's only suggestive. But—you see the difficulty?'

'I do,' returned Elliot grimly.

'If somebody in this house did it, who could have done it? Joe Chesney was out on a case; if he didn't leave the case until midnight, he's certainly out of it. Wilbur Emmet was nearly killed by the real murderer. There's nobody else except a couple of maids and a cook, who could hardly qualify. The only other alternative—yes, I know this sounds fantastic—but there's only one other possibility. This would mean that the murderer was one of the three persons who were supposed to be watching the show in this room. It would mean that this person crept out of here in the dark, coshed poor Emmet, put on the clothes, gave Chesney a poisoned pill, and crept back in here before the lights went up.'

'No, sir, it doesn't sound likely,' agreed Elliot dryly.

'But what else have we got?'

Elliot did not reply.

He knew that they must not theorise now. Until the post-mortem, they could not even say with definiteness how Marcus Chesney had died, except that it had probably been by one of the cyanides in the prussic-acid group. But the Chief Constable's final possibility had already occurred to him.

He looked round the Music Room. It was about fifteen feet square, panelled in grey picked out with gilt. The French windows were closed in with heavy velvet curtains of a dark grey colour. As for furniture, the room contained only the grand piano, the radio-gramophone, a tall Boule cabinet beside the door to the hall, four light arm-chairs upholstered in brocade, and two footstools. Thus the centre was comparatively clear; and a person—if he took care to avoid the grand piano by the windows—could cross the room in the dark without bumping into anything. The carpet, they had already seen, was so thick as to prevent any footstep being heard.

'Yes,' said the Chief Constable. 'Test it.'

The electric switch was behind the Boule cabinet beside the door to the hall; Elliot pressed it down, and darkness descended like an extinguisher-cap. The lights had been so bright that a ghost-pattern of the electric candles in the chandelier still wove and shrank in front of Elliot's eyes in the dark. Even with the curtains open, it was impossible to distinguish anything against the overcast sky outside. There was a faint rattle of rings as someone drew the curtains close.

'I'm waving my hands,' came the Chief Constable's voice out of the dark. 'Can you see me?'

'Not a thing,' said Elliot. 'Stay where you are; I'm going to open the double-doors.'

He groped his way across, avoiding a chair, and found the doors. They opened easily and almost without noise. Shuffling forward some eight or nine feet until he found the table, he felt for the bronze lamp. He turned the switch, and the dead white glare sprang up against the opposite wall. Then Elliot backed away to study it from the Music Room.

'H'm,' said Major Crow.

The only living thing in that 'office' was the clock. They saw it, ruthless and busy, on the mantelpiece of dark polished wood behind the head of the dead man. It was a fairly large ormolu clock, having a dial fully six inches across, and a small brass pendulum which switched and swung in moving gleams. Beneath it sat the dead man, undisturbed. The time was five minutes to one.

The table was of mahogany, with a brown blotter; and the bronze lamp stood towards the front of it slightly to (their) right. They saw the chocolate-box with its design of blue flowers. By standing on tiptoe, Elliot could see the pencil lying on the blotter, but there was no trace of the pen Marjorie Wills had described.

In the wall towards their left, they could make out one of the French windows. Against the wall to their right stood a roll-top desk, closed, with a green-shaded lamp over it; and a very long filing-cabinet in steel painted to represent wood. That was all, except for one more chair and a pile of magazines or catalogues spilled on the floor. They saw it framed in the proscenium arch of the doors. Judging by the position of the chairs in the Music Room, the witnesses had been sitting about fifteen feet away from Marcus Chesney.

'I don't see much there,' observed Major Crow doubtfully. 'Or do you?'

Elliot's eye was again caught by the folded piece of paper he had seen before, stuck behind the handkerchief in the pocket of the dead man's jacket.

'There's that, sir,' he pointed out. 'According to what Miss Wills told us, that must be the list of questions Mr. Chesney prepared.'

'Yes, but what about it?' almost shouted the Chief Constable. 'Suppose he did prepare a list of questions? What difference—?'

'Only this, sir,' said Elliot, feeling tempted to shout himself. 'Don't you see that this whole show was designed as a series of traps for the witnesses? There was probably a trick in half the things they saw. And the murderer took advantage of it. The tricks helped him; covered him; probably still cover him. If we could find out exactly what they saw, or thought they saw, we should probably have a line on the murderer. Not even a lunatic is going to commit such a slap-dash, crash-bang, open murder as this unless there was something in Mr. Chesney's plan that afforded him protection, threw the police dead wrong, provided him with an alibi, God knows what! Isn't that clear?'

Major Crow looked at him.

'You will excuse me, Inspector,' he said with sudden politeness, 'if I still think your manner has been odd all evening. I am also curious to know how you knew the surname of Miss Wills's *fiancé. I* hadn't mentioned it.'

(Oh, hell!)

'Sorry, sir.'

'Not at all,' returned the other, with the same formality. 'It doesn't matter in the least. Besides, with regard to the list of questions, I am inclined to agree with you. Let's see if we learn anything from them. You're right: if there are any catch questions, or questions about catches, they will be here.'

He pulled the paper out of the dead man's pocket, unfolded it, and spread it out on the blotter. Here is what they read, in neat copper-plate handwriting.

ANSWER CORRECTLY THE FOLLOWING QUESTIONS:

1. *Was there a box on the table? If so, describe it.*

2. *What objects did I pick up from the table? In what order?*

3. *What was the time?*

4. *What was the height of the person who entered by the French window?*

5. *Describe this person's costume.*

6. *What was he carrying in his right hand? Describe this object.*

7. *Describe his actions. Did he remove anything from the table?*

8. *What did he give me to swallow? How long did it take me to swallow it?*

9. *How long was he in the room?*

10. *What person or persons spoke? What was said?*

N.B.—The LITERALLY *correct answer must be given to each of the above questions, or the answer will not count.*

'It looks straightforward enough,' muttered Major Crow, 'but there are catches. See the N.B. And you certainly seem to be right about the fake swallowing, Inspector. See question 8. Still—'

He folded up the paper and handed it to Elliot, who put it carefully away in his notebook. Then Major Crow backed away towards the double-doors, his eyes fixed on the clock.

'Still, as I was saying—'

A shaft of light cut across the Music Room as the door to the hall opened. The silhouette of a man was framed there, and they saw a bald head gleam against the light.

'Hullo!' said a voice, sharp and going a little high. 'Who's in there? What are you doing there?'

'Police,' said Major Crow. 'It's all right; come in, Ingram. Put the lights on, will you?'

After fumbling a moment on the wrong side of the door, the newcomer groped behind the Boule cabinet and switched them on. And Elliot realised that his first brief impression of

Professor Gilbert Ingram, gained in a courtyard at Pompeii, would have to be revised a little.

Professor Ingram's round, shining, amiable face, his tendency towards portliness and his somewhat bouncing movements, gave the impression that he was short and tubby. This was aided by the twinkle of a guileless-seeming blue eye, a button nose, and two tufts of dark hair ruffled out over the ears on either side of his baldness. He had a trick of lowering his head and looking up with a quizzical expression which matched his attitude towards life. But all this looked subdued now; subdued, and a trifle scared. His face was mottled with colour; his shirt-front, which had a deep crease, bulged out round the waistcoat like dough rising in an oven; and he brushed the fingers of his right hand together as though to remove chalk from them. Actually, Elliot saw, he was of middle height, and he was not noticeably fat.

'Reconstructing, eh?' he suggested. 'Good evening, Major. Good evening, Superintendent.'

His manner had a casual courtesy which included everybody in the flick of a smile, like the flick of a whip over a team of horses. Elliot's chief impression was of a strong and penetrating intelligence looking out of that guileless face.

'And this, I suppose,' he added hesitantly, 'is the Scotland Yard man Joe Chesney was telling me about? Good evening, Inspector.'

'Yes,' said Major Crow. He went on with some abruptness. 'Look here, you know—we're depending on you.'

'Depending on me?'

'Well, you're a professor of psychology. *You* wouldn't be fooled by tricks. You said you wouldn't. You can tell us what really happened in this damned show. Can't you?'

Professor Ingram took a quick look through the double-doors. His expression altered still more.

'I think so,' he said grimly.

'Well, there you are!' said Major Crow, with a gesture of rising argumentativeness. 'Miss Wills has told us there was some jiggery-pokery intended.'

'Oh. You've seen her?'

'Yes. And, from what we can gather, this whole show was designed as a series of traps—'

'It was more than that,' said Professor Ingram, looking him straight in the eyes. 'I happen to know it was designed to show how the chocolates at Mrs. Terry's shop were poisoned without anyone seeing the murderer do it.'

II

Second View Through the Spectacles

'She is dying.'
'Sh! There are ladies present.'

DR. EDWARD PRITCHARD,
GLASGOW, 1865

VI

TO HIDE THE ASSOCIATION OF SEVERAL NEW THOUGHTS, Elliot walked into the office before anybody commented. He switched on the green-shaded lamp over the roll-top desk there, and turned off the Photoflood bulb on the table. By contrast the ordinary light seemed feeble, but it still showed Marcus Chesney huddled in his last chair.

So? Two days before he was murdered—according to Superintendent Bostwick—Marcus Chesney had been asking the police questions about the exact size of the chocolate-box at Mrs. Terry's shop. A box of cheap chocolates lay on the table now, and had figured in the 'show.' But how?

Elliot returned to the Music Room, where Major Crow was attacking the same problem.

'But how,' inquired the Chief Constable, 'could he illustrate how somebody had poisoned the chocolates at Mrs. Terry's by having this bogey-man—whoever it was—shove a green capsule into his mouth?'

Professor Ingram lifted his shoulders slightly. His eyes remained strained when he glanced into the other room.

'I can hardly tell you that,' he pointed out. 'But, if you want my guess, Chesney meant this green-capsule incident to be only a side-line; a part of the show; perhaps not even a necessary part of it. My guess is that the real incident we were to watch was something to do with a box of chocolates in there on the table.'

'I think,' said the Chief Constable, after a pause, 'that I shall keep out of this. You carry on, Inspector.'

Elliot indicated one of the brocaded arm-chairs, and Professor Ingram sat down gingerly.

'Now, sir. Did Mr. Chesney tell you that the purpose of this performance was really to show how chocolates could be poisoned without anybody noticing it?'

'No. But he hinted at it.'

'When?'

'Shortly before the performance began. I taxed him with it. "Taxed him with it!" There's a phrase for you: it sounds like farce comedy.' Professor Ingram shuddered a little, and then his guileless look became shrewd. 'Look here, Inspector. I knew at dinner there was something queer about Chesney's sudden and headlong desire to give us a show. The subject seemed to be introduced casually, and to work up by an argument among us to his final challenge. But he meant to introduce that challenge all along. He meant it before ever we sat down at the dinner table. I could see that; and young Emmet was grinning like a wolf whenever he thought nobody saw him.'

'Well, sir?'

'Well! That is why I objected to his postponing the show until so late, and taking nearly three mortal hours after dinner before he was willing to get down to business. I will interfere with no man's vanities, which I hold are sacred things; but that seemed to be carrying it too far. I said frankly, "What's the game? Because there is one." He said to me privately, "Watch with care, and you may see how Mrs. Terry's chocolates were poisoned, but I'm betting you won't."'

'He had a theory?'

'Evidently.'

'A theory which he was going to prove in front of all of you?'

'Evidently.'

'And,' asked Elliot casually, 'he suspected who the poisoner was?'

Professor Ingram glanced up briefly. There was a thick shade of worry in his eyes; if the term had been applicable to so genial a face, you might almost have said that he looked haunted.

'That was the impression I gathered,' he admitted.

'But didn't he tell you—give you any hint?'

'No. Otherwise it would have spoiled the show.'

'And you think the poisoner killed him because he knew?'

'It seems probable, yes.' Professor Ingram stirred in his chair. 'Tell me, Inspector. Are you an intelligent man? A man of some understanding?' He smiled curtly. 'One moment, please. Let me explain why I ask that. With all due deference to our good friend Bostwick, I hardly think that this affair so far has been handled in a way that will do any credit to him.'

Major Crow's expression became bleak and stiff.

'The Superintendent,' he said slowly, 'has been trying to do his duty—'

'Oh, stop that balderdash,' said Professor Ingram without offence. 'Of course he has. God help us, so have all of us! But doing our duty doesn't mean getting at the truth; sometimes it means just the reverse. I don't say there is any police plot against Marjorie Wills. I know there isn't, though it seems a pity that the niece of a friend of mine cannot even walk down the High Street without danger of having mud thrown in her face by the very children. What real effort has been made to solve the problem of those poisoned chocolates? What approach has been made to it? What kind of crime is it? *Why* were those chocolates poisoned at Mrs. Terry's?'

He struck the arm of the chair.

'Superintendent Bostwick,' he went on, 'supports the soothing, sweeping doctrine that loonies are loonies; and there you are. And to bolster up their accusation against Marjorie, they cite the parallel case—a fine parallel, by gad!—of Christiana Edmunds.'

Major Crow did not comment. Professor Ingram went on:

'Similar? There never were two cases more wildly dissimilar, on the only grounds that are important: motive. Christiana Edmunds was mad, if you like, but she had as sound a motive as most murderers. This young lady, in the Brighton of 1871, fell violently in love with a married doctor who gave her no encouragement. She first attempted unsuccessfully to poison the doctor's wife with strychnine. It was discovered; she was forbidden the house, and went away in a frenzy. To show that she was innocent, as she claimed—to prove there was a poisoner at work in the town, who could not be Miss Christiana Edmunds—she conceived the idea of doctoring the chocolate creams in a sweet-shop, and killing people wholesale. Very well; where's the parallel? Has anything like that ever been suggested about Marjorie? In heaven's name, where is the motive? On the contrary, her own *fiancé*, after coming to Sodbury Cross and hearing what is being said about her, is on the point of getting cold feet and slipping away.'

At this point Professor Ingram's expression was what can only be called cherubically murderous, emphasised by the crackling of his shirt-front. He laughed a little, and grew more quiet.

'Never mind,' he said. '*You* were asking the questions.'

'Has Miss Wills,' Elliot asked unexpectedly, 'ever been engaged to anybody before?'

'Why do you ask that?'

'Has she, sir?'

Again Ingram gave him that brief, indecipherable glance. 'No, not that I am aware of. I believe Wilbur Emmet was and is intensely fond of her. But Wilbur's red nose and his general—I am sorry—his general unattractiveness would hardly recommend him, even if Marcus had favoured it. I hope I am speaking in confidence?'

Here Major Crow intervened. 'Chesney, I am told,' he observed in a colourless voice, 'used to discourage *all* possible suitors from coming here to see her.'

Professor Ingram hesitated.

'In a sense that is true. What he called caterwauling disturbed his smooth life. He didn't exactly discourage them, but—'

'I was wondering,' said Major Crow, 'why this boy Marjorie met abroad got Chesney's approval so easily.'

'You mean,' the professor spoke bluntly, 'you mean Chesney was becoming anxious to get her off his hands?'

'I did not say that.'

'My friend, the devil you didn't. In any case you're wrong. Marcus liked young Harding; the boy has prospects; and his exaggerated deference towards Marcus may have helped. But may I ask why we are arguing about this? Whatever else is true or false in this world'—here Professor Ingram's shirt-front gave a sharp crackle—'it is absolutely certain that Marjorie had nothing to do with killing her uncle.'

Again it was as though the temperature of the room altered. Elliot took charge.

'You know what Miss Wills thinks about it herself, sir?'

'Thinks about it?'

'That someone knocked out Mr. Emmet, played Mr. Emmet's part, and used a poisoned capsule in the performance?'

Ingram looked at him curiously. 'Yes. That seems the most feasible explanation, doesn't it?'

'Consequently, some person overheard what plans Mr. Chesney and Mr. Emmet were making in this room after dinner? Some person outside the door or outside the windows?'

'I see,' murmured the professor.

For a moment there was a faint, fixed half-smile on his face. He was leaning forward, his plump fists on his knees and his elbows outspread like wings. He wore that oddly witless expression assumed by intelligent people when their thoughts turn inwards, and arrange facts with swift certainty into a pattern. Then he smiled again.

'I see,' he repeated. 'Now let me ask your questions for you, Inspector!' He waved his hand in the air, mesmerically. 'Your next question is, "Where were you between nine-fifteen and midnight?" And, "Where were Marjorie and George Harding between nine-fifteen and midnight?" But you'll go further. "Where were all of you at the time the performance took place?" That's the important thing. "Is it possible that one of you spectators could have slipped out in the dark, and played the part of the sinister bogey in the top-hat?" That's what you want to know, isn't it?'

Major Crow's eyes narrowed.

'Yes,' he said.

'It is a fair question,' replied Professor Ingram comfortably. 'And it deserves a fair answer, which is this. I will swear before any court in the world that not one of us left this room during the performance.'

'H'm. Pretty strong statement, isn't it?'

'Not at all.'

'You know how dark it was in here?'

'I know perfectly well how dark it was. In the first place, with that Photoflood lamp blazing in the other room, not quite so dark as you seem to think. In the second place, I have other reasons, which I hope my companions will corroborate. In fact, we might ask them.'

He got up from his chair, and gestured towards the hall door like a showman, as Marjorie and George Harding came in.

And Elliot inspected the new *fiancé*.

At Pompeii he had seen only the back of Harding's head, and he was now vaguely irritated with the full view. George Harding could not have been more than twenty-five or twenty-six. He had a good-natured, straightforward, hearty manner; he was without self-consciousness, and moved among people as naturally as a cat among ornaments on a sideboard. He was rather handsome in a somewhat Southern European manner: black crinkled hair that looked wiry, broad face, and dark eyes of singular expressiveness. It was this appearance which Elliot found difficult to reconcile with his hearty minor-public-school manner. He was probably welcome company anywhere, and knew it.

Then Harding caught sight of Marcus Chesney's body beyond the folding doors, and his air became full of solicitude.

'Could we have those doors closed?' he asked, taking Marjorie's arm under his. 'I mean, do you mind?'

Marjorie disengaged her arm, to his evident surprise.

'It's quite all right,' she said, looking straight at Elliot nevertheless.

Elliot closed the doors.

'Marjorie told me you wanted to see me,' Harding went on, looking round in the friendliest possible way. His face clouded. 'Just tell me what I can do to help. All I can say is that this is a rotten bad business, and—oh, you know!'

(Now we are seeing him through Elliot's eyes, not necessarily as he actually was; and therefore it would be unfair to stress the sour impression made on Elliot by this straight-from-the-shoulder speech, and the straightforward gesture with which he accompanied it. To Major Crow and Superintendent Bostwick, who liked him, Harding sounded quite sincere.)

Elliot indicated a chair.

'You're Mr. Harding?'

'That's right,' agreed the other, now friendly as a puppy and as anxious to please. 'Marjorie says you want us all to tell what happened here when—well, when the poor old boy got his.'

'He wants more than that,' chuckled Professor Ingram. 'He suspects that you or Marjorie or I—'

'Just a moment, sir,' said Elliot sharply. He turned to the others. 'Sit down, please.' A shade of uneasiness went through the room. 'Yes, we shall want a statement. But I want to ask you some other questions, and the replies may be more valuable than any statement. You knew that Mr. Chesney had prepared a list of questions for you about this show of his?'

It was Marjorie who answered, after a pause.

'Yes, of course. I told you so.'

'If you were asked those same questions now, could you answer them accurately?'

'Yes, but look here,' said Harding. 'I can do better than that, if you want to know what happened. I've got a film of it.'

'A colour-film?'

Harding blinked.

'Colour? Good Lord, no! Just the ordinary kind. A colour-film for indoor photography, particularly in that light, would be—'

'Then I'm afraid it won't help us with some of our troubles,' said Elliot. 'Where is the film now?'

'I shoved it inside that radio-gramophone over there when all the row started.'

He seemed disappointed by the way Elliot took his announcement, as though there were an anti-climax hovering somewhere. Elliot went to the gramophone and raised the lid. A leather camera-case, its flap open and the camera inside it, lay on the green-felt-covered disc of the gramophone. Behind him the three witnesses had taken chairs rather awkwardly, and were looking at him; he could see them reflected in the glass of a picture hanging on the wall over the gramophone. He also caught (in the glass) the puzzled, inquiring glance which Major Crow directed towards Superintendent Bostwick.

'I have the list here,' Elliot explained, taking it out of his pocket-book. 'They are better questions than any I could ask, because they're expressly designed to cover the important points.'

'What points?' asked Marjorie quickly.

'That's what we're here to find out. I'm going to ask each of you the same question in turn, and I should like each of you to answer it as fully as you can.'

Professor Ingram raised his almost invisible eyebrows. 'Aren't you afraid, Inspector, that we may have concocted a story for you?'

'I shouldn't advise you to, sir. And I don't think you have, because Dr. Chesney tells me you've already contradicted each other all over the place. If you go back on that now, I'll learn about it. Now, then: do you honestly think you can live up to your boasts and answer these questions with absolute accuracy?'

'Yes,' said Professor Ingram with a curious smile.

'Yes!' said Marjorie fiercely.

'I'm not sure,' said Harding. 'I was more concentrated on getting everything in the picture than keeping tabs on details of it. But all the same, I think so, yes. In my business we've got to keep our eyes—'

'What is your business, Mr. Harding?'

'I'm a research chemist,' replied Harding, as bluntly as though he were uttering a defiance. 'But never mind that. Fire away.'

Elliot closed the lid of the gramophone and spread out his notebook on it. It was as though a conductor had lifted his baton, a wheel had begun to spin, a curtain had parted at the rising of the lights. In his bones and soul, Elliot knew that this list of questions contained all the clues to the truth— provided he had the wit to grasp not only the significance of the answer, but the significance of the question.

'The first question,' he said; and there was a sharp creaking from the chairs as his listeners braced themselves.

VII

'THE FIRST QUESTION. *WAS THERE A BOX ON THE TABLE? If so, describe it.* Miss Wills?'

Marjorie's soft mouth grew stern. She had kept her eyes fixed on Elliot, and they showed anger.

'If you say this is important, I'll answer,' she told him. 'But this is rather ghastly, isn't it? Sitting here and asking q-questions as though this were a game, with him—' She looked towards the closed door, and away again.

'It's important, Miss Wills. *Was there a box on the table? If so, describe it.*'

'Of course there was a box on the table. It was on Uncle Marcus's right-hand side, towards the front. A two-pound box of Henrys' Chocolate Caramels. I didn't see the label, because I was sitting down, but I know they were Henrys' Chocolate Caramels because the box had a design of bright green flowers on it.'

George Harding turned round and looked at her.

'Nonsense,' he said.

'What is nonsense?'

'The colour of the flowers,' said Harding. 'I don't know about the chocolates, and I agree it was a two-pound box, and it had flowers on it. But the flowers were not bright green. They were dark blue. Definitely blue.'

Marjorie's expression did not alter; she turned her head round with an arrogant and almost classic grace. 'Darling angel,' she muttered, 'to-night has been horrible enough already without your getting on my nerves and making me want to scream. Please don't. Those flowers were green. Men are always mistaking green for blue. Don't, don't, don't—not to-night.'

'Oh, all right, if you say so,' said Harding, between contrition and sulkiness. 'No, I'm damned if it is!' he added, hopping up. 'We're supposed to be telling the truth. Those flowers were blue, dark blue, and—'

'Darling angel—'

'Just a moment,' Elliot interposed sharply. 'Professor Ingram should be able to settle this. Well, sir? Which is right?'

'They are both right,' answered Ingram, crossing his plump legs in leisurely fashion. 'And consequently, at the same time, they are both wrong.'

'But we can't *both* be wrong!' protested Harding.

'I think you can,' said Professor Ingram politely. He turned to Elliot. 'Inspector, I am telling you the literal truth. I could explain now, but I should prefer to wait. One of the later questions will explain what I mean.'

Elliot raised his head.

'How do you know what the later questions will be, sir?' he asked.

There was a silence which seemed to creep out and extend itself as though every corner of the room were being filled. You almost imagined that you could hear, through closed doors, the clock ticking in the office.

'I do not know, of course,' Professor Ingram returned blandly. 'I am merely anticipating a question which is certain to appear later in the list.'

'You haven't seen this list before, sir?'

'I have not. Inspector, for the love of heaven try not to tangle me up with trifles at a moment like this. I am an old war-horse, an old trickster, an old showman. These tricks are old stuff: I have tried them out myself on a thousand of my classes. I know exactly how they work. But, just because I can't be deceived by them, don't fall into the error that I am trying to deceive you. If you go on with that list, you will see exactly what I mean.'

'It was green,' said Marjorie, with her half-closed eyes fixed on a corner of the ceiling. 'It was green, green, *green*. Please go on.'

Elliot picked up his pencil.

'The second question, then. *What objects did I pick up from the table? In what order?* What objects,' he translated, 'did Mr. Chesney pick up from the table when he first sat down, and in what order did he pick them up. Miss Wills?'

Marjorie spoke promptly.

'I've already told you that. When he sat down he picked up a pencil, and pretended to write with it on the blotter, and put it down. Then he picked up a pen, and pretended to write with that. He put it down just before the thing in the top-hat came in.'

'What do you say, Mr. Harding?'

'Yes, that's true,' admitted Harding. 'At least, the first part of it is. He first picked up a pencil—a bluish or blackish kind of pencil—and put it down. But the second object wasn't a pen. It was another pencil: about the same colour, but not as long.'

Again Marjorie turned her head round. 'George,' she said, with no change in her voice, 'are you doing this deliberately, to torment me? Please, I want to know. Must you take me up on every single thing I say?' Then she cried out: 'I *know* it was a pen. I saw the little nib, and the head of the pen; it was blue or black; a small pen. Please don't go on trying to—'

'Oh, if you put it like that,' said Harding, with a kind of hurt superciliousness. He turned round his 'expressive' dark eyes on her; and, to Elliot's supreme annoyance, her expression changed and grew anxious. In Elliot's mind was a Picture of a Pair of Lovers, in which Harding's boyish charm spread its tyranny over an intelligent but adoring woman, and played the very devil.

'I'm sorry,' observed Marjorie. 'All the same, it was a pen.'

'Pencil.'

'What do you say, Professor Ingram. Pen or pencil?'

'As a matter of fact,' replied the professor, 'it was neither.'

'Goddelmighty!' whispered Major Crow, growing suddenly human.

Professor Ingram held up his hand.

'Don't you see it?' he inquired. 'Aren't you beginning to understand that all these things are tricks and traps? What else did you expect?' He sounded mildly irritated. 'Marcus simply set one of the ordinary traps for you, and you tumbled into it. First of all—as you quite rightly say—he picked up an ordinary pencil and pretended to write with it. That prepared your mind. He then picked up what was neither a pen nor a pencil (though in size and shape not unlike the pencil), and pretended to write with that. You immediately suffered from the psychological illusion that you had seen either a pen or a pencil. Of course it was nothing of the sort.'

'What was it, then?' demanded Elliot.

'I don't know.'

'But—'

Ingram's guileless eye twinkled. 'Steady, Inspector. Whoa!' he suggested, in somewhat un-professorial tones. 'I guaranteed to tell you where the trick lay. I guaranteed to spot what was wrong. But I did not guarantee to tell you *what* he picked up—and I confess I don't know.'

'But can't you describe it?'

'To a certain extent, yes.' The professor seemed badly bothered. 'It was something like a pen, but narrower and much smaller; dark blue in colour, I think. Marcus had some difficulty in picking it up, I remember.'

'Yes, sir, but what kind of object looks like that?'

'I don't know. That's what bothers me. It—stop!' Here Ingram's hands closed very firmly round the arms of the chair, and he held himself poised as though he were going to jump up. Then a wave of relief or some other emotion flooded over his face; he relaxed with a kind of 'whoosh!' and stared at them. 'I've got it,' he added. 'I know what it was now.'

'Well, sir?'

'It was a blow-pipe dart.'

'What?'

'I think so,' the professor told them, as though some huge hurdle were surmounted. 'We had some in the Natural History Museum at the University. They were under three inches long, thin slivers of wood, blackish, sharp-tipped. South American or Malayan or Bornese or something of the sort; my notions of geography have always been muddled.'

Elliot looked at Marjorie. 'Had your uncle any blow-pipe darts in the house, Miss Wills?'

'No, certainly not. At least, not that I ever heard of.'

Major Crow intervened, with interest. 'You mean,' he said to Professor Ingram, 'a poisoned dart?'

'No, no, no, not necessarily. We have here, I suspect, a beautiful example of how suggestion can run away with the imagination until none of us can remember what we did see. In a moment we shall have somebody remembering that he saw poison on the dart, and then we shall be nowhere. Control yourselves!' said Ingram. He got his breath, and made a spreading gesture. 'All I said was that I saw something which Looked Like a blow-pipe dart. Is that clear? Then go on with the questions.'

George Harding nodded.

'Yes,' he agreed—and on his face Elliot surprised a curious look as Harding glanced at the professor. It was gone in a flash, nor could Elliot interpret it. 'We don't seem to be getting a great deal further. Fire away with the questions.'

Elliot hesitated. The new suggestion disquieted him, and he would have liked to attack it. But that could wait.

'The next question,' he glanced at his list, 'presumably refers to the entrance of the muffled-up figure through the French window. Take it as you like, though. *What was the time?*'

'Midnight,' said Marjorie promptly.

'About midnight,' admitted George Harding.

'To be completely exact,' said Professor Ingram, fitting the palms of his hands together, 'it was just one minute to midnight.'

Here he paused as though inquiringly, and Elliot put the query he seemed to expect.

'Yes, sir. But I've got a question of my own. Do you actually know that it was one minute to midnight—from your own watch, that is—or do you only know it was one minute to midnight by that clock on the mantelpiece in the office? I know the clock is right now; but was it necessarily right then?'

Professor Ingram spoke dryly.

'The question had occurred to me,' he said. 'I wondered whether Marcus might have altered the clock and given a false time to stare us in the face, so that we should swear to it later. But I claim fair play.' Again he looked annoyed. 'A trick of that sort would not come within the rules. This was to be an observation test. Marcus ordered the lights turned out, and consequently we could not see our own watches. Therefore, if he gives us a clock to judge by, the only way we can judge time is by that clock. I regarded that as in the agreement. I can tell you the various times when things happened by that clock. But I can't tell you whether it had the correct time to start with.'

Marjorie said:

'Well, *I* can. Of course the clock was right.'

She spoke with violence and surprise and perplexity. It was as though she had expected every development except this, or as though the hopelessness of making anyone see reason had driven her even beyond weariness.

'I have the best of reasons for knowing,' she informed them. 'Oh, it isn't a question of observation, my observation! I can prove it. Easily. Of course the clock was right. But what difference does it make anyway?'

'It might make all the difference,' said Major Crow, 'to the alibi of somebody who wasn't here.'

'Joe Chesney,' murmured Professor Ingram, and whistled. 'I beg your pardon,' he added formally.

As once before he had been able to reach everyone with the flick of a smile, so he now (evidently by a slip of the tongue) reached everyone with a flick of something else altogether. Elliot wondered how the dictionary defined the word 'suggestion.' Whatever else it might be, it was a stirring of the waters.

'Uncle Joe?' cried Marjorie. 'What about him?'

'Go on with the questions,' invited the professor, and gave her a reassuring grin.

Elliot, after making a quick note, decided to increase the tempo.

'We can thrash out these things later, if you don't mind. Just give me the answers as briefly as you can. Next: *What was the height of the person who entered by the French window?*'

'Six feet,' replied Marjorie instantly. 'Anyway, he was just the same height as Wilbur, and we all know Wilbur's height. Just the same height as Wilbur and Uncle J—' She stopped.

'Six feet is about right,' decided Harding, after reflection. 'If anything I'd have said a bit more than that, but it may have been the effect of that wild-looking hat.'

Professor Ingram cleared his throat.

'Nothing, I know,' he said, 'is more exasperating than to be constantly contradicted over these points—'

And under this quiet exterior it was clear that tempers were getting ready to boil clear up to the roof. To this extent had the waters of suggestion been stirred. Marjorie's eyes were extraordinarily bright.

'Oh, I can't stand this! Surely you're not going to tell us he was short and fat?'

'No, my dear. Easy now.' Professor Ingram looked at Elliot. 'Inspector, here is the answer. The person who came in by that window was about five feet nine inches tall—about the height, say, of Mr. Harding or myself. Or else (mark this) he was a man of six feet walking with his knees bent under that long coat to suggest a somewhat shorter person. In any case, his height was roughly five feet nine.'

There was a silence.

Major Crow, who had fitted on a pair of shell-rimmed spectacles which somewhat destroyed his military appearance, wiped a hand across his forehead. He had been making notes on the back of an envelope.

'Look here,' he began.

'Yes?'

'Now I ask you,' said the Chief Constable with angry reasonableness, 'I ask you, man to man, what kind of an answer is that? Either he was five feet nine inches, or else possibly he might have been six feet. Look here, Ingram. It strikes me you're the one who's been planting notions in everybody's head. Wherever it's possible to contradict somebody, you've contradicted 'em. Would you like to hear the score so far?'

'With pleasure.'

'Well, you all agree that there was a two-pound chocolate-box on the table, and that the first of the two objects Chesney picked up was a pencil. But look at the rest of it. I've scored my own questions.'

He flung the envelope across to Professor Ingram, who inspected it and then passed round the following remarkable document:

WHAT I SAW

What was the colour of the chocolate-box?	MISS WILLS: It was green. MR. HARDING: It was blue. PROF. INGRAM: It was both.
What was the second object Chesney picked up?	MISS WILLS: A pen. MR. HARDING: A pencil. PROF. INGRAM: A blow-pipe dart.
What was the time?	MISS WILLS: Midnight. MR. HARDING: About midnight. PROF. INGRAM: One minute to 12.
How tall was the bloke in the hat?	MISS WILLS: Six feet. MR. HARDING: Six feet. PROF. INGRAM: Five feet nine.

'The only rough agreement there,' Major Crow went on, 'is about the time. And that's probably the most thoroughly wrong of the lot.'

Professor Ingram got to his feet.

'I don't think I quite understand you, Major,' he said. 'You ask me, as an expert witness, to tell you what really happened. You expect discrepancies. You want to find discrepancies.

And then for some reason you seem annoyed with me when I point them out to you.'

'I know, and that's all very well,' argued Major Crow, pointing the envelope at him. 'But what about that business of the chocolate-box? A box may be green or it may be blue; but it ruddy well can't be both, and that's what you say it is. Now it may interest you to know'—here, despite Elliot's and Bostwick's frantic signals, he tossed police discretion overboard—'it may interest you to know that the box in that room is *blue*. Blue flowers on it. And the only other object on that table is a flattish pencil. There's no sign of any second object: either a pen, or another pencil, or a blow-pipe dart. One blue box of chocolates; one pencil; nothing else. May I ask what you've got to say to that?'

Professor Ingram sat down again, wearing a satirical smile.

'Only,' he said, 'that, given half a chance, I shall explain it in just one moment.'

'All right, all right,' growled Major Crow, lifting his hands as though he were beginning a salaam. 'Have it your own way, and explain when you like; I'll retire. Carry on, Inspector. Sorry I butted in. It's your show.'

And, during the next few minutes, Elliot began to feel that their disputes were at an end. The next two questions and half of the following one were answered with almost complete agreement. These questions, with regard to the goblin from the French window, were: *Describe this person's costume. What was he carrying in his right hand? Describe this object. Describe his actions.*

Out of it emerged a picture of that grotesque dummy-figure which seemed to have made so powerful an impression on them all. From top-hat through brown wool muffler, sun-glasses, raincoat, and black trousers with evening-shoes, not a detail was missed by anyone. Each person correctly described the black bag, painted with the white letters *R. H. Nemo, M.D.*, and carried in the visitor's right hand. The only new detail was that the visitor had been wearing rubber gloves.

This unanimity disturbed and puzzled Elliot, until he remembered that all of the witnesses had had more than a fair opportunity to study the costume. Most of Nemo's properties, including the black bag, had been flung down outside the office window. The witnesses had not only seen them during the performance. They had seen them afterwards, when they went out to look for Wilbur Emmet.

Yet, even so, they had missed nothing of the visitor's actions on the stage. The figure of the black-blind Nemo, bowing and nodding under his own huge shadow in the white light, seemed to fill the screen of their minds like a nightmare. They described his entrance. They described how, at an incautious jeer of George Harding's from the audience, Nemo had turned round and looked at them. They described how he had put down his bag on the table, turning his back to them. They then told how he had gone to the right of the table, taken a pill-box out of his pocket, extracted a capsule, and—

But where in all the raving blazes was the clue?

That was what Elliot wanted to know. He was nearly at the end of the list, and so far he could see nothing to give him a lead. There had been contradictions among the witnesses, yes; but how would these help?

'We're getting on,' he told them. 'So we'll wind up this question. *Did he remove anything from the table?*'

Three voices spoke almost at once.

'No,' said Marjorie.

'No,' said George Harding.

'Yes,' said Professor Ingram.

In the uproar that followed, Harding spoke firmly. 'Sir, I'll swear he didn't. He never touched that table. He—'

'Of course he didn't,' said Marjorie. 'Besides, what could he have removed? The only thing that seems to be gone is one pen—or pencil, or blow-pipe dart, whatever you two call it—and I know he didn't take that. Uncle Marcus put it down on the blotter in front of him. And that thing in the top-hat never went near the blotter in front of Uncle Marcus. So what could he have removed?'

Professor Ingram called for silence. He looked a trifle grim now.

'That,' he said, 'is what I have patiently been trying to tell you. To be specific: He removed a green-flowered box of Henrys' Chocolate Caramels, and for it he substituted the blue-flowered box of Henrys' Chocolate Peppermint Creams which is there now. You wanted the literal truth. There you are. Don't ask me how he did it! When he put down his black bag on the table, he put it down in front of the green box. When he took the bag away again, and walked out of the room, the box on the table was blue. I repeat: Don't ask me how he switched the boxes. I am not a conjuror. But I think that the answer to the problem of several very ugly poisonings is contained in that little action. I suggest you exercise your wits on it. I also trust that this removes some of Major Crow's doubts as to my sanity or good faith; and, before any more tempers are lost this evening, can anyone oblige me with a cigarette?'

VIII

WHETHER OR NOT PROFESSOR INGRAM GOT HIS cigarette, Elliot never knew. For the explanation of some of this sleight-of-hand had suddenly come to him.

'Excuse me; back in a moment,' he said. And, moving round the piano, he went out through one of the French windows.

As an afterthought he closed the thick velvet curtains behind him. It was colder here, in the narrow aisle of grass between the house and the spectral yellow chestnut trees. It was also darker, now that some lights were dimmed and only an ordinary bulb burned in the office. He felt the effect of that dead hour of the night when flesh and bone seem brittle. He also thought he heard a bell ringing faintly somewhere. But he paid no attention to it, for his attention was concentrated on Dr. Nemo's properties lying outside the office windows.

That black satchel—

Now he knew why its appearance had seemed vaguely familiar. Larger than a doctor's medicine-case, though of much the same shape, and yet not large enough for an ordinary valise. Such a bag was one of the exhibits on display in the Black Museum at Scotland Yard.

He knelt down by the bag, which stood near the hat and the raincoat. It was of varnished leather, and looked new. Dr. Nemo's name had been painted on the side, rather crudely, with a stencil. Using his handkerchief, Elliot opened the bag. Inside was a two-pound box of Henrys' Chocolate Caramels, designed with bright green flowers.

'That's got it,' he said aloud.

This bag was the Shop-Thief's Friend. He picked it up and looked at the bottom. Originally used for conjuring entertainments, its principle had been adopted by the gentry who raid department-stores, jewellers, any shop in which valuable goods are exposed openly.

You entered a shop, carrying this innocent-looking bag. You put it down casually on the counter, while you looked at something else. But you put the bag down over what you wanted to steal. The bottom was equipped with the conjuror's 'spring-grip' device, which snapped up into the bag what lay underneath. You then—having made no suspicious move of any sort—picked up your bag and left the shop.

Dr. Nemo's genial course became clear. He had entered the office, put his bag on the table, and, when doing so, had turned his back to the audience. He had put down the spring-grip bag not in front of the green box, but on top of it. The bag would deal with much heavier objects than a comparatively small and light chocolate-box. In the deep pocket of his raincoat he had a blue box of chocolate peppermints. Either while bending over to put down the bag, or when bending over to pick it up again, he had slipped the other box behind the satchel under cover of turning his back. Before an already be-dazzled and flurried audience, it would require no great skill. And all this had been done with Marcus Chesney's aid, at Marcus Chesney's direction, as a part of Marcus Chesney's scheme to trick the witnesses wherever they turned their eyes...

But how did this fact help towards a solution of this crime, or of the crime at the sweet-shop? Did it mean that at Mrs. Terry's one whole box of chocolates had been substituted for another?

'Hoy!' whispered a voice.

Elliot jumped. It was a hoarse voice, whispering fiercely, and it came from directly above his head. He peered up, to see Dr. Joseph Chesney's face looking down at him from a window on the floor above. Doctor Joe was leaning so far out of the window that Elliot wondered whether that great weight would come tumbling down like a laundry-bag.

'Are you all deaf down there?' whispered Doctor Joe. 'Don't you hear the doorbell ringing? Why don't somebody answer it? It's been ringing for five minutes. Curse it all, I can't do everything. I've got a patient here—'

Elliot woke up. That, of course, would be the police-surgeon, the photographer and fingerprint-man, who had to be summoned from twelve miles away.

'And—hoy!' roared Doctor Joe.

'Yes?'

'Send Marjorie up here, will you? He's calling for her.'

Elliot looked up quickly. 'Is he conscious? Could I see him?'

A rusty, hairy fist, its loose sleeve dangling, was shaken at him from the window. Illuminated from below, Doctor Joe's gingery beard had an aspect almost Mephistophelian.

'No, my lad, he's not conscious; not in the way you mean. And you can't see him to-night, or to-morrow, or maybe for weeks or months or years. Got that? And send Marjorie up here. These maids are no good. One of 'em drops things, and the other's hiding in bed. Oh, for God's sake—!'

The head was withdrawn.

Very slowly Elliot gathered up Dr. Nemo's properties. The distant ringing had ceased. A chilly wind was beginning to stir at the turn of the night; it moved in the tattered leaves; it brought up from the earth the rich scent and decay of autumn; and then, as at the insistence of the breeze or the opening of a door, it brought another and sweeter odour. It was like the faint scent which seemed to pervade the house itself. Then Elliot remembered, somewhere close, half an acre of green-houses in the darkness. It was the scent of the peach tree, the almond tree, whose fruit ripens between July and November, the almond tree of bitter almonds, haunting Bellegarde.

He carried Dr. Nemo's properties into the office as the office door (to the hall) opened, and Superintendent Bostwick brought in two newcomers whom he introduced as Dr. West and Sergeant Matthews. Major Crow followed them. Matthews was given the routine instructions as to fingerprints and photographs, and Dr. West bent over Marcus Chesney's body.

Major Crow looked at Elliot.

'Well, Inspector?' he asked. 'Why did you decide to dash off all of a sudden? And what did you find?'

'I've found how the chocolate-boxes were exchanged, sir,' said Elliot, and explained.

The other was impressed. 'Neat,' he conceded. 'Devilish neat. But even so—look here, where did Chesney get a trick bag like that?'

'You can buy them at some of the magical supply houses in London.'

'You mean he sent away specially for it?'

'Looks like it, sir.'

Major Crow went over and inspected the bag. 'Which would mean,' he reflected, 'that he's had this performance in mind for some little time. You know, Inspector'—he seemed to resist an impulse to give the bag a hearty kick—'the more and more we go on, the more and more important this confounded show becomes; and the less and less it seems to help us. Where are we? What have we got? Wait! Are there any more questions in Chesney's list?'

'Yes, sir. Three more.'

'Then go in there and get on with it,' said the Chief Constable, giving a bitter glance towards the closed double-doors. 'But before you go, I want to ask you whether you've noticed something that's struck me particularly in all this flummery.'

'Yes?'

Major Crow took up his stance. He extended a bony wrist and forefinger as though he were uttering a denunciation. 'There's some jiggery-pokery about that clock,' he declared.

They looked at it. Dr. West had turned on the blazing white light so as to look at the body, and again the derisive white face of the clock, with its brass trimmings and marble frame, stared back at them from the mantelpiece. The time was twenty minutes to two.

'Hullo! I've got to get home,' observed Major Crow suddenly. 'But anyway—look at it. Suppose Chesney altered that clock? He could have done it before the show. Then, when the show was over (you remember?) he closed those double-doors on them, and didn't go into the Music Room until Ingram rapped on the doors and told him to come out for a curtain-call. During that time he could have altered the clock back to the right time. Couldn't he?'

Elliot was doubtful.

'I suppose he could, sir. If he wanted to.'

'Of course he could. Nothing easier.' Major Crow went to the mantelpiece, edging behind the dead man's chair. He turned the clock round, bumping it a little, until its back was towards them. 'You see those two gadgets? One is the key you wind the clock by. The other is the head of the little pin you twist round to alter the position of the hands—hullo!'

He stared, bending closer, and Elliot joined him. There, true enough, was the small brass key in the back of the clock. But where the other pin or spindle should have been there was only a tiny round hole.

'The pin to set the hands has been broken off,' said Elliot, 'and broken off inside the outer case of the clock.'

He bent closer. Inside the microscopic hole he could just see a microscopic bright stump, and there was a fresh scratch round the hole on the somewhat grimy metal back of the clock.

'It's been damaged recently,' he explained. 'That's probably what Miss Wills meant when she said she was certain the clock was right. You see, sir? Until a clockmaker gets at this, nobody can alter the position of the hands even if he tries to.'

Major Crow stared at it.

'Nonsense,' he said. 'Nothing easier. Like this.'

He turned the clock round again with its face outwards. Opening the round glass door protecting the face of the clock, he laid hold of the hands.

'All you've got to do,' he continued, 'is simply push—'

'*Steady on, sir!*' said Elliot.

Even Major Crow left off, and knew himself beaten. The metal hands were too delicate. To attempt to push them in either direction was only to bend them in half or break them off; quite plainly, their position could not be altered by the fraction of a second. Elliot stood back. He began to grin in spite of himself. The hands continued their derisive course, the metal screw holding them fast winked back at him, and the ticking of the clock touched in him such a deep inner chord of amusement that he almost laughed in the Chief Constable's face. Here was a symbol. He was looking at the fiction-writer's nightmare—a clock that could not be tampered with.

'So that's that,' he said.

'That is not that,' said Major Crow.

'But, sir—'

'There is some jiggery-pokery about that clock,' declared the other, with such slow and measured emphasis that he seemed to be making a vow. 'I admit I don't know what it is. But you'll see it proved before we're many hours older.'

It was at this point that the Photoflood bulb, after flaring up with a dense and smoky glare, abruptly burned itself out. It startled them all, and the green-shaded lamp over in the corner now seemed dusky by contrast. But Dr. West had already drawn back; he was an elderly man with a pince-nez, who looked tired.

'What would you like me to tell you about this?' he said to Major Crow.

'Well, what killed him?'

'It is prussic acid or one of the cyanides. I will do a post-mortem in the morning and let you know.'

'"One of the cyanides?" Joe Chesney said it was cyanide.'

Dr. West looked apologetic. 'You are probably thinking of potassium cyanide. That is one of a group of cyanide salts derived from prussic acid. But I agree it is the most common.'

'Let me acknowledge my ignorance,' said Major Crow. 'I read up on strychnine for that other business, but I'm out of my depth here. Well, say someone killed Chesney with prussic acid or its cyanide derivative. Where does the stuff come from? How would you go about getting it?'

'I have some notes here,' the doctor told him, fumbling in his pocket with what can only be called a sort of slow hurry. He spoke with modest satisfaction. 'It's not often we get the opportunity to see a case of prussic-acid poisoning, you know. It is rare, very rare. I made some notes in the case of Billy Owens, and I thought I had better bring them along.'

He went on in his grateful way:

'Pure prussic acid (HCN) is almost inaccessible to the layman. On the other hand, any good chemist could easily prepare it from non-poisonous (I mean unscheduled, not on the poison-list) substances. Its salt, potassium cyanide, is used in a variety of ways. It is used in photography, as you probably know. It is sometimes used as an insecticide on fruit trees—'

'Fruit trees,' muttered Major Crow.

'It is used in electro-plating. It is used in killing-bottles—'

'What's a killing-bottle?'

'Entomology,' said the doctor. 'Catching butterflies. The painless killing-bottle contains five per cent of KCN; they can be bought at a taxidermist's. But for all these things, of course, the buyer would have to sign a poison-book.'

Elliot interposed. 'May I ask a question, doctor? It's true, isn't it, that there is prussic acid in peach-stones?'

'Yes, that is true,' agreed Dr. West, rubbing his forehead.

'And that anybody could distil prussic acid by crushing ordinary peach-stones and boiling them?'

'I have been asked that question before,' said Dr. West, rubbing his forehead still harder. 'It is certainly true. But I have estimated that to produce a lethal dose from peach-stones would require the kernels of approximately five thousand six hundred peaches. This hardly seems practicable.'

After a pause Superintendent Bostwick spoke heavily. 'That poison came from somewhere,' he pointed out.

'It did. And this time you're going to trace it,' said the Chief Constable. 'We missed the strychnine, but we're not going to miss the cyanide if we have to comb through every poison-book in England. That's your job, Superintendent. But, incidentally, doctor—you know those big green capsules, castor-oil capsules?'

'Yes?'

'Suppose you were going to give a dose of cyanide in one of those. How would you get the stuff into the capsule? A hypodermic needle?'

Dr. West reflected. 'Yes, that would be practicable. Unless too much were put in, the gelatine and the oil would contain it firmly. It would also conceal odour and taste. Nine-tenths of a grain of anhydrous prussic acid has been fatal. The pharmaceutical preparation of potassium cyanide is, of course, weaker. But two or three grains, I feel justified in saying, would do the work.'

'And how long would it take to kill?'

'I do not know the size of the dose,' observed Dr. West apologetically. 'Ordinarily, I should expect to see symptoms come on within ten seconds. Here, however, the gelatine would have to melt, and the castor-oil would retard the absorption of the poison. Let us say that it might take anything up to two minutes for the symptoms to appear strongly. For the rest, everything would depend on the size of the dose. Complete prostration would quickly follow. But death might occur in three minutes, or it might not occur for half an hour.'

'Well, that squares with what we know,' said Major Crow. He made a gesture of exasperation. 'Anyhow, Inspector, I suggest you go back there and pitch into that gang again.' He nodded malevolently towards the closed double-doors. 'Find out if they're certain that what they saw was really a castor-oil capsule. It may be another piece of hocus-pocus. Find out—oh, get the guts out of all the foolery, and then we shall know where we are.'

Elliot, glad of an opportunity to work alone, went into the Music Room and pulled shut the doors behind him. Three pairs of eyes were fixed on him.

'I won't detain you much longer to-night,' he told them pleasantly. 'But if you wouldn't mind clearing up the rest of these points?'

Professor Ingram studied him. 'One moment,' he suggested. 'Could *you* clear up a point, Inspector? Did you find out that the chocolate-boxes really were switched in the way I said?'

Elliot hesitated. 'Yes, sir, I don't mind telling you they were.'

'Ah!' said Professor Ingram, with a rich and evil satisfaction. He sat back, while Marjorie and George Harding looked at him in a puzzled way. 'I was hoping for that. Then we are already on the way towards a solution.'

Marjorie was about to speak, but Elliot gave her no chance.

'Here is Mr. Chesney's eighth question, about the man in the top-hat. *What did he give me to swallow? How long did it take me to swallow it?* You're all agreed, now, that it was a castor-oil capsule?'

'I'm positive,' answered Marjorie. 'It took two or three seconds for him to swallow it.'

'It certainly had that appearance,' Professor Ingram said more cautiously. 'And he had some difficulty in getting it down.'

'I don't know anything about these capsules,' said Harding. His face was white and restless and doubtful: Elliot wondered why. '*I* should have said it was a grape, a green grape, and I wondered why he didn't choke on it. But if you both recognised it, all right. I agree.'

Elliot switched the attack. 'We'll return to that. Now a question of very great importance. *How long was he in the room?*'

He spoke so gravely, and the satiric expression had become so broad across Ingram's face, that Marjorie hesitated.

'Is there a catch in it?' she inquired. 'You mean how long was it between the time he walked in through the French window and the time he walked out again? Certainly not very long. Two minutes, I should think.'

'Two and a half minutes,' said Harding.

'He was in the room,' said Professor Ingram, 'exactly thirty seconds. Over and over again—with such uniformity that it becomes almost boring—people will overestimate time wildly. Actually, Nemo ran little risk. You had almost no opportunity to study him, although you think you had. If you like, Inspector, I will give you the entire time-schedule of the performance, including Chesney's movements. Shall I?'

At Elliot's nod, Professor Ingram closed his eyes.

'Let's begin with the time when Chesney slipped through those doors and I turned out the lights in here. After I had turned out the lights, about twenty seconds elapsed before Chesney pulled open the doors to begin the show. Between the time Chesney opened the doors and the time Nemo entered, fully forty seconds elapsed. There is a full minute before Nemo's entrance. Nemo's part was over in thirty seconds. After his departure, Chesney sat for another thirty seconds before he flopped forward in pretended death. He rose and closed the doors again. I had some difficulty in getting the lights on: I always grope on the wrong side of the door for that infernal switch. Say another twenty seconds. But the whole performance, from extinguishing the lights to turning them on again, took just two minutes and twenty seconds.'

Marjorie looked doubtful, and Harding shrugged his shoulders. They did not contradict, but a settled rebellion had got into them. Both were looking white and tired. Marjorie shuddered a little, and her eyes were strained. Elliot knew that the spring could not be pressed much harder to-night.

'And now the final question,' he said. 'Here it is. *What person or persons spoke? What was said?*'

'I'm glad it's the last one,' observed Marjorie, swallowing. 'And this time at least I know I can't be wrong. The thing in the top-hat never spoke at all.' She faced Professor Ingram fiercely. 'You don't deny that, do you?'

'No, my dear, I don't deny it.'

'And Uncle Marcus only spoke once. It was just after the thing in the top-hat had put down that black bag on the table and walked over to the right-hand side of the table. Uncle Marcus said, "You have done now what you did before; what else will you do?"'

Harding nodded. 'That's right. "You have done now what you did before; what else will you do?" Or something like that, anyway. I won't swear to the exact order of the words.'

'And that's all that was said?' persisted Elliot.

'Absolutely everything.'

'I disagree,' said Professor Ingram.

'Oh, *damn* you,' Marjorie almost screamed. She leaped to her feet. Elliot was startled and rather shocked at the way her soft face, a face of almost Victorian placidity, could change. 'Blast your soul to hell!'

'Marjorie!' shouted Harding. Then he coughed, and began to make embarrassed gestures in Elliot's direction, like an adult who wishes to distract the attention of a baby by making faces.

'There is no need to carry on like that, my dear,' Professor Ingram told her mildly. 'I am only trying to help you. You know that.'

Marjorie stood irresolute during a few bad moments. Then tears came into her eyes, and the colour in her face gave her a very real beauty which was not even destroyed by the twitching of her mouth.

'I'm s-sorry,' she said.

'For instance,' pursued Professor Ingram, as though nothing had happened, 'it is not literally true to say that nothing else was said during the show.' He looked at Harding. '*You* spoke, you know.'

'I spoke?' repeated Harding.

'Yes. When Dr. Nemo entered, you moved forward to get a better view for your camera, and you said, "Shh! The Invisible Man!" I think that is correct?'

Harding rubbed his wiry black hair. 'Yes, sir. I may have tried to be funny. But dash it all!—the question doesn't refer to that. It only refers to what the people on the stage said, doesn't it?'

'And you,' continued Professor Ingram to Marjorie, 'you also spoke, or whispered. When Nemo was giving your uncle that castor-oil capsule, and forced back his head to tilt it down his throat, you uttered a kind of cry or sound of protest. You said or whispered, "Don't! Don't!" It was not loud, but it was distinct.'

'I don't remember saying anything,' answered Marjorie, blinking. 'But what of it?'

The professor's tone grew more easy.

'I am preparing you against Inspector Elliot's next line of attack. I tried to tell you a long time ago: He has already been wondering whether one of us three could have slipped out of here and murdered your uncle during the two minutes while the lights were out. Now, I am in a position to swear that I both saw and heard you—both of you—all the time Nemo was on the stage. I can swear you never left this room. If you are in a position to do the same for me, we shall present a triple alibi which all the weight of Scotland Yard cannot break. Are you in a position to swear it? What do you say?'

Elliot braced himself. He knew that the next few minutes would bring him to the crux of the case.

IX

THIS TIME HARDING WAS ON HIS FEET. HIS LARGE EYES—
'cow-like,' Elliot called them, having already gone through a
whole series of animals in finding his similes about Harding—
looked alarmed. He retained his mechanical expression of
good nature, nor did his deference towards authority lessen;
but his hairy hands twitched a little.

'But I was taking the picture!' he protested. 'Look, there's
the camera. Didn't you hear it going? Didn't you—'

Then he laughed, with very genuine charm. He seemed to
hope that someone would laugh with him, and was annoyed
when nobody did.

'I see,' he added, looking far away. 'I read a story once.'

'Did you, now?' inquired Professor Ingram.

'Yes,' said Harding quite seriously. 'Chap had an alibi
because they swore they could hear him working his typewriter all the time. It turned out he had a mechanical gadget
which made a noise like a typewriter when he wasn't there.
Great snakes, do you think there's something that will run a
ciné-camera for you while you're not there?'

'But that's absurd,' cried Marjorie, as though this were the last point of bedevilment. 'I *saw* you. I know you were there. Is that what you think, Inspector?'

Elliot assumed his stolidest grin.

'Miss Wills, I haven't said anything. It's the professor here who has made all the suggestions. All the same, we might consider the point, even if we only,'—he was broadly sympathetic—'clear it up. It was very dark in here, though, wasn't it?'

Professor Ingram answered him, before the others could speak.

'It was very dark for perhaps twenty seconds, up to the time Chesney opened those double-doors. Afterwards there was enough reflection thrown back from the Photoflood bulb on the far wall of the office so that it could hardly be called altogether dark. Outlines were perfectly clear, as I think my companions will tell you.'

'Just a moment, sir. How were you sitting?'

Professor Ingram got up, and carefully arranged three arm-chairs in a row about three feet apart. The chairs faced the double-doors from a distance of some eight or nine feet, so that their full distance from Marcus Chesney would have been about fifteen feet.

'Chesney arranged the chairs before we got here,' Professor Ingram explained, 'and we didn't disturb them. I sat here, on the right-hand end nearest the lights.' He laid his hand on the back of the chair. 'Marjorie was in the middle. Harding sat at the other end.'

Elliot studied the position. Then he turned to Harding.

'But what were you doing so far over to the left?' he asked. 'Couldn't you have got a better picture from the middle? From this position you couldn't have photographed Nemo as he stepped in through the window.'

Harding wiped his forehead.

'Now, I ask you: how the devil did I know what was going to happen?' he demanded, man to man. 'Mr. Chesney didn't explain what we were to look out for. He just said, "Sit there;" and I hope you don't think I was going to argue with him. Not little Georgie. I was sitting—or, rather, I was standing, about *here*; and I had a good enough view.'

'Oh, what's the good of this arguing?' said Marjorie. 'Of course he was here. I saw him move back and forth to get the picture in. And I was here. Wasn't I?'

'You were,' Professor Ingram confirmed blandly. 'I felt you.'

'Eh?' said Harding.

Professor Ingram's face grew murderous. 'I felt her presence, young man. I heard her breathe. I could have reached out and touched her. It is true she is wearing a dark dress; but she has, you observe, a very white skin, and her hands and face were as plain in the dark as the front of your shirt.' Clearing his throat, he turned to Elliot. 'What I am trying to tell you, Inspector, is that I will swear neither of these two left the room at any time. Harding was always at the corner of my eye. Marjorie was within touch of me. Now, if they will say the same of me—?'

He inclined his forehead politely, keenly, towards Marjorie. His manner, Elliot felt, was that of a physician testing a patient's pulse; and there was a quiet concentration in his face.

'Of course you were,' cried Marjorie.

'You're sure of that?' Elliot insisted.

'I'm perfectly sure of it. I saw his shirt and his bald head,' she went on with emphasis, 'and—oh, I saw everything! I heard him breathe too. Weren't you ever at a spiritist séance? Wouldn't you have known if anybody had left the group?'

'What do you say, Mr. Harding?'

Harding hesitated.

'Well, to tell you the truth, I had my eye glued on the view-finder most of the time. So I didn't get much chance to look about. Hold on, though!' He struck his fist into the palm of his left hand, and such an expression of relief came into his face that it was as though a wheel went round behind his eyes. 'Haa! Now wait: don't hurry me. Just after this top-hatted bloke stepped out of the picture, I looked up, and stepped back, and shut off the camera. I bumped into a chair as I stepped back; I looked round'—he was following this with turns of his wrist—'and I could see Marjorie right enough. I could see her eyes shine, in a way. That isn't scientifically correct, but you know what I mean. Of course I knew she was there all the time, because I'd heard her speak out and say "Don't." But I also saw her; and anyway,' his broad grin cheered the room, 'you can be ruddy well certain *she's* no more five feet nine inches tall than she is six feet. What's got into us, anyway?'

'And did you see me?' questioned Professor Ingram.

'Eh?' said Harding, whose eyes were on Marjorie.

'I say, did you see me in the dark?'

'Oh, definitely. I think you were trying to look at your watch, bending over it. You were there, all right.'

Harding had regained such an extraordinary sparkle and animation that it was as though he were about to strut up and down with his thumbs hooked in his waistcoat.

But Elliot had begun to feel that he was groping in an even worse fog. The case was a psychological morass. Yet he was willing to swear that these people were telling the truth, or thought they were telling the truth.

'You see before you,' explained Professor Ingram, 'a corporate alibi of truly remarkable soundness. It is impossible for one of us to have committed this crime. That is the bedrock on which you must build your case, whatever it is. Of course, you may choose to doubt our stories; but nothing is easier to test. Reconstruct! Sit us down here in a row, as we were before; turn out the lights; turn on that Photoflood bulb in the other room; and you will see for yourself that it is absolutely impossible for any of us to have left the room without being seen.'

'I'm afraid we can't do that, sir, unless you've got another Photoflood bulb,' said Elliot. 'The other one has just burned out. Also—'

'But—!' exclaimed Marjorie. She checked herself, staring with puzzled eyes at the closed doors.

'—also,' continued Elliot, 'you may not be the only persons with alibis. There's one thing in particular I'd like to ask you, Miss Wills. A little while ago you said you were certain that clock in the office had the right time. Why are you certain of it?'

'I beg your pardon?'

Elliot repeated the question.

'Because it's broken,' replied Marjorie, drawing her attention back. 'I mean, the little thingummyjig you set the hands by was broken clean off, so you can't alter the clock at all. And it's an accurate time-keeper; it's never been a second out since we've had it.'

Professor Ingram began to chuckle.

'I see. When was it broken, Miss Wills?'

'Yesterday morning. Pamela—that's one of the maids—broke it off when she was tidying up Uncle Marcus's office. She was winding the clock, and carrying an iron candlestick in the other hand, and she bumped it against that other little pin and broke it clean off. I thought Uncle Marcus would be furious. You see, we're only allowed to tidy up his office once a week. He's got all his business accounts in there, and particularly a manuscript he's working on that we mustn't touch. But he didn't.'

'Didn't what?'

'He wasn't furious, I mean. Just the opposite. He walked in in the middle of it. I said we could send the clock down to Simmonds' in town and get it mended. He stood looking at the clock for a minute, and all of a sudden he burst out laughing. He said, No, no, let it alone: it was now set with the right time, couldn't be altered, and was a joy to behold. (It's an eight-day clock; it was wound up then.) He also said Pamela was an excellent girl, and would be a blessing to her parents in their old age. That's how I remember so well.'

Now why, reflected Detective-Inspector Elliot, does a man stand in front of a clock and suddenly roar with laughter? But he had no time to consider. As though to overload his troubles to the breaking-point, Major Crow appeared from the door to the hall.

'May I see you for a moment, Inspector?' he requested in a curious voice.

Elliot went out and shut the door. It was a spacious hall, panelled in light oak, with a broad, low staircase and a floor so highly polished that it reflected the edges of the rugs. One bridge-lamp was burning, making a pool of light beside the staircase and shining on a telephone on its stand.

Major Crow kept his deceptively mild appearance, but his eye looked wicked. He nodded towards the telephone.

'I've just been talking to Billy Emsworth,' he said.

'Billy Emsworth? Who's that?'

'The fellow whose wife had a baby to-night. The one Joe Chesney attended: you know? I know it's very late, but I thought Emsworth would probably be still sitting up celebrating with a friend or two. He was, and I talked to him. I didn't give anything away; I was only offering congratulations, though I hope it doesn't occur to him to wonder why I should ring up at two o'clock in the morning to do it.' Major Crow drew a deep breath. 'Well, if that clock in the office is right, Joe Chesney has an absolutely cast-iron alibi.'

Elliot said nothing. He had expected it.

'The brat was born about a quarter past eleven. Afterwards Chesney sat down and talked with Emsworth and his friends until close on midnight. They all looked at their watches as he was leaving. When Emsworth saw him to the door, the church clock was just striking twelve; and Emsworth stood on the front steps and made a speech about the dawn of a newer, fairer day. So the time of his going is established. Now, Emsworth lives at the other side of Sodbury Cross. It's absolutely impossible for Joe Chesney to have been here at the time of the murder. What do you think of that?'

'Only, sir, that they all have alibis,' said Elliot—and told him.

'H'm,' said Major Crow.

'Yes, sir,' said Elliot.

'This is awkward.'

'Yes, sir.'

'*Damned* awkward,' amplified the Chief Constable, with a slight roar. 'Do you think they're telling the truth about it's not being too dark to follow everybody's movements?'

'We must test it out, naturally.' Elliot hesitated. 'But I noticed myself that that brilliant light in the other room makes all the difference. I honestly don't think it was dark enough so that one could have slipped out without being seen. To tell you the honest truth, sir—I believe them.'

'You don't think the three of them concocted the story among themselves?'

'Anything is possible. Still—'[1]

'You don't think so?'

Elliot was cautious. 'At least,' he decided, 'it would seem that we can't just concentrate attention on members of this household. We've got to go much farther afield. That phantom outsider in the dinner-jacket is probably real after all. Hang it, why shouldn't he be?'

'I'll tell you,' said Major Crow coolly. 'Because Bostwick and I have just found evidence—evidence, mind—which shows that the murderer is either a member of this household or closely connected with it.'

While Elliot experienced again that irrational sensation that something was vitally wrong, that he was looking at the case through distorted eyeglasses, the Chief Constable drew him towards the stairs. Major Crow, in fact, had assumed a somewhat guilty manner.

---

1   'No device,' Dr. Fell once said, 'is more useless or exasperating than deceit by conspiracy to tell the same lie.' Therefore I think it only fair to state that there was no conspiracy of any kind among the three witnesses. Each spoke independently, and without collusion with either of the other two.—J.D.C.

'It was irregular. Most irregular,' he said, clucking his tongue hollowly; 'but it's done now and a good job too. When Bostwick went upstairs to see whether this fellow Emmet was well enough to have a word with us, he thought he would just have a look in the bathroom. In the medicine-chest of that bathroom he found a box of castor-oil capsules—'

Here he looked inquiring.

'Not necessarily important, sir. I understand they're pretty common.'

'Granted. Granted! But wait. Tucked away at the back of the shelf beside the mouth-wash, he found a one-ounce bottle a quarter full of pure prussic acid...

'I thought that would knock you in a heap,' said Major Crow with some satisfaction. 'I know it did me, particularly when you now tell me everybody in the house has got an alibi. It was *not*, mind you, the weaker solution of potassium cyanide; it was the simon-pure article, the fastest-working poison on earth. At least, that's what we think it is. West is going to have it analysed for us, but he's fairly certain now. It was standing there in a bottle actually labelled, "Prussic Acid, HCN". Bostwick took one look at it and couldn't believe his eyes. He took the cork out of the bottle, but when he caught one faint whiff of it he stuck the cork back again faster than he's ever moved before in his life. He had heard that one good deep inhalation of pure prussic acid will kill; and West says that's true. Look at this beauty.'

Very gingerly he felt in his pocket. He produced a tiny bottle in which the cork had been pushed down almost level with the neck, and he tilted it to show a colourless liquid inside. To the bottle had been fastened a gummed piece of paper on which the words 'Prussic Acid, HCN' were crudely printed in ink. Major Crow put it down on the telephone-table under the light and backed away as though he had just lit a particularly dangerous firework.

'No fingerprints,' he explained. 'Don't get too close to it,' he added nervously. 'Can't you smell it even now?'

Elliot could.

'But where did anybody get the stuff?' he said. 'You heard what Dr. West said. Pure prussic acid is practically inaccessible to a layman. The only person who could get it would be—'

'Yes. A technician. Say a research chemist. What's this fellow Harding, by the way?'

It was here, either by good or by bad fortune, that Harding walked out of the Music Room.

He had seemed in a particularly cheerful, bouncing frame of mind when Elliot left him. This did not greatly lessen, though he was not far away from the bottle on the table and must have been able to read its label. He leaned one hand against the door-post, as though he were about to have his photograph taken. Then he came over, smiling and respectful, and addressed the Chief Constable.

'HCN?' he inquired, pointing to the bottle.

'That's what the label says, young man.'

'Do you mind my asking where you found it?'

'In the bathroom. Did you put it there?'

'No, sir.'

'But you use this stuff in your business, don't you?'

'No,' said Harding promptly. 'No, I honestly don't,' he added. 'I use KCN—potassium cyanide—and lots of it. I'm working out an electro-plating process which will make imitation silver indistinguishable from the real thing. If I can market it myself, and get sufficient backing so that I don't have to tie up with sharks, I'm going to revolutionise the industry.' He spoke without any hint of boasting; he was stating a fact. 'But I don't use HCN. It's no good to me.'

'Well, frankness is frankness,' said Major Crow, unbending a little. 'All the same, you could make HCN, couldn't you?'

Harding spoke with such intensity, and such an intense shaking of the jaws as he formed his words, that Elliot wondered whether he had been born with an impediment in his speech: which, like other disadvantages, he had overcome. Harding said:

'Of course I could make it. So could anyone else.'

'Don't follow you, young man.'

'Well, look here! What do you need to manufacture HCN? I'll tell you. You want prussiate of potash; not poisonous; buy it anywhere. You want oil of vitriol, which is better known as sulphuric acid; take some out of the nearest motor-car battery, and who's the wiser? You want plain water. Put those three elements together in a distilling process that a little golden-haired child could manage with implements out of grandma's kitchen, and you get—the stuff in that bottle. Anybody, with an elementary book on chemistry propped up in front of him, could do it.'

Major Crow glanced uneasily at Elliot. 'And that's all you've got to do to get prussic acid?'

'That's all. But don't take my word for it. The trouble is— well, sir, there's something wrong. D'you mind telling me: you say you found that stuff in the bathroom. I'm not surprised; I'm past surprise; but do you mean you just picked it up in the bathroom, like a tube of toothpaste or something?'

Major Crow spread out his hands. The same thought had occurred to him.

'This house is mouldy,' said Harding, studying the fine and gracious hall. 'It looks all right; but there's something chemically wrong with it. I'm an outsider. I can tell. And now—er—if you'll excuse me, I'm going out to the dining-room to get a drink of whisky; and I'm praying to the saints there's nothing chemically wrong with that.'

His footsteps clacked loudly on the bare parquetry, defying bogles. The pool of light trembled by the staircase, the pool of poison trembled in the small bottle; upstairs a man with concussion of the brain lay muttering, downstairs two investigators looked at each other.

'Not easy,' said Major Crow.

'No,' admitted Elliot.

'You have two leads, Inspector. Two solid, definite leads. To-morrow young Emmet may be conscious and able to tell you what happened to him. You have that ciné-film—I'll have that developed for you by to-morrow afternoon; there's a chap in Sodbury Cross who does that kind of work—and you will be able to tell exactly what happened during the show. Beyond that, I don't know what you have, and notice that I say "you." I have my business to attend to. To-morrow, I promise you on my word of honour, I butt in no longer. It's your case, and I wish you joy of it.'

Elliot had no joy in it, for private reasons. But for public reasons the matter had been squeezed down into one issue that stood out as clear and black as a fingerprint:

The murder of Marcus Chesney had probably been committed by someone in this house.

Yet everyone in this house appeared to have an unshakable alibi.

Who, therefore, had committed it?

And how had it been committed?

'I can see all that,' the Chief Constable agreed. 'So go your virtuous way and clear it up. All the same, there are four questions of my own that I'd give twenty pounds to have answered, here, now, and on the nail.'

'Yes, sir?'

Major Crow put off his official dignity. His voice rose in a kind of wail.

'Why were those chocolate-boxes changed from green to blue? What is wrong with that confounded clock? What was the real height of the bloke in the top-hat? And why, oh, why was Chesney fooling about with a South American blow-pipe dart that nobody has seen before or since?'

III

Third View Through the Spectacles

'And what did you do after you had done the murder?'
'Why, of course, then I went to sleep.'

ARTHUR WARREN WAITE,
NEW YORK, 1915

X

At eleven o'clock on the following morning Inspector Elliot drove into Bath and pulled up near the Beau Nash Hotel, which is in the court just opposite the entrance to the Roman baths.

Whoever said that it is always raining in Bath basely slanders that noble town, where the tall eighteenth-century houses look like tall eighteenth-century dowagers, and turn blind eyes to trains or motor-cars. But (to be strictly accurate) it was pouring torrents on this particular morning. Elliot, when he ducked into the entrance to the hotel, was in such a hideously dispirited frame of mind that he had to confide in somebody or throw up the case and tell his Superintendent why.

True enough he had had little sleep the night before. And he had been again at routine inquiries since eight o'clock this morning. But he could not get out of his mind the picture of Wilbur Emmet—with his plastered hair, his red nose and blotchy complexion—twisting in delirium and muttering words not one of which became audible. It had been the final bedevilment of last night.

Elliot went to the hotel desk, and inquired for Dr. Gideon Fell.

Dr. Fell was upstairs in his room. Despite the hour, it is regrettable to state, Dr. Fell was not yet up and about. Elliot found him sitting by the breakfast-table in a flannel dressing-gown as big as a tent, drinking coffee, smoking a cigar, and reading a detective-story.

Dr. Fell's eyeglasses on the broad black ribbon were clamped firmly to his nose. His bandit's moustache bristled with concentration, his cheeks puffed in and out and gentle earthquakes of deep breathing animated the huge purple-flowered dressing-gown as he attempted to spot the murderer. But at Elliot's entrance he rose in a vast surge that almost upset the table, like Leviathan rising under a submarine. Such a radiant beam of welcome went over his face, making it shine pinkly and transparently, that Elliot felt better.

'Wow!' said Dr. Fell, wringing his hand. 'This is excellent. By all that's holy, this is wonderful! Sit down, sit down, sit down. Have something. Have anything. Hey?'

'Superintendent Hadley told me where to find you, sir.'

'That's right,' agreed Dr. Fell, giving a spectral chuckle, and sitting back broadly to contemplate his guest as though Elliot were some refreshing phenomenon he had never seen before. His delight animated the whole room. 'I am taking the waters. The term has a fine, spacious, adventurous sound. *Cras igens iterabimus aequor*. But the actual performance falls short of the swashbuckling; and I am seldom tempted to strike up a drinking-song after my tenth or fifteenth pint.'

'But are you supposed to take it in that quantity, sir?'

'All drinkables are supposed to be taken in that quantity,' said Dr. Fell firmly. 'If I cannot do the thing handsomely, I am not going to do it at all. And how are you, Inspector?'

Elliot tried to screw up his courage.

'I have been better,' he admitted.

'Oh,' said Dr. Fell. The beam left his face, and he blinked. 'I suppose you've come about that Chesney business?'

'You'd heard about it?'

'H'mf, yes,' said Dr. Fell, sniffing. 'My waiter, a very good fellow who is too stone-deaf to hear a bell but has lip-reading down to a fine art, told me all about it this morning. He got it from the milkman, who got it from I forget precisely whom. Besides, I—well, I knew Chesney in a way.' Dr. Fell looked troubled. He scratched the side of a small and glistening nose. 'I met Chesney, and I met his family, at a reception six months or so ago. And then he wrote me a letter.'

Again the doctor hesitated.

'If you know his family,' said Elliot slowly, 'that makes it easier. What I've come to you about isn't only the case; it's a personal problem. I don't know what in hell's got into me, or what to do about it, but there it is. Do you know Marjorie Wills, Chesney's niece?'

'Yes,' said Dr. Fell, fixing him with a small sharp eye.

Elliot got to his feet.

'I've fallen for her,' he shouted.

He knew that he was cutting a weird figure, standing up and yelling the news as though he were throwing a plate in the doctor's face; and his ears felt on fire. If Dr. Fell had chuckled in that moment, if Dr. Fell had told him to lower his voice, he would probably have stood on his peevish Lowland dignity and walked out of the room. He could not help it; that was how he felt. But Dr. Fell merely nodded.

'Quite understandable,' he rumbled, with a broad and rather surprised agreement. 'Well?'

'I've only seen her twice before,' shouted Elliot, facing him and determined to have this out. 'Once was at Pompeii, and once was at—never mind that, for the minute. As I say, I don't know what in hell has got into me. I don't idealise her. When I saw her again the other night, I could hardly remember what she looked like from the first two times. I have certain knowledge that she's probably a poisoner and a pleasant sleek bit of treachery. But I walked in on that crowd in a place at Pompeii—you don't know about that, but I was there—and she was standing in a kind of garden, with her hat off and the sun on her arms; and I just stood there and looked at her, and then I turned round and walked out. It was the way she moved or spoke or turned her head: something, nothing, I don't know what.

'I wouldn't have had the cheek to follow their party and try to scrape an acquaintance, though that's what this fellow Harding evidently did. I don't know why I couldn't have forced myself to do it. It wasn't merely because I had just heard them all arranging things about her being married to Harding. So help me, I didn't even think of that. If I thought about Harding at all, I supposed it was just my cursed luck, and let it go at that. All I knew was, first, that I had fallen for her, and, second, that I would have to get the idea out of my head; because it was all nonsense. I don't suppose you understand.'

The room was quiet except for the wheezing of Dr. Fell's breath, and the splash of the rain outside.

'You have a very low opinion of me,' said the doctor gravely, 'if you suppose I don't understand. Go on.'

'Well, sir, that's all. I didn't get the idea out of my head.'

'Not all, I think?'

'All right; you want to know about the second time I saw her. It was a fatality. I knew in my bones it was bound to happen. See a person once, try to forget it or get away from that person, and you bump into the person every time you turn around. The next time I saw her was just five days ago, at a little chemist's shop near the Royal Albert Docks.

'When I saw them at Pompeii, I overheard Mr. Chesney mention the name of the ship they were travelling back by, and the sailing date. I left Italy the next day, overland, and got home well over a week before they did. Last Thursday, the 29th, I happened to be in the neighbourhood of the Royal Albert Docks on a case.' Elliot stopped. 'I can't even tell you the truth, can I?' he asked bitterly. 'Yes, I made the excuse to be there on that particular day, but the rest of it must have been coincidence—or you shall judge for yourself.

'This chemist's poison-register had been called into question. He seemed to have been getting rid of more drugs than was natural or normal; that was why I was there. I went in and asked to see his poison-register. He showed it to me quickly enough, and sat me down to look at it in a little dispensary at the back of the shop, screened off from the counter by a wall of bottles. While I was looking at it, a customer came in. I couldn't see the customer, and she couldn't see me; she thought there was nobody else in the shop. But I knew that voice right enough. It was Marjorie Wills, wanting to buy cyanide of potassium "for photographic purposes".'

Again Elliot stopped.

He did not see a room at the Beau Nash Hotel. He saw a dingy shop in the dingy afternoon light, and breathed the dim chemical smell he would always associate with this case. There was creosote on the floor; the tops of squat glass jars were faintly luminous; and across the shop, in shadow, was a fly-blown mirror. In that mirror he saw Marjorie Wills's reflection, her eyes upturned, when she edged along the counter requesting potassium cyanide for photographic purposes.

'Probably because I was there,' Elliot went on, 'the chemist began to ask her questions about why she wanted it, and the use of it. Her answers showed that she knew about as much about photography as I know about Sanskrit. There was a mirror across the shop. Just as she got to the point of being badly confused, she happened to glance in the mirror. She must have seen me, though I didn't think at the time she got a proper look, and I'm still not sure. All of a sudden she called the chemist a—well, never mind—and ran out of the shop.

'Yes; a pretty business, eh?' he added savagely.

Dr. Fell did not comment.

'I think that chemist is a wrong 'un,' Elliot said slowly, 'though there was nothing I could find. But on top of this, Superintendent Hadley handed me—*me*—the Sodbury Cross poisoning case: of which (thank you) I had already read up every detail in the back files of the newspapers.'

'You didn't refuse the case?'

'No, sir. Could I have refused it anyway? At least, without telling the Superintendent what I knew?'

'H'm.'

'Yes. You're thinking I ought to be kicked out of the Force; and you're quite right.'

'Good God, no,' said Dr. Fell, opening his eyes wide. 'That confounded conscience of yours will be the death of you yet. Stop talking such rubbish and get on with it.'

'Driving down here last night, I thought of every possible way out. Some of them so daft that they make me squirm when I think of it this morning. I thought of systematically ditching the evidence against her. I even thought of taking her and running off to the South Seas with her.'

He paused; but Dr. Fell only nodded sympathetically, as though he understood the sound reason of such courses; and it was with an enormous sense of relief flooding through him that Elliot continued.

'I hoped the Chief Constable—Major Crow, his name is—wouldn't notice anything. But I must have acted queerly from the start, and I put my foot in it time after time. The worst was when the girl almost recognised me. She didn't quite recognise me: that is, she didn't connect me with the mirror in the chemist's shop. But she knows she's seen me before, and she's still trying to remember where.

'For the rest of it, I tried to go into the case without prejudice—compromise again, eh?—and treat it exactly as I would treat an ordinary case. Whether I succeeded or not, I don't know, but you notice I'm here to-day.'

Dr. Fell considered. 'Tell me. Putting aside the chocolate-shop murder, did you find anything last night that led you to believe she might be guilty of killing Marcus Chesney?'

'*No!* That's just it: quite to the contrary. She's got an alibi as big as a house.'

'Then what in the name of Beelzebub are we arguing about? Why aren't you carolling like a lark?'

'I don't know, sir, and that's a fact. It's only that the case is too queer and funny and fishy to be taken at one swoop. It's a box of tricks right from the start.'

Dr. Fell leaned back, taking several puffs at his cigar, an expression of fierce concentration on his face. He shook his shoulders loose and took several more puffs at the cigar, as though for great weightiness of utterance. Even the ribbon on his eyeglasses was agitated.

'Let us,' he said, 'examine your emotional problem. No; don't shy away from it. This may be infatuation or it may be the real thing, but in either case I want to ask you a question about it. Suppose this girl is a murderess. One moment! I say: suppose this girl is a murderess. Now, these crimes are not crimes for which we can readily find an excuse. Even I find it necessary to concentrate tensely before being able to excuse them. They are not natural crimes; they are calculated abnormalities, and the person who perpetrated them is about as safe to have about the house as a king cobra. Very well. Supposing this girl to be guilty—do you want to know it?'

'I don't know.'

'Still, you agree that it might be just as well to find out?'

'I suppose so.'

'Good,' said Dr. Fell, taking a few more puffs at his cigar. 'Now let us look at it the other way. Suppose this girl is completely innocent. No; do not loose me a strangled breath of relief; be practical in your romanticism. Suppose this girl is completely innocent. What are you going to do about it?'

'I don't understand, sir.'

'You say you have fallen for her?'

Then it dawned on Elliot.

'Oh, leave me out of it,' he said. 'I don't flatter myself that *I* would ever stand a chance with her. You should see the expression on her face when she looks at Harding. I saw it. I tell you, sir, the hardest thing I had to do last night was to be fair to Harding. I've got nothing against the fellow; he seems decent enough. I can only say that there's something in my upbringing which, whenever I talk to Harding, sets my teeth on edge.'

He felt his ears tingling again.

'I had all sorts of visions about that, too, last night. I imagined myself dramatically arresting Harding for the murder—yes, handcuffs and all—and her looking at me, and all the claptrap that just naturally comes into a bloke's head. But emotional knots don't get cut as easily as that. Not for any human being they don't. Harding is a red herring if I ever saw one. You ruddy well can't commit a murder when you're in one room with two people looking at you, and the real murderer is also in sight in another room. Harding may be a fortune-hunter (I think he is) but that's just the line of human cussedness that things take in this world. Harding had never heard of Sodbury Cross until he met the Chesneys in Italy. So forget Harding and, in particular, forget me.'

'In addition to your conscience,' observed Dr. Fell critically, 'you must also get rid of your confounded humility. It is an excellent spiritual virtue; but it is a virtue that no woman can endure. However, we'll pass that. Well?'

'Well, what?'

'How do you feel now?' asked Dr. Fell.

And Elliot suddenly realised that he felt better: so much better that he wanted a cup of coffee and something to smoke. It was as though his wits focused and clarified. He did not understand it; yet even the room seemed in different colours.

'Harrumph,' said Dr. Fell, scratching the side of his nose. 'So what shall we do? You forget, you know, that I have been given only the barest outline of the case; and in your natural enthusiasm you have fired most of the arrows clear over my head. But what will you do? Will you make a fool of yourself by going back and explaining to Hadley? Or shall we have a go at the facts and see what happens? I am at your service.'

'Yes!' roared Elliot. 'Yes, by the living—'

'Good. In that case, sit down there,' said Dr. Fell grimly, 'and kindly tell me just what in blazes did happen.'

It took half an hour, for Elliot, clothed in hard-headedness again yet somehow not ashamed of himself, kept his mind busy with the smallest facts. He concluded with the little bottle of prussic acid in the medicine-chest of the bathroom.

'—and that's about all, though we didn't get away from the house until three o'clock. Everybody denied having anything to do with the prussic acid; swore they knew of no such thing in the bathroom; and said it wasn't there when they dressed for dinner that night. I also looked in on this fellow Wilbur Emmet, but naturally he was in no shape to be any good to us.'

He had a vivid recollection of that bedroom, as tidy yet as unattractive as Emmet himself. He remembered the lanky form twisted in the bed-clothes, the harsh electric light, the elaborate array of hair-creams and neckties on the dressing-table. On the work-table there was a pile of letters and receipted bills. Beside it stood the little straw suitcase in which Emmet carried an assortment of syringes, tiny shears, and curious articles which to Elliot's eye resembled surgical tools. Even the wall-paper was of a yellowish-red pattern which suggested peaches.

'Emmet was talking a lot, but you couldn't make out one intelligible word he said: except that he would sometimes say, "Marjorie!" and they would have to quiet him. That's all, sir. I've now told you every single thing I know, and I wonder if you can make any sense of it. I wonder if you can explain what's so infernally wrong about it.'

Dr. Fell nodded slowly and emphatically.

'I think I can,' he said.

XI

'But before I do,' continued Dr. Fell, pointing aggressively with the cigar, 'I should like to clear up one point on which I either cannot have heard you correctly, or else somebody has committed a bad howler. It deals with the end of Chesney's performance. Chesney (imagine) has just opened those double-doors to announce that the show is over. Got the scene?'

'Yes, sir.'

'Professor Ingram then says to him, "By the way, who was your hideous-looking colleague?" To which Chesney replied, "Oh, that was only Wilbur; he helped me plan the whole thing." That is correct?'

'Yes, that's right.'

'You have other testimony on the point besides Miss Wills's?' insisted the doctor. 'The others confirmed it?'

'Yes, sir,' returned Elliot, puzzled. 'I went over all that with them just before I left the house.'

Dr. Fell's colour had changed slightly. He sat with his mouth open, the cigar poised in the air, while he stared at his companion with widening eyes. He said, with a kind of thunderous whisper like wind along an underground tunnel: 'Oh, Bacchus! Oh, Lord! Oh, my sacred hat! This won't do.'

'But what's wrong?'

'Get out that list of Chesney's ten questions,' urged Dr. Fell excitedly. 'Cast your eye over it. Study it. Be appalled by it. Don't you see anything wrong?'

Elliot stared from Dr. Fell's face to the list, made uneasy by the other's intense eagerness. 'No, sir, I can't say I do. Maybe my brain isn't working properly—'

'It isn't,' the doctor assured him seriously. 'Look at it, man! Concentrate! Don't you see that Chesney has asked a totally unnecessary and even absurd question?'

'Which one?'

'Question number four. *"What was the height of the person who entered by the French window?"* Hang it all! That was one of a short list of questions he was carefully preparing to ask them; shrewd questions, catch questions, questions to take them by surprise. Yet, before he even begins to ask those questions, he calmly announces to them *just who the person was*. You follow that? As you quote Miss Wills as saying, they all knew Wilbur Emmet's height. They lived with him; they saw him every day. So, when they heard beforehand who the visitor was, they couldn't possibly go wrong on question four. Why, therefore, does Chesney spill the beans all over the floor by presenting them with the answer before he even asks the question?'

Elliot swore uneasily. Then he began to reflect.

'Steady, though. What about a catch in that, sir?' he suggested. 'Suppose Emmet had instructions—Professor Ingram suggested this—to hunch down inside the raincoat, so that his height appeared three inches less than it actually was? So Mr. Chesney set a trap for them like that. When he carefully told them it was Emmet, he expected them to fall into the trap and give what they knew to be his height: six feet. Whereas actually the height of the man hunched down inside the raincoat was to be only five feet nine.'

'It is possible.' Dr. Fell scowled. 'I will agree, with my hand on my heart, that there may have been more traps in that little show than even you seem to realise. But as for having Emmet crouch down—you know, Inspector, I can't quite believe it. You describe the raincoat as long and tight-fitting. The only way a person could take away three inches from his height would be to bend his knees and shuffle across the stage with short steps. Now, I will almost defy anyone to do that without his knees jutting out like pistons under the coat, carrying himself oddly and making obvious to the audience just what he is doing. Everyone seems, on the contrary, to convey a kind of tense straightness and rigidity about the fellow's bearing. Anything is possible, I admit; but—'

'You mean the man was five feet nine after all?'

'Or,' said Dr. Fell with some dryness, 'there is the startling and unusual possibility that he really was six feet. Two witnesses say so, you know. At every point where Professor Ingram disagrees with them, you automatically believe the professor. Probably you are right to do so; but we mustn't—h'mf—we mustn't fall into the error of treating Professor Ingram as an oracle or an augur or a mouthpiece of Holy Writ.'

Again Elliot reflected.

'Or,' he suggested, 'Mr. Chesney may have been nervous or rattled, and blurted out Emmet's name without intending to.'

'Hardly,' said Dr. Fell, 'when he immediately called Emmet in and made a row when Emmet didn't appear. H'mf, no. It's difficult to believe that, Inspector. The conjuror doesn't spill his cards all over the floor so easily, or get rattled and call the audience's attention to the particular trap-door through which he dropped his assistant. Chesney never struck me as that sort of chap.'

'I shouldn't have thought so myself,' Elliot admitted. 'But where does it leave us? This gives us only one more puzzle to add to the rest. Do you see any actual light in the business?'

'Quite a good deal. It is now clear, isn't it, how Chesney thought the chocolates were poisoned at Mrs. Terry's?'

'No, sir, I'm hanged if it is! How?'

Dr. Fell shifted in his chair. An expression of Gargantuan distress went over his face; he made vague gestures and mysterious internal noises.

'Look here.' He spoke in a tone of protest. 'I most emphatically do not wish to sit here myself like a stuffed oracle, blandly tut-tutting and being so dashed superior at your expense. I have always detested that sort of snobbery; I will fight it to the last ditch. But I insist that these emotional disturbances have not been good for your intelligence.

'Now let us consider the problem of the poisoned chocolates at Mrs. Terry's. What are the terms of it? What are the facts that we must accept? First: that the chocolates were poisoned at some time during the day of June 17th. Second: that they were poisoned either by some visitor to the shop on that day, or by Miss Wills in a sleight-of-hand exchange through Frankie Dale. For it is established that there was nothing wrong with the chocolates on the night of the 16th, since Mrs. Terry took a handful or so for a children's party. These are correct assumptions?'

'Yes.'

'Not at all,' said Dr. Fell. 'Rubbish!

'I deny,' he went on, fiery with earnestness, 'that the chocolates were necessarily poisoned on June 17th. I also deny that they were necessarily poisoned by someone who visited the shop on that day.

'Now, Major Crow (if I understand you) outlined a method by which a murderer could easily hocus an open chocolate-box on a counter. The murderer enters with a number of poisoned sweets concealed in his hand or in his pocket. He misdirects Mrs. Terry's attention, and drops the doctored sweets into the box on the counter. True, true, true! Easy enough. It could have been done in that way. But isn't it, when you reflect, an incredibly simple-minded approach for a murderer who has shown himself as nimble as this one? What does it do? It immediately shows that the poisoning was done on a definite given day, and limits the field of suspects to those who were in the shop on that day.

'With your permission, I can suggest a much better way.

'Prepare an exact duplicate of that *open* box of chocolates on the counter. Don't (like a fool) poison the top layer of chocolates in your duplicate box. Instead poison six or ten of them fairly well down into the box. Go into Mrs. Terry's and substitute one open box for another. Unless there is a fairly large demand for chocolate creams, nobody will get the poisoned ones on that day. On the contrary!—children, as a rule, don't go in much for chocolate creams. They infinitely prefer liquorice or bull's-eyes, where they get more quantity for their money. So it is likely that the poisoned creams will be in the shop one, two, three, four days, perhaps a week, before anyone reaches the poisoned layer. Therefore the real murderer will most certainly not be in the shop on the day the damage is done. And, at whatever date those creams were poisoned, I will lay you odds it was well before the fatal 17th of June.'

This time Elliot cursed loudly. He walked to the window, stared out at the rain, and turned round.

'Yes, but—well, for one thing, you can't walk about the country hiding an *open* box of chocolates, can you? And juggling it with another open box?'

'You can,' said Dr. Fell, 'if you have a spring-grip bag. I'm sorry, my lad, but I'm afraid that spring-grip bag rather tears it. Those bags (correct me if I am wrong) are controlled by a button in the leather handle. Press the button; the bag snaps up whatever is underneath. Or it can, of course, be used conversely. Place something inside the bag; press the button to open the jaws of the spring, and it deposits what is inside the bag in whatever place you want it.'

Here Dr. Fell made a mesmeric pass; sniffed; looked disconsolate; and finally spoke earnestly.

'Yes, my lad. I'm afraid that's just what happened, or there would be no point whatever to the spring-grip bag bobbing and tumbling through this case. The murderer, as you say, couldn't juggle with open boxes unless he had something to hold them quite steady so that they wouldn't spill in the juggling. Hence the Thief's Friend.

'He walked into Mrs. Terry's shop with a box of hocussed creams in the bottom of his bag. While he misdirected Mrs.

Terry's attention, he released this box on the counter. He then put the bag down over the real box; snapped it up into the bag out of sight; pushed the poisoned box into place: all in the space of time it took him to receive fifty Players or Gold Flake across the tobacco-counter opposite. And Marcus Chesney tumbled to the trick. To illustrate how the boxes were changed, he imported a similar spring-grip bag from London. Chesney then had the same trick performed last night—and nobody spotted it.'

Elliot drew a deep breath in the silence that followed.

'Thank you,' he said gravely.

'Eh?'

'I said thank you,' repeated Elliot, grinning. 'You're pulling my wits back to normal, sir; or giving them a kick in the pants, if you know what I mean.'

'Thanke'e, Inspector,' said Dr. Fell, with vague gratification.

'But do you realise, all the same, that this explanation leaves us still worse off than before? I believe it. I think it's the one that best fits all the circumstances. But it upsets the only facts we had before. We don't even have an idea as to when the chocolates might have been poisoned, except that it probably wasn't the only day the police have been concentrating on for nearly four months.'

'I am sorry to upset the apple-cart,' said Dr. Fell, rubbing his head vigorously but apologetically. 'But—hang it all! If you have a crooked mind like mine, such a course seems as inevitable as a cat in the salmon-tin. And I don't agree with you that it leaves us worse off than before. On the contrary, it ought to lead us straight to the truth.'

'How?'

'Tell me, Inspector. Were you brought up in a village, or at least in a small community?'

'No, sir. Not exactly. Glasgow.'

'Ah. But I was,' said Dr. Fell, with rich satisfaction. 'Now let us postulate our situation. The murderer, carrying what appears to be a small harmless satchel, walks into the shop. We assume that the murderer is someone known to Mrs. Terry; we must assume that. Have you never had any experience with the ripe, healthy, and instinctive curiosity of shopkeepers in a small community, particularly of the bustling sort Mrs. Terry is? Suppose you walked in carrying a satchel. It would be, "Going away, Mr. Elliot?" "Off to Weston, Mr. Elliot?"—or she would think that even if she didn't say it, because the sight of you with a satchel would be an unusual sight. It is not a customary appendage of yours. The memory would stick in her mind. If anyone with a small valise went into her shop during the week preceding the chocolate-murder, she will probably have some recollection of it.'

Elliot nodded. But he had a feeling that there was another step to be taken, another groping to be made, for Dr. Fell was watching him with massive concentration.

'Or else—?' the doctor prompted.

'I see,' muttered Elliot, staring at the rain-washed window. '*Or else the murderer was someone who usually carries a bag of that type, and the sight was so ordinary Mrs. Terry never thought twice about it.*'

'It is a tenable hypothesis,' said the other, sniffing.

'You mean Dr. Joseph Chesney?'

'Perhaps. Is there anybody else who usually goes about with a bag or case or something of the sort?'

'Only Wilbur Emmet, they tell me. He's got a little straw semi-suitcase affair; I saw it in his room, as I told you.'

Dr. Fell shook his head.

'Only Wilbur Emmet,' he observed. '"Only" Wilbur Emmet, the man says. Archons of Athens! If a leather bag can be turned into a spring-grip bag through the ingenuity of a magic supply-house, is there any reason why the same shouldn't apply to a straw suitcase? Surely it is obvious that, when Major Crow and Superintendent Bostwick recover from their present *idées fixes*, they will certainly fasten on Emmet? Professor Ingram, I suspect from what you tell me, has already done so; and will greet us with the theory as soon as we poke our noses into Bellegarde. We must be inordinately careful of traps. Therefore, on the basis of the evidence as it stands now, I assure you that the only person who can possibly be guilty is Wilbur Emmet. Would you care to hear my reasons?'

XII

DR. FELL, ELLIOT HAS SOMETIMES THOUGHT, WOULD BE a bad person with whom to hold a conversation on a morning (say) when you were suffering from too many whiskies the night before. His mind moved so fast that it was round the corner and in at the window before your mental eyesight could follow it. You were conscious of a whir of wings, a capping of tall words; and then, before you quite knew what had happened, a whole edifice had been reared by steps which seemed completely logical at the time but were difficult to remember afterwards.

'Steady on, sir!' Elliot urged. 'I've heard you do this sort of thing before, and—'

'No, hear me out,' said the doctor with fierce earnestness. 'You must remember that I started life as a schoolmaster. Every minute of the day the lads were attempting to tell me some weird story or other, smoothly, plausibly, and with a dexterity I have not since heard matched at the Old Bailey. Therefore I start with an unfair advantage over the police. I have had much more experience with habitual liars. And it occurs to me that you accepted Emmet's innocence much too tamely.

'It was foisted on you, of course, by Miss Wills, before you had time to think. Kindly don't rise in wrath; the foisting was probably unconscious. But what was the state of affairs there? You say, "Everybody in that house had an alibi,"—which isn't true. Explain, if you will, how Emmet had an alibi.'

'H'm,' said Elliot.

'Nobody, in fact, saw Emmet at all. You found him lying unconscious under a tree, with a poker handy. Someone immediately said, "He has clearly been lying here like this for a long time." But what medical evidence did you have (or could you have) as to how long he had been lying there? It was not like a post-mortem report as to the time of death. It could just as well have occurred ten seconds before as two or three minutes before. A prosecuting counsel might call it the double-bluff.'

Elliot reflected. 'Well, sir, I won't say I hadn't thought of it. By that theory, the man in the top-hat was really Emmet after all. He played his own part, except that he gave Mr. Chesney a poisoned capsule. Then he arranged to get himself a crack over the head—self-mutilation to prove incapacity isn't a new thing—and showed he couldn't have been Dr. Nemo.'

'Exactly. And further?'

'It would have been easier for him than anybody else,' Elliot acknowledged. 'No hocus-pocus. No putting on or off the props. All he had to do was play his own part in his own good time. All he had to do was substitute a prussic-acid capsule for the harmless one. He knew all the details. He was the only person who knew all the details. He—' The more Elliot thought of it, the more he was impelled and pushed into belief. 'The trouble is, sir, that as yet I don't know anything *about* Emmet. I've never talked to him. Who is Emmet? What is he? There's been no breath of suspicion against Emmet so far, by anybody. How would it profit him to kill Mr. Chesney?'

'How would it profit him,' asked Dr. Fell, 'to spread strychnine among a group of children?'

'We're getting back to pure lunacy, then?'

'I don't know. But it might pay you to consider motive a bit more. As for Emmet—' Dr. Fell scowled, and stubbed out his cigar. 'I remember meeting him at the same party where I met Chesney. Tall, dark-haired, red-nosed chap, with a voice and manner rather like Hamlet's father's ghost. He stalked about, intoning; and spilled an ice over his knee. The leit-motif was "poor old Wilbur." As for his appearance—what about the mechanics? The top-hat, raincoat, and so on? Were they of a size to be worn only by Emmet, or what?'

Elliot took out his notebook.

'The top-hat was size 7; it was an old relic belonging to Marcus Chesney himself. The raincoat, which belongs to Emmet, was an ordinary Men's Large Size; they don't make raincoats in a list of carefully graded sizes like suits. The rubber gloves, a sixpenny pair from Woolworth's, I found expertly rolled up in the right-hand pocket of the raincoat—'

'So?' said Dr. Fell.

'And here are the various measurements; Bostwick got them for me. Emmet is 6 feet tall; weight 11 st. 8; wears size 7 hat. Dr. Joseph Chesney is 5 ft. 11½ inches tall; weight 13 st.; size 7 hat. George Harding is 5 ft. 9 inches tall; weight 11 st.;

size 6⅞ hat. Professor Ingram is 5 ft. 8 inches tall; weight 12 st. 2; wears size 7¼ hat. Marjorie Wills is 5 ft. 2 inches tall; weight 7 st. 8—but you don't want to hear that, *She's* out of it,' said Elliot, with quiet and firm satisfaction. 'Any of the others could have worn the stuff without looking queer in it: the only point being that every one of 'em except Emmet has an unbreakable alibi. We can't say too much at the moment; but just at present it looks as though it's got to be Emmet. Why, I wonder?'

Dr. Fell looked at him curiously. He was to remember that look long afterwards.

'Our psychologist friends,' the doctor declared, 'will doubtless say that Emmet is the downtrodden one who suffers from the Lust for Power. It is a common complaint among poisoners, I admit. Jegado, Zwanziger, Van de Leyden, Cream: the list is endless. I have also heard that Emmet suffers from (let us give it the capitals) a Hopeless Passion for Miss Wills. Oh, any arrangement of the dark cells is possible, I grant you. But it is possible, too'—here he stared very hard at his companion—'that Emmet figures in still another role: as scapegoat.'

'Scapegoat?'

'Yes. For (do you see?) there is still another interpretation of the spring-grip bag and the murderer in the chocolate-shop.' Dr. Fell considered. 'It has seemed curious to me, Inspector, that so many references have been made to the case of Christiana Edmunds in 1871. It always seemed to me that there was a moral in that story.'

Doubt struck Elliot again as quick and sharp as a dart in a board.

'You mean, sir, that—'

'Eh?' said Dr. Fell, waking up and looking genuinely startled out of his heavy musings. 'No, no, no! Good God, no! Perhaps I don't make myself clear.' He made flurried gestures; he seemed anxious to change the subject. 'Well, let's apply your own theory and get down to business. What are we going to do? What's our next move?'

'We are going to see that ciné-film,' Elliot told him. 'That is, if you'd care to come along. The chemist in Sodbury Cross, Major Crow tells me, is an enthusiast on amateur film-work, and does his own developing. Major Crow knocked him up at a quarter past three this morning and made him promise to have the film ready by lunch-time to-day. The chemist has a private projector above his shop; Major Crow says he's to be trusted. We're meeting there at one o'clock to run the film through. Lord!' said Elliot violently, and shook his fist. 'This might solve our problems. The real story of what happened, down in black and white that can't lie! Everything we want to know! I tell you, it seems almost too good to be true. Suppose something went wrong with the film? Suppose it didn't come out? Suppose—'

He did not know that within the next hour he was to get one of the greatest shocks of his life. While Dr. Fell dressed, while they drove the short distance to Sodbury Cross under a clearing sky, while they pulled up in the grey High Street outside the chemist's shop of Mr. Hobart Stevenson, Elliot anticipated the shock from every direction except the right one. Dr. Fell, a great bandit figure in box-pleated cape and shovel hat, uttered thunderous reassurances from the rear seat. Elliot's chief fear was that the chemist had bungled the developing; by the time they arrived he had almost convinced himself that this was the case.

The shop of Mr. Hobart Stevenson, in the middle of the rather grim-lipped High Street, had a distinctly photographic flavour. Its shop-windows displayed pyramids of small yellow boxes of films; a camera looked out from among the cough-mixtures, and behind it was a poster displaying enlargements of impossibly ecstatic photographs. From here you could look along the High Street to the boarded windows that marked Mrs. Terry's shop: to a garage and filling-station, a long array of shops displaying nothing but eatables, several pubs, and the Jubilee drinking-fountain in the middle of the road. It seemed deserted, despite the main traffic that hummed through in a series of lonely swishes; and despite figures that were stricken motionless as they peered out of shop-windows. From here to The Blue Lion, Elliot was conscious of being watched.

The bell over the shop door gave a sharp *ping* as they went in. Hobart Stevenson's shop was gloomy, full of that dim chemical smell which brought back sharply to Elliot the memory of another shop. But it was a tidy little box, a kind of bottle walled in by bottles, from the brisk diploma framed on the wall to the weights of a weighing-chair beside the counter. Hobart Stevenson—a plump, lip-pursing young man in a neat white jacket—wormed out from behind the counter to meet them.

'Inspector Elliot?' he said. He was obviously so weighed down by the importance of the occasion that his eye strayed to the door, and considered locking it against customers. Every strand of his flat hair seemed to quiver with it; Elliot studied him, and decided that he could be trusted.

'This is Dr. Gideon Fell,' said Elliot. 'Sorry we had to get you out of bed last night.'

'Not at all, not at all. I didn't mind,' said Stevenson, who clearly didn't.

'*Well? Have you got that film?*'

'All ready for you.'

'But is it—all right? I mean, how did it come out?'

'Not bad; not at all bad,' answered Stevenson, speaking cheerfully after considering this. From an amateur photographer, it was a handsome concession. He rubbed his hands together, as one who soothes. 'A little under-exposed; a little.' He cocked his head on one side, considering again. 'But not bad. Not at all bad. No.' Then he could not quite control his excitement. 'I hope you don't mind, Inspector. I ran the print through once on my projector, just to make sure it was all right. I'm ready for you as soon as the Major gets here. If you don't mind my saying so, you've certainly got some remarkable things there. Clues, I suppose you'd call them.'

It is a sober fact that the hair stirred on the back of Elliot's neck. But he spoke casually.

'Oh? What in particular?'

'Clues,' repeated Stevenson, with immense respect. He looked round. 'For instance, that second article Mr. Chesney picked up from the table, and pretended to write with—'

'Yes?'

'As I say, I hope you don't mind. I had to go over and take a magnifying-glass to the screen before I was dead certain. And then it was so simple that I started to laugh; and I haven't quite stopped yet.'

'Yes? What was it?'

'You'd never guess in the world,' Stevenson assured him, but without laughing. 'It was a—'

'S-HH!' roared Dr. Fell.

This thunderous hiss merged into the *ping* of the bell over the door, as the door opened and Professor Gilbert Ingram walked in.

Professor Ingram did not appear surprised. On the contrary, he showed an expression of great satisfaction. He wore a cap and dark-coloured suit of tweed plus-fours, which did not flatter his somewhat portly figure. But Elliot noticed less his straight glance, or his courteous gesture of greeting, than the atmosphere which entered with him. As he stood in the open door it was as though all the fierce watching of Sodbury Cross, all the attention concentrated on this shop, blew in through the doorway like a draught. Outside it was growing darker with approaching rain.

Professor Ingram closed the door.

'Good morning, Inspector,' he said. 'And this, I think, will be Dr. Fell?' (Dr. Fell acknowledged the greeting with a cordial roar, and Professor Ingram smiled.) 'I have heard a great deal about you, sir; though I am not sure whether we met or did not meet at a dinner or some such thing six months ago. Anyhow, I've heard Chesney speak of you. He wrote you a letter only a few days ago, I think?'

'He did.'

'However.' Professor Ingram became businesslike. He turned to Elliot. 'If I overslept this morning, Inspector, I don't suppose anybody will blame me. I've just come pelting in from my cottage.' He puffed humorously, indicating that he was out of breath. 'It seems to me I overheard you last night making plans for the—er—pre-view of a certain film here at Stevenson's—(morning, Mr. Stevenson!). I don't suppose there will be any great objection if I join you at the pre-view?'

Again the atmosphere subtly changed. Elliot was stolid.

'Sorry, sir. I'm afraid that's impossible.'

The other's cordial air grew puzzled. 'But surely, Inspector—?'

'Sorry, sir. We haven't seen it yet ourselves. You'll probably have an opportunity to see it all in good time.'

There was a pause.

'Don't you think, Inspector, that's being just a little unfair?' asked Professor Ingram, with a very slight change in his voice. 'After all, you came to me as an expert witness; I helped you to the best of my ability, which you will be the first to admit was a good deal; and I am naturally anxious to see whether I was right.'

'Sorry, sir.'

Elliot moved back to the counter. He bumped against the weighing-machine, whose weights rattled. Glancing to the left, he caught his own reflection in a gloomy mirror on the wall; and he would have fought out against these coincidences if he had not suddenly realised that most chemists must have such mirrors, to see whether a customer had come into the shop when the chemist himself was behind the dispensary. But most of all he studied Professor Ingram—who peered out from under the tweed cap, and chuckled.

'Well, it's of no consequence,' said the professor, bouncing and bustling and quizzical again. 'I shall have to restrain my natural curiosity, that's all, though you've punctured my vanity confoundedly.' He stopped to consider. 'Yes, that's it: vanity. However, if you don't mind, I really do want to buy several things; and after that I promise to clear out. Mr. Stevenson! A packet of the usual razor-blades. And a box of Strymo throat-tablets; the small size; yes, over there. Oh, and you might give me—'

He moved along the counter, and went on speaking more seriously:

'I must get along to Bellegarde. There will be funeral arrangements after the post-mortem, and I understand Vickers is coming over from Bath this afternoon or this evening to read the will. Also, I've been wondering whether Wilbur Emmet will be conscious yet.'

'I say,' observed Dr. Fell.

Dr. Fell spoke with such casualness that they all jumped a little. It was as though he had put out his hand to speak to somebody in the street.

'Have you got a theory?' he inquired with ghoulish interest.

'Ah!' said Professor Ingram. He had been bending down to point to some article in a lower show-case, but he straightened up. 'If I had, sir, this would hardly be the place or time to indicate it: would it?'

'Still—'

'Still, as you say! Now, sir, you are an intelligent man; I think I can depend on you.' (Elliot was suddenly as completely ignored as though he were the life-size cardboard figure of the young lady advertising soap at his elbow.) 'I told the Inspector last night, I several times told them all, that they would not approach this affair in the right direction; that they would not take into consideration the only factors that are of any importance. I mean, of course, motive.' His face grew red, as though by concentration. 'I needn't discuss it now. But I need only say this. *You* have heard of a motive for murder, one of the most powerful known to criminal psychology, which may roughly be called the lust for power?'

'Oh, my hat,' said Dr. Fell.

'I beg your pardon?'

'No; I beg yours,' said Dr. Fell, earnestly and rather guiltily. 'It was only that I hardly expected it to tumble on my neck quite so soon.'

'You deny it? Tell me: do you believe the poisoning at Mrs. Terry's and the poisoning last night were done by different persons?'

Dr. Fell scowled. 'No. On the contrary, I'm almost certain they were done by the same person.'

'Good. Then where is there another possible link? Where is there another possible motive?'

The cash-register rang sharply. Professor Ingram, receiving a parcel into his hands, turned round a little and eyed it as though it had started a new thought. 'I can only repeat: it's the only motive that applies to both crimes. The murderer gained nothing out of killing poor Frankie Dale and nearly killing the Anderson children. Nor did he gain anything out of killing Marcus Chesney. I mean in a material way. Both Marjorie and Joe Chesney, as we all know, will inherit very large sums. But the murderer'—here he opened his eyes—'gained nothing. Well, I mustn't stand here talking and keep you away from your proper work. Good morning, Dr. Fell. Good morning, Mr. Stevenson. Good morning.'

He did not completely close the door when he went out. There was a faint tingling of glass as a lorry thundered by in the High Street; a scent of cool wet air and cool wet trees blew in, stirring chemical odours. Dr. Fell was whistling "Aupres de Ma Blonde" under his breath. Elliot, who knew the signs, hesitated.

Then the doctor lifted his crutch-handled stick and pointed towards the door.

'I assure you I am not unduly suspicious,' he said. 'But that gentleman *has* got an alibi?'

'A cast-iron one. That's the trouble. The alibis here don't consist in the possibility that somebody, by fooling about with train-connections or motor-cars, might have made a sleight-of-hand jump from one place to the other. The alibis, except in one case, consist of people being actually seen and identified by other people. In the one other case, the alibi is proved by a clock that can't be tampered with.'

Elliot checked himself, suddenly realising that he was talking before an outsider in the person of Hobart Stevenson. He could also have sworn that at some point in his previous remarks there had been a flicker of honest delight in Stevenson's face. The chemist, professionally solemn again, was trying to cork down a huge secret.

So Elliot spoke sharply. 'You were telling us something a minute ago, Mr. Stevenson?'

'Honestly, Inspector, I'd rather you saw it for yourself. If you believe—'

'Hoy!' said Dr. Fell.

The doctor had lumbered and poked round to the dispensary behind the counter. Stevenson, evidently fascinated by this enormous visitor, followed him. Dr. Fell peered round with interest.

'How are you off for poisons here?' he asked, like a man inquiring after the drainage.

'The usual lot, sir.'

'Got any prussic acid or potassium cyanide?'

For the first time Stevenson seemed a trifle nervous. He smoothed back his hair with both hands, cleared his throat, and prepared to be businesslike.

'No prussic acid, no. I've got one or two preparations of potassium cyanide; but, as I was telling Mr. Bostwick this morning—'

'Do a brisk trade in 'em?'

'I haven't sold any of them for eighteen months. Er—I suppose it's all right to tell you?' He looked doubtfully at Elliot, who had joined them in the narrow and dusky aisle between the bottles. 'As I say, I was answering the Superintendent's questions this morning. And if you're thinking (I said, just among ourselves) if you're thinking anybody up at Bellegarde ever bought KCN anywhere, from anybody, to use on the fruit trees—well, I said, it would hardly do. With the temperature in those greenhouses kept between fifty and eighty degrees Fahrenheit all the year round, it would be plain suicide to take a KCN spray inside the door.'

This was an aspect of the matter which had not struck Elliot.

'I can show you my register, if you like,' Stevenson added.

'No, no. To tell you the truth,' said Dr. Fell, 'I'm rather more interested in photography. This seems to be a house of photography.' He blinked round. 'Tell me: you sell Photoflood lamps, don't you?'

'Photoflood lamps? Certainly.'

'Now, tell me,' argued Dr. Fell. 'Suppose I shoved one of those bulbs into a socket, and turned it on, and kept it burning steadily. How long would it go on before it burned out?'

Stevenson blinked at him.

'But you aren't supposed to do that,' he pointed out with an air of shrewdness. 'You only keep it on while you're taking a picture.'

'Yes, yes, I know. But suppose I'm an eccentric. Suppose I shove the blighter into a socket and keep it there. How long will it last?'

The chemist considered this.

'I should say well over an hour, anyhow. But—'

'You're sure of that, now?'

'Yes, sir, quite sure. Those things are the best value for the money I know.'

'H'mf. So. Did anybody from Bellegarde buy a Photoflood bulb from you yesterday morning?'

Stevenson looked fussed. 'Yesterday morning? Let me think.' (He did not really need to think, Elliot decided.) 'Yes; Miss Wills did. She came in about ten o'clock in the morning and bought one. But, if you don't mind, I hope you're not going to quote everything I say. *I* don't want to say anything about anybody up at Bellegarde—'

'Did Miss Wills frequently buy them?'

'Not frequently, but sometimes.'

'For herself?'

'No, no, no. For Mr. Chesney. They sometimes took indoor photographs at the greenhouses. The peaches, you see; specimens, and advertising, and things like that. He told her to get the bulb yesterday.'

Dr. Fell blinked round at Elliot. 'You quoted her as saying, Inspector, that the bulb last night was a new bulb she had bought herself.' He turned to Stevenson again. 'Miss Wills doesn't dabble in photography herself, then?'

'No, no, no. She never bought anything here—for photographic purposes.'

Andrew Elliot looked up, stung by memory. And for the second time, as at the return of a wheel, he saw Marjorie Wills looking at him in a mirror.

They had heard no *ping* from the bell over the door. The door still stood ajar, moving and creaking a little. They had heard no tap of footsteps. What they did hear, as Elliot looked up and found himself staring full into the girl's face in a mirror not five feet away, was the chemist's clear, soft, e-nun-ci-ating voice.

It was as though that reflection had slid out from behind the scenes of nowhere. Her lips were partly open, and she was wearing the same soft grey hat. One gloved hand was half raised, as though to point. Looking straight into her eyes in the dim mirror, Elliot saw recognition come into them as clearly as though a new face were taking shape.

She knew.

Marjorie Wills put one finger to her mouth, like a child.

And it was at this moment that there was a bursting crash of glass from the front door, the rattle of falling fragments and a last slow tinkle in silence, as someone flung a stone at her from the street.

XIII

ELLIOT VAULTED OVER THE COUNTER AND PLUNGED FOR the door. It was instinctive, the training of the Force. But it was also because he did not want to meet Marjorie Wills's eyes.

He threw open the door, his feet crunching in broken glass. He was suddenly so furious at the malice of that stone that he almost dodged out through the shattered panel. Then he stood looking up and down the street.

The street was empty. The only person in sight—too far away to have thrown the stone—was a delivery-boy on a bicycle, who toiled along on plodding pedals and stared virtuously up at the sky. The High Street lay serene and righteous in its proper business.

Steady, now.

Even with the blood in his head, he felt the cool of the wind and got a grip on himself. He must not make a false move. He must not go rushing wildly about, or he would only make a fool of himself; and then they would have an opportunity to laugh as well as to throw stones. Should he shout after the boy? Or rout out the greengrocer across the street? No; better not, for the moment. When in doubt, play a waiting game and let the other fellow wonder what you are up to: that alarms him more than anything else. But for the first time he knew the force of the secret, dumb-faced dislike centring round Marjorie Wills. For perhaps twenty seconds, Elliot stood looking quietly up and down the street.

Then he went back into the shop.

Marjorie Wills was leaning against the counter with her hands over her eyes.

'But why?' she said piteously. 'I—I haven't done anything.'

'They can't smash my windows like that,' said Stevenson, who was rather pale. '*I* haven't done anything either. They can't smash my windows like that. I don't call it right. Aren't you going to do anything about it, Inspector?'

'Yes,' said Elliot. 'But just now—'

Stevenson hesitated, confused between several ideas. 'Er—would you like to sit down, Miss Wills? A chair? In the back room? Or upstairs? That is,' his caution slipped up, 'I hadn't realised it was quite as bad as it is. I don't think it would be very wise for you to go out again.'

This was too much for Elliot.

'Oh, wouldn't it?' he said. 'Where are we, anyhow? In England? Or Germany? What are we?—a bunch of non-Aryans cooped up in a citadel? Just tell me where you want to go; and, if anybody as much as looks crooked at you, I'll have him in the cooler before you can say Dr. Nemo.'

She looked at him, turning her head quickly; and certain things were made as clear as though they had been printed on all the endless cardboard containers round the shop. It was not what he had said. It was that atmosphere which the emotions give out as palpably as the body gives out heat. Again he became intensely aware of her: of every detail of the face, from the line of the eye to the brushing of her hair back from the temple. It is what is called communication.

'Steady,' said Dr. Fell.

The doctor's quiet, rumbling tones restored sanity. He sounded almost cheerful.

'After all,' he continued, 'I hardly think we're as badly off as all that. Does Miss Wills want to sit down? By all means! Does she want to go anywhere? By all means! Why not, hey? Did you come here for anything, ma'am?'

'Did I—?' She was still looking at Elliot, with fixed eyes; now she roused herself.

'Soap, toothpaste, bath-salts?'

'Oh. I—I came to get the Inspector.' She did not look at him now. 'Major—Major Crow wants him at Bellegarde. At once. They—couldn't find him from eleven o'clock on, and nobody knew where he was. We tried to get Stevenson's on the 'phone, because Major Crow said you—he—was to be here at one o'clock; but there wasn't any answer; and in my state of mind I thought it would be a kind of spiritual exercise to drive through Sodbury Cross. My car's outside, if they haven't cut the tyres.'

'Major Crow? But why at Bellegarde? He was supposed to be here at one o'clock.'

'You mean you haven't *heard*? Nobody's told you?'

'Told us what?'

'Wilbur's dead,' said Marjorie.

Dr. Fell reached up to the brim of his shovel-hat and pulled it a little farther forward over his eyes. His big hand remained there, shading the eyeglasses.

'I am sorry,' he growled from behind it. 'The concussion was fatal, then?'

'No,' said Marjorie. 'Uncle Joe says someone came into the room in the middle of the night, with a hypodermic with prussic acid in it; and—and injected it into his arm; and he died in his sleep.'

There was a silence.

Dr. Fell extricated himself from behind the dispensary. He lumbered towards the door, where he stood with his head lowered; then he got out a large red bandana handkerchief and blew his nose violently.

'You must excuse me,' he said. 'I have met the powers of hell before; but never where they moved with such reasoned and loving care. How did it happen?'

'I don't know; nobody knows.' Marjorie was evidently holding tight to her nerves. 'We didn't get to bed until very late, and we weren't up until nearly eleven this morning. Uncle—Uncle Joe said it wouldn't be necessary for anybody to sit up with Wilbur. This morning Pamela went into his room and just—just found him.'

She lifted her hands slightly from the sides of her skirt, and dropped them.

'I see. Mr. Stevenson!'

'Doctor?'

'Is your telephone out of order?'

'Not that I know of,' replied the other, worried. 'I've certainly been here all morning, and I don't understand it.'

'Good.' Dr. Fell turned to Elliot. 'Now I will offer a suggestion. You must ring up Bellegarde. You must tell Major Crow that, far from your going to Bellegarde, he must come here at once—'

'Hold on! I can't do that, sir,' protested Elliot. 'Major Crow is the Chief Constable, you know. Bostwick—'

'*I* can do it,' said Dr. Fell mildly. 'I happen to know Crow very well, since that case of the Eight of Swords. In fact, to tell you the strict and guilty truth,' here his red face became more conspicuous, 'Crow asked me to look into the Mrs. Terry affair when the first of these damnable things happened. I declined. I declined because the only explanation I could think of at the time sounded so wild and wool-gathering that I didn't even put it forward. But now, by thunder, I begin to see it wasn't wild at all. It was the obvious: the plain, dull, dead obvious. That, I fear, is why I was so immediately and infernally ready with explanations for you this morning.'

He shook his fist savagely.

'And, because I emulated the modest violet—*hrrr!*—two more persons have died. I want you here. I want Crow here. I want to see that film, now, more than anything else I can think of. I want to point out to you, in cold black and white on a screen, just what I think happened. Therefore I am going to telephone and issue orders like a buccaneer. But while I am telephoning'—here he ceased to thunder; he looked very steadily at Elliot—'I suggest you ask Miss Wills what happened at another chemist's shop.'

Marjorie stiffened. Elliot appeared not to notice; he spoke to Stevenson.

'You live above the shop here? Have you got a room you could turn over to me for a few minutes?'

'Yes, of course. It's the room where I'm going to show you the film.'

'Thanks. Lead the way, will you? Miss Wills, will you go on ahead?'

She did not comment. Stevenson led them upstairs to a comfortable, old-fashioned sitting-room overlooking the street. Double-doors (again) communicated with what was presumably a bedroom; they were open, but a sheet had been fastened in the space with drawing-pins to form a motion-picture screen. The heavy curtains were half drawn, and there was a bright fire in the grate. A large ciné-projector, its round film-spools in place, stood on the table.

Still without comment, Marjorie went over to a sofa and sat down. Elliot was now suffering from a severe reaction; his conscience was at work again.

Marjorie looked round the firelit room, as though to make sure they were alone. Then she nodded and said coolly:

'I told you we had met before.'

'Yes,' agreed Elliot. He sat down by the table and took out his notebook, which he flattened out with great deliberation. 'To be exact, last Thursday, Mason & Son, Chemists, 16 Crown Road, where you tried to buy cyanide of potassium.'

'And yet you never told anybody.'

'What makes you think I didn't, Miss Wills? Why do you suppose I was sent down to this part of the country?'

This was a stinger. He did it deliberately, throwing more meat to his conscience. He wondered how much he had betrayed himself downstairs; how much she had noticed; whether she would try to make use of it, as she seemed to be doing by that abrupt, inspired guess; and he was not standing any of that.

If he hoped for an effect, he got one. The colour drained out of her face. Her eyes, which had been fixed widely and steadily on him, now blinked; she could not make him out; and afterwards would come anger.

'Oh. So you *did* come down to arrest me?'

'That depends.'

'Is it a crime to try to buy cyanide even when you don't get it?'

Elliot picked up his notebook and let it fall flat on the table.

'Honestly, Miss Wills, and between ourselves, what's the good of talking like that? What sort of interpretation could anybody put on it?'

She was extraordinarily acute. Elliot admired her intelligence even when he cursed it. She was still watching, waiting, wondering what to make of him; and her ear had instantly caught that faint shade of come-on-hang-it-why-don't-you-help-me which he could not help putting into the last exasperated question. The rapid rise and fall of her breast grew slower.

'If I tell you the truth, Inspector—if I tell you really and truly why I wanted that poison—will you believe me?'

'If you tell me the truth, yes.'

'No, but that isn't the point. That isn't the real thing. If I tell you the real honest truth, will you promise, *promise* not to tell anyone else?'

(That, he thought, was genuine.)

'Sorry, miss. I'm afraid I can't make any promises like that. If it concerns this investigation—'

'But it doesn't.'

'All right: what did you want with the cyanide?'

'I wanted it to kill myself with,' said Marjorie calmly.

There was a slight pause, while the fire crackled.

'But why should you want to kill yourself?'

She drew a deep breath. 'If you must know, because I was so utterly and horribly sick at the idea of being home again. Now I've told you. I've told somebody.' She looked at him curiously, as though she wondered why she had told him.

Unconsciously Elliot had slipped from the attitude of a detective asking official questions into an attitude somewhat different; but neither of them noticed it.

'Yes, but look here! Was there any reason why you should want to kill yourself?'

'Try being exposed to what I was exposed to—here. Poisoning people; poisoning them like that; expecting to be arrested every minute of the day, and only getting out of it because there wasn't enough evidence. Then try going away on a gorgeous Mediterranean cruise, the sort of thing you've never had in your life in spite of the fact that your uncle is a millionaire. Then try coming back again—to what you left. Try it. Try it! And see what you feel.'

She clenched her hands.

'Oh, I've got over it now. But all I felt, the minute I stepped off that ship, was that I simply could not go through with it. I didn't stop to think. If I had, I could have got some plausible story together, so that I didn't stammer and stumble and go panicky when the chemist started to ask me questions. I thought of that afterwards. But all I thought of at the time was that I'd heard potassium cyanide was so quick and it was painless; all you had to do was taste it and you were dead. And I thought that in the East End of London they'd never know or remember me. I think it was coming back up the river on the ship that did it—seeing the houses, and everything.'

Elliot put down his pencil. He asked:

'But what about your *fiancé*?'

'My *fiancé*?'

'Do you mean to tell me you wanted to buy poison to kill yourself with when you were coming home to be married?'

She made a despairing gesture. 'I told you it was a mood! I told you. Besides, that was another thing. Everything had been so wonderful before all this happened, and I hoped things were turning out right for me. When I met George in London—'

Elliot said:

'When you met him in *London*?'

'Oh, damn,' whispered Marjorie, and put her hand over her mouth. She remained staring at him; then an expression of weariness and cynicism came into her face. 'Never mind. Why shouldn't you know? It's doing me a lot of good—a lot of good—to get this off my chest.

'I've known George for ages and ages and ages. I met him at a party in London, one of the rare occasions when Uncle Marcus let me go to town alone, and I fell for him terribly. I used to sneak up to town to meet him. Oh, we didn't do anything about it. I suppose I didn't have the nerve: that's me.'

She stared at the floor.

'But we decided it wasn't wise to introduce George to Uncle Marcus just yet. In the first place, Uncle Marcus never—never—encouraged—people; that is, people to come and see me. I'm a really good housekeeper, and it was much more convenient and everything to keep me—you know what I mean.' She flushed. 'In the second place, George knew all about Uncle Marcus's reputation. There would be a dreadful row if Uncle Marcus knew what had been going on behind his back. You can see that?'

'Yes. I can see it.'

'It would be better if we seemed to meet casually. Preferably abroad; and, besides, George said he needed a holiday anyway. Of course George hasn't got much money, especially for a trip like that. But I had a couple of hundred in insurance, that my mother left me, and I got rid of that and so George was able to take the trip.'

(Swine, said Andrew Elliot to himself. Damned swine. Clever swine.)

She opened her eyes.

'He isn't!' cried Marjorie. 'I mean, he's clever, but he isn't the other thing. He's the most brilliant man I ever met, and sure of himself: that's what I loved: sure of himself.'

'Sorry,' Elliot was beginning—when he stopped short with an uncanny feeling that the world had slipped its moorings. 'Swine, damned swine, clever swine.' He had not said those words aloud. He had seen them in his mind as clearly as though they were written on moving teletype, but he had not spoken them. This girl might be intelligent, except as concerned Mr. George Harding. But she was not a mind-reader.

Marjorie herself appeared to be unconscious of it.

'And how I hoped,' she said, with a kind of violence, 'that George would give Uncle Marcus back as good as he sent! Oh, I wanted him to make a good impression. Naturally. But this—this *humble* tail-wagging was too much. There was a day in Pompeii when Uncle Marcus decided to have the whole thing out, just like that (in front of Wilbur and Professor Ingram too), and right in a public place where anyone might have walked in. He as good as gave George his orders, exactly how everything was to be managed for the future; and George took it like a lamb. And you ask me why I felt low and dispirited and ready to scream when I stepped off that ship! I saw there wasn't going to be any change. I saw my life was going on exactly as it always had before. Everywhere I turned it would be nothing but Uncle Marcus, Uncle Marcus, Uncle Marcus.'

Elliot pulled himself up.

'You didn't like your uncle?'

'Of course I liked him. I loved him. But that isn't the point. Do you understand?'

'Ye-es, I suppose so.'

'He was wonderful, in his own way. He's done everything for me, and he went out of his way to give me a wonderful holiday when I needed it. But if you could only have heard him talk for five minutes! And then these eternal, non-stop arguments with Professor Ingram about crime—even when there was real, true crime right here among us—and his "criminological" manuscript...'

Elliot abruptly picked up his pencil again.

'Criminological manuscript?'

'Yes; I told you. He was always working at some scholarly effort or another, but mostly to do with the science of the mind. That's why he was so thick with Professor Ingram. He used to say, "Well, you maintain that a practising psychologist would make the greatest criminal alive. Why not be a pioneer in the interests of science? Commit a purely disinterested crime and prove your theory." Brr!'

'I see. And what did Professor Ingram say to that?'

'He said no, thanks. He said he wouldn't commit a crime until he could devise a perfect alibi—'

(Elliot had heard this somewhere before.)

'—and, so far as even a practising psychologist could see, it was still impossible for a man to be in two places at the same time.' Marjorie crossed her knees and leaned back against the sofa. 'What gave me the shivers was that they were always so cool and calm about it. Because, you see, it has happened. All these horrible things are going on, and we don't know how or who or why. And now Wilbur is dead. *Wilbur*, who never did anybody the least harm, any more than Frankie Dale or the Anderson children or Uncle Marcus himself. I'm nearly at the end of my string, es-especially when they begin throwing stones at *me* and heaven knows what else that might happen to me. Like lynching or burning or I don't know what. Help me. Please help me!'

She paused.

Such a soft and vital directness had come into her voice, such a strength of appeal, that Elliot came near losing his official calm. She was leaning forward, her hand outstretched as though she were asking to be helped up from the sofa; and her eyes never left his. It was here that they heard outside the closed door a continued noise like an elephant stumping and pawing the ground, and a trumpeting sound like a challenge at feeding-time. After this there was a loud knock; Dr. Fell, navigating the doorway sideways, turned round and blinked down at them.

'I don't want to interrupt,' he said, 'but I think you'd better postpone questioning until a little later. Crow and Bostwick are on their way up. I think it would be better for you to go, Miss Wills. Mr. Stevenson is locking up the shop; but his assistant will drive you home in the car. Then—'

He fastened his eyes on the cinema-projector.

XIV

Major Crow and Superintendent Bostwick passed Marjorie in the doorway as she was going out. But Major Crow did not speak until the door had closed. He was himself again.

'Good morning, Inspector,' he said politely. 'Or, rather, good afternoon. We were unable to find you this morning.'

'Sorry, sir.'

'It is of no consequence,' said the other, still politely. 'I only wanted to tell you that there is the small matter of another death to be considered.'

'I said I was sorry, sir.'

'Since you went to my friend Fell, I've got no objection. You had more luck than I had. *I* tried to interest him in this business last June. But no. Wasn't sensational enough for him, it seems. No hermetically sealed rooms. No supernatural elements. No funny business at the Royal Scarlet Hotel. Only a brutal murder by strychnine, and several near-murders. But now we've got a broad range of evidence, and two more victims—one of whom, Inspector, it might be worth your while to examine—'

Elliot picked up his notebook.

'I've told you twice I was sorry, sir,' he replied slowly. 'I don't see that I need to say it again. And furthermore, if you want the truth, I don't admit I've neglected anything I should have attended to. By the way, are there any constables in Sodbury Cross?'

Bostwick, who had also taken out a pipe and pouch, stopped in the act of unscrewing the stem of the pipe.

'There are, my lad,' he said. 'And why do you want to know that, now?'

'Only because I didn't see any. Somebody smashed a plate-glass door downstairs with a stone, and made a noise you could hear as far as Bath; but I didn't see any.'

'Dash my buttons,' said Bostwick, suddenly blowing down the stem of the pipe and then looking up again. It was an optical illusion; but his face seemed to swell to a startling extent. 'What do you mean by that, now?'

'What I say.'

'If you mean,' said Bostwick, 'that I think—mind, I say I think—that pretty soon we'll be able to arrest a certain young lady who needn't be named—why, yes, I do think it.'

'Hey!' roared Dr. Fell.

It was a blast that shook the window-frames, making all the contestants turn round.

'This has got to stop,' said Dr. Fell seriously. 'You are row-ing over nothing, and you know it. If there is anybody to be blamed, blame me. The real reason for all this tempest (and you know this too) is that each of you has a different, definite, preconceived, and stubborn notion as to who is guilty. For the love of Mike, come off it, or we shall get nowhere.'

Major Crow broke the tension by chuckling. It was an honest, homely sound; both Elliot and Bostwick grinned.

'The old blighter's quite right,' agreed Major Crow. 'Sorry, Inspector. The fact is (you could add) we've got our nerves so much on edge that we can't see straight. And we've got to see straight. We've *got* to.'

Bostwick extended his tobacco-pouch to Elliot. 'Have a fill,' he invited.

'Thanks. I don't mind if I do.'

'And now,' said Dr. Fell murderously, 'now that the amenities are preserved and a general warmth of cosiness reigns o'er all—'

'I don't admit I have a definite, preconceived notion,' said Major Crow with dignity. 'I haven't. All I know is that I'm right. When I saw that poor devil Emmet lying there—'

'Hah!' muttered Superintendent Bostwick, with such a sceptical and sinister inflection that Elliot was surprised. He wondered in what direction they were headed now.

—'but there's nothing to go on, Inspector. Nothing to hold to. There Emmet is: bang. Someone walked in during the night and put a hypodermic into his arm. Nobody heard, or will admit having heard, anything suspicious in the night. Anybody could have done it. Even an outsider could have done it, because they never lock doors at Bellegarde. Very few people hereabouts do lock doors at night. I say even an outsider could have done it, though I know what I think. Oh: and I've seen West, by the way, for the medical report. Chesney was killed with pure prussic acid, about a grain of it. That is, there were no traces of other ingredients to show he was killed with a preparation of the stuff like potassium cyanide or mercury cyanide. And that's all we've got.'

'No, it isn't,' said Dr. Fell with satisfaction. 'Here's Mr. Stevenson. Now, my lad. We're ready. Touch her off.'

An uneasy silence settled on the group.

Stevenson, conscious of his own importance, trod lightly and had a tendency towards fussiness. After mopping his forehead, he inspected the fire. He glanced at the windows. He studied the sheet hung in the space between the double-doors. After a prolonged scrutiny of the table, he hauled it back, bumping, until it was almost against the wall opposite the sheet. Then he pushed it forward some inches. From a book-case he dragged out a number of volumes of the *Encyclopaedia Britannica*, which he piled up on the table to make a higher platform for the projector. All four investigators were now smoking pipes, so that a cloud of smoke rose in the dusky room. They had a tendency to prowl.

'This won't work,' said Major Crow suddenly. 'Something'll go wrong.'

'But what can go wrong?' demanded Elliot.

'I don't know. Some damned thing. This is too easy. You'll see.'

'I assure you it's all right, sir,' said Stevenson, turning a perspiring face. 'Ready in just a second.'

The silence lengthened, except for an occasional mysterious tinkling sound in Stevenson's operations, or a mournful whish of traffic from the High Street. Stevenson edged the sofa to one side so that there was an uninterrupted line to the screen. He arranged chairs. There was a slight wrinkle in the screen, so he altered the position of a drawing-pin and smoothed that out.

Finally, while a vast breath of relief came from the spectators, he moved back slowly on his heels towards the windows.

'Now, gentlemen,' he said, groping for one curtain. 'Ready. If you'll just take chairs before I close these curtains?'

Dr. Fell lumbered over to the sofa. Bostwick sat down gingerly on the edge beside him. Elliot drew a chair to a position closer to the screen but at one side of it. There was a rattle of rings as one set of curtains swept together.

'Now, gentlemen—'

'Stop!' said Major Crow, taking the pipe out of his mouth.

'Oh, my ancient hat,' howled Dr. Fell, 'what is it now?'

'No need to get excited about it,' protested the other. He pointed with the stem of his pipe. 'Suppose—well, suppose nothing does go wrong.'

'That's what we're waiting to see, you know.'

'Suppose it comes out as we hope. There are certain things we're bound to get: Dr. Nemo's actual height, for instance. It's only fair to take a show of hands now. What are we going to see? Who was Dr. Nemo? What do you say, Bostwick?'

Superintendent Bostwick turned round a moon-face over the back of the sofa. He held his pipe in such a way that it seemed to be poised in the air behind his head.

'Well, sir, if you ask me—I haven't got much doubt we shall find he was Mr. Wilbur Emmet.'

'Emmet! Emmet? But Emmet's dead!'

'He wasn't dead then,' the Superintendent pointed out.

'But—never mind, then. What's your view, Fell?'

'Sir,' said Dr. Fell with polished courtesy, 'my view is this. My view is only that I wish to be allowed to have a view. On some points I am certain what we shall see. On other points

I am uncertain what we shall see. On still further points I am beginning not to give a curse what we see, provided only that we are ultimately permitted to get on and see it.'

'Right-ho!' said Stevenson.

The remaining curtains swept shut. Now the darkness was broken only by the faint glow of the fire, or the uncertain goblin gleam of a pipe. Elliot became conscious of the dampness which clings to old stone houses; of stuffiness, and smoke. He had no difficulty in making out the shapes or faces of any of his companions: even of Stevenson at the back of the room. Stevenson moved round, stepping gingerly to avoid the electric flex attached to the projector. He switched it on. Chinks and gleams of light sprang up from the box, illuminating him like an alchemist over a crucible; and the beam of the projector, which the smoke caught and followed, appeared on the screen in a blank white patch some four feet square.

From the back of the room came a series of rattling, tinny sounds, and a click as of something opened or shut. The projector began to hum, rising to a steady whirring noise. The screen flashed, flickered, and then went dead black.

There was nothing wrong, for the whirring noise still filled the room. The blackness continued, shot a little with grey, and wavering slightly. It seemed to go on interminably. Then a faint blur of light appeared, becoming a dazzle. It was as though a vertical crack were opening down the centre of the screen, with a vague black blur pushing and stretching it open. Elliot knew what it was. They were back in the Music Room facing the office; and Marcus Chesney was pushing open the double-doors.

Someone coughed. The picture jumped a little; then they saw, as though cut off from them by a lawn of darkness, the back part of the office at Bellegarde. A moving shadow wavered along the edge of it, evidently that of a man walking back to the table. Harding had taken the picture from slightly too far to the left, so that you could not see the French windows. The light was vague and rather bad despite its sharpness of shadow. But you could distinctly see the glimmering mantelpiece, the face of the clock whose pendulum threw back gleams, the back of a desk-chair, the broad table-top, the chocolate-box whose pattern showed grey, and the two tiny pencil-like articles lying on the blotter. Then there was a stir at the edge of the light—and Marcus Chesney's face stared out from the screen.

Marcus Chesney was not a pleasant sight. Due to the placing of the light, the absence of make-up, the jumpy flickering world created by the unsteady camera, he looked already dead. His face was bloodless, his eyebrows accentuated and eye-sockets hollowed out, his cheeks streaked with darkness whenever he turned his head. But he wore an expression of high and lofty calmness. He bobbed into the picture, moving leisurely…

'Look at the clock,' someone said with shattering loudness from behind Elliot's shoulder. It drowned out the steady whirring of the projector. 'Look at the clock! What's the time?'

'Gawdlummycharley—' said Bostwick's voice.

A stir went through the room, as though it were the furniture that had moved rather than the people.

'What's the time there? What do you say?'

'They were all wrong,' said Bostwick's voice, 'that's what it is. One of 'em said midnight; one said about midnight; and Professor Ingram said one minute to midnight. They're all wrong. It's one minute *past* midnight.'

'Sh-h-h!'

The little mimic world was unaffected. With great deliberation Marcus Chesney drew out the desk-chair and sat down. He reached out and pushed the chocolate-box a little to his own right, with great nicety as contrasted to the flickering of the film. Next he picked up a flattish pencil, and with it he industriously and rather self-consciously pretended to write. Next—having to dig his finger-nails a little into the blotter, and showing some difficulty in picking it up—he took the other tiny article. They saw it clearly, straight against the light.

Professor Ingram's description of it flashed into Elliot's mind. The professor had described it as something like a pen, but narrower and much smaller. He had described it as a thin sliver, under three inches long, blackish, sharp-tipped. And this was a correct description.

'I know what that is,' said Major Crow.

There was the scrape of a chair. Major Crow walked quickly out of the group, edged sideways, and stuck his head into the beam of light to get a better look. His shadow blotted out half the screen; and a series of fantastic pictures, of Marcus Chesney writhing wildly, danced in faint outline across the back of his raincoat.

'Stop the picture,' said Major Crow, turning round full in the beam from the projector. His voice was going high.

'I know what it is right enough,' he repeated. 'It's the minute-hand of a clock.'

'The what?' demanded Bostwick.

'The minute-hand of that clock on the mantelpiece,' shouted Major Crow, raising his finger as though to illustrate. 'We noticed the clock had a dial six inches in diameter. Don't you see it? It's the long minute-hand as opposed to the short hour-hand. All Chesney had to do before the performance was unscrew the head of the spindle holding the hands (we saw it had a screw-head), remove the minute-hand from the spindle, and replace the screw-head. That left only one hand on the clock: the short hour-hand pointing dead to twelve.

'Gad, take my—don't you see it yet? There was only one hand on the clock. The witnesses all thought they saw two hands. What they really saw was the hour-hand; and a sharp, black shadow of the hour-hand thrown above and beside it on the white face of the clock by that brilliant light shining up on it from below.'

He pointed his finger; he seemed to fight down a tendency to dance.

'It even accounts for all the differences in the testimony, don't you see? The witnesses differ according to the direction in which they saw the shadow fall. Professor Ingram, sitting to the extreme right, saw the shadow fall at one minute to twelve. Miss Wills, sitting in the centre, saw it dead on midnight. This film, taken from the extreme left, shows it at one minute past twelve. After the performance—when Chesney carefully closed the double-doors on them—all he had to do was replace the minute-hand on the clock: which would take about five seconds. And the clock showed the right time again. But during the performance Chesney had the colossal cheek to sit there holding the minute-hand under their very eyes; and not one of 'em saw it.'

There was a silence.

From the gloom came the sound of Bostwick apprecia-tively slapping his thigh, of an approving grunt from Dr. Fell, and of Stevenson muttering as he struggled with a jammed film. Major Crow added, more mildly, but bursting with pride:

'Didn't I tell you there was some jiggery-pokery about that clock?'

'You did that, sir,' said Bostwick.

'It's sound psychology,' admitted Dr. Fell, nodding with vigour. 'You know, I would offer a small wager that the trick would have deceived them even if there had been no shadow. When the hands of a clock are on midnight we see only one hand; we glance no further; custom deceives us. But our good Chesney went even further and made his scheme triple fool-proof. That, we begin to see, was why he insisted on holding the show round about midnight. The shadow illu-sion, granted, would work with the hands at any position on the dial. But by getting the hour-hand vertical at midnight he made sure that three different witnesses in three different positions saw three different, sharply emphasised times on the clock. And he would catch them out in no less than two questions out of his ten. But look here! The question is— steady—the question now is, what was the *real* time?'

'Ah,' said Bostwick.

'That hour-hand is vertical, isn't it?'

'It is,' affirmed Major Crow.

'Which means,' scowled the doctor, 'which means, if I recall anything of my own various tinkerings with clocks, that the position of the minute-hand could have been any-thing from five minutes before midnight to five minutes past midnight. The hour-hand stays more or less vertical during those times, depending on the size and mechanism of the clock. The time before midnight does not concern us. The time after midnight does concern us. It means—'

Major Crow put away his pipe in his pocket.

'It means,' he said, 'that Joe Chesney's alibi is shot to blazes. Everything depended on his leaving Emsworth's house at just midnight, the same time (we supposed) that Dr. Nemo was in the office at Bellegarde. Joe Chesney really did leave the Emsworths' at midnight. But Dr. Nemo didn't walk into the office and kill Chesney at midnight. No: the real time was past midnight. Probably five or six minutes past midnight. Joe Chesney could easily have driven from the Emsworths' to Bellegarde in three minutes. Q.E.D. Open those curtains, somebody. I've got nothing against Joe Chesney; but I'm inclined to think he's the lad we want.'

XV

IT WAS ELLIOT WHO THREW BACK THE CURTAINS ON ONE window. Daylight came in with grey pallor, paling the beam from the projector, showing Major Crow standing before a picture still twisted and stuck faintly on the sheet hung between the doors.

And Major Crow's excitement was growing.

'Inspector,' he said, 'I never fancied myself much in the analytical way. But this is so plain we can't overlook it. You know? Poor old Marcus Chesney actually planned the way in which another person could kill him.'

'So?' observed Dr. Fell thoughtfully.

'Joe Chesney could have known all about the clock and the shadow-illusion. You see that? Either he could have hung about Bellegarde after dinner: Marcus and Wilbur Emmet were in the study, with windows open, for nearly three hours. Or else, which seems more likely, Marcus and Emmet were planning this show for days ahead; and Joe could have known all about it beforehand.

'He knew Marcus wouldn't start the show until the hand of that clock was vertical. In the ordinary way, you know, that clock couldn't be tampered with; Marcus couldn't re-set the position of the hands. If Joe could get himself an alibi at the Emsworths'—if he could get back to Bellegarde—and if Marcus chose to put on the show at a time after midnight rather than a time before midnight, Joe Chesney would be in clover. And wait! There's one thing (by Jove, I've just thought of this) there's one thing he would certainly have to do afterwards.'

'Which is?' said Elliot.

'He'd have to kill Wilbur Emmet as well,' said the Major. 'Emmet knew all about the trick with the clock. And how many other people hereabouts, do you think, know how to use a hypodermic needle?' He let this sink in. 'Gentlemen, it's as plain as anything I ever saw. He's got a head, that chap has. Who would suspect him?'

'You would,' said Dr. Fell.

'What's that?'

'In fact, you did,' the doctor pointed out. 'It was the very first thing you thought of. I suspect that in your correct Woolwich head there has long been stirring a profound distrust of Joseph Chesney's too-roaring manners. But continue.'

'Gad, I've got nothing against the fellow!' protested Major Crow rather querulously. He became formal again, and turned to Elliot. 'Inspector, this is your case. After this morning, I will have nothing more to do with it. But it strikes me you've got some very good grounds here. It's well known that Joe Chesney hates work, as he would; and that Marcus somehow kept him at it or bullied him into it; and that, so far as grounds for arrest are concerned—'

'What grounds?' interrupted Dr. Fell.

'I don't follow you.'

'I said what grounds?' repeated Dr. Fell. 'In your highly intelligent reconstruction you seem to have forgotten one small but possibly important fact. It was not Joseph Chesney who hoaxed you with the clock. It was his brother Marcus. You have got the direction of the evidence mixed. You are robbing Peter to hang Paul.'

'Yes; but—'

'And therefore,' said Dr. Fell with emphasis, 'by some mental sleight-of-hand you have convinced yourself that you ought to arrest a man simply because you have broken an alibi which somebody else constructed for him. You do not even suggest that he constructed it. You want to arrest him simply because he has no alibi. I will make no comment on the other glaring weaknesses in your hypothesis; I will confine myself to the simple observation that you cannot do that there here.'

Major Crow was offended.

'I didn't say anything about arresting him. I know we've got to have evidence. But what do you suggest?'

'What about getting on with it, sir,' suggested Bostwick, 'and finding out?'

'Eh?'

'This chap in the top-hat. We haven't *seen* him yet.'

'—and is it understood,' Dr. Fell said savagely, when order was restored and the curtains drawn again, 'that this time nobody interrupts until the film is finished? Is it agreed?

Good! Then kindly bite on a bullet and restrain yourselves and let us see what is happening. Fire away, Mr. Stevenson.'

Again the click and hum of the projector filled the room. The mimic scene silenced them to coughs and rustlings. Now, as Elliot looked at the screen, the thing seemed so obvious that he wondered how mind co-related with eyesight could have gone so far astray. The larger hand on that clock clearly was a shadow: nothing more. Marcus Chesney, holding the real clock-hand and industriously pretending to write with it, wore an expression that betrayed nothing.

Marcus Chesney dropped it on the blotter. He seemed to hear something. He turned round a little way, to his right. His face, bony and unpleasantly hollowed with shadow, swung round so that they had an even better view of it.

And into the picture stepped the murderer.

Dr. Nemo, in fact, turned round slowly and looked at them.

He was a dingy figure. The nap of the tall hat was badly rubbed and looked moth-eaten. The raincoat, a muddy light grey, had its collar turned up to where the ears might have been. A fuzzy greyish blob, which might have been the face of an insect or the windings of a muffler, filled up the space between; and the black spectacles stared at them opaquely.

Their first view of him was a fairly full view, though taken from the left. He was standing within the radius of light; but at the moment he was standing too far to the front, and the light was placed too high, so that his trousers and shoes were too dim to be made out. The fingers of his gloved right hand, smooth and jointless as a dummy's, held the black bag with its painted name towards them.

Then he moved with blinding swiftness.

Elliot, on the alert for it, saw what he did. His back was partly turned to them when he looked back at Marcus Chesney, and the movement was easier to follow. Approaching the table, he put down the bag. He put it down just behind the chocolate-box there. Instantly, as though altering his intention, he picked it up again and put it down on top of the chocolate-box. By his first movement he had released the duplicate chocolate-box on the table from the spring-grip bag. By his second movement he snapped up the original box into the bag.

'So that's how he changed 'em over!' said Major Crow's voice out of the gloom.

'Sh-h-h!' roared Dr. Fell.

But there was not time to think, for the whole affair was over too soon. When Nemo circled the table outside the range of light he became a sort of exploding blur, unpleasantly as though he had no existence and were de-materialising.

Then they saw a man murdered.

Nemo reappeared on the other side of the table. Marcus Chesney spoke to him soundlessly. Nemo's right hand—which they could see because he was now partly facing them—was in his pocket. It came out; the movement of the hands flickered a little, but he was taking something out of what looked like a tiny cardboard box.

Hitherto his movements had been swift and precise. Now they became charged with a kind of malignancy. The fingers of his left hand fastened lightly round Marcus Chesney's throat; they moved, and tilted up the chin. Even in the hollows of the eye-sockets you could see the startled gleam of Marcus Chesney's eyes. Nemo's right hand wormed over his captive's mouth; it pressed a capsule inside, and flattened out.

Superintendent Bostwick spoke out of the gloom.

'Ah,' he said. 'That was where the lady cried out, "*Don't, don't!*"'

Nemo disappeared again.

Circling back round the table in a shadowy dazzle, he picked up the black satchel. But this time he moved back to the extreme rear of the room as he was going out. Dimly but clearly, the light picked up his full figure. It showed the dress trousers and the evening shoes. It also showed the distance of the bottom of the raincoat from the floor. In one flash they could estimate his height almost as clearly as though they held a measure.

'Stop the film!' said Major Crow. 'Stop it right there! You can see—'

It was unnecessary to stop the film. It had come to its end. With a series of flapping noises from the projector, the screen flickered, darkened, and grew blankly white.

'That's all,' said Stevenson's voice rather huskily.

For a brief time it was only Stevenson who moved. He shut off the machine, wormed his way from behind it, and went to open the curtains. He disclosed a kind of tableau. Major Crow radiated satisfaction. Superintendent Bostwick was smiling quietly and secretly to his pipe. But on Dr. Fell's face was such an expression of utter and thunderstruck consternation that the Major burst out laughing.

'Someone has received a jolt, I notice,' he remarked. 'Now, Inspector, I appeal to you. What was Dr. Nemo's height?'

'At least six feet, I should say,' Elliot conceded. 'Of course, we shall have to take a magnifying glass to the film and do some measuring. He was dead in line with that mantelpiece, so it ought to be easy. Comparative measurements will do it. But it looked like six feet.'

'Ah,' agreed Bostwick. 'Six feet it was. And did you notice the chap's walk?'

'What do *you* say, Fell?'

'I say no,' roared Dr. Fell.

'But don't you believe your own eyes?'

'No,' said Dr. Fell. 'Certainly not. Definitely not. Observe the mess in which we have already landed by believing our own eyes. We are travelling in a house of illusions, a box of tricks, a particularly devious sort of ghost-train. When I think of that trick with the clock, I am filled with a kind of reverent awe. The clock couldn't have been tampered with: but it was. If Chesney could think of a stunt as ingenious as that, he could think of others as good—or better. I don't believe it. By thunder, I won't believe it.'

'But is there any reason to suppose this is a trick too?'

'There is,' affirmed Dr. Fell. 'I call it The Problem of the Unnecessary Question. But here we are only supplied with huger and fresher problems.'

'Such as?'

'Well, observe how our expert witness was snookered,' argued Dr. Fell, drawing out his bandana handkerchief and flourishing it. 'Three witnesses answered that question as to the height of Dr. Nemo. Marjorie Wills is not a particularly good witness. Harding is a rotten witness. Professor Ingram, on the other hand, is a very good witness indeed. Yet, in this question of height, both the unobservant ones got it right and Professor Ingram got it hopelessly wrong.'

'Still, why are you so insistent that he wasn't six feet?'

'I'm not insistent on it. I only say something is fishy some-where. For all the time, all the prickly, scrambled, uneasy time since I have heard about this case, one question has been bothering me like blazes. It still bothers me worse than any; and it is this. Why wasn't that film destroyed?'

'I repeat,' said Dr. Fell, flourishing the handkerchief, 'why wasn't that film destroyed by the murderer? After Chesney's death, when they carried Emmet upstairs, the whole ground floor of the house was deserted. There was ample opportu-nity, easy opportunity, to destroy it. You yourselves found the Music Room empty when you arrived. The camera had been shoved away carelessly under the lid of a gramophone. All the murderer would need to do would be open the camera, expose the film to the light, and pop goes the weasel. You can't tell me the murderer *wanted* a picture of himself in action floating about for the police to put under a microscope. No, no, no.'

'But Joe Chesney—' began Major Crow.

'All right: suppose the murderer was Joe Chesney. Suppose he killed Marcus, depending on the clock trick for his alibi, exactly as you say he did. But the man can't be a complete lunatic. If he played the part of Dr. Nemo, he knew Harding was there filming the whole thing for dear life. He must have known an examination of this film would immediately dis-close the missing minute-hand, the hocussed clock, and upset the whole scheme with a crash: as it did. Now, what time did he telephone to you at the police station?'

'At twenty minutes past twelve.'

'Yes. And what time did you get to Bellegarde?'

'About twenty-five minutes past.'

'Yes. Exactly. So, if he telephoned you, he was downstairs

within three steps of the Music Room door. The others were upstairs. Why didn't he take two seconds off, walk into the Music Room, and destroy the evidence that could hang him?'

Major Crow had grown rather red.

'That's got you, sir,' observed Bostwick dryly.

'What the devil do you mean, it's got me?' said Major Crow, with inordinate stiffness. 'I don't know. Maybe he couldn't find the camera.'

'Tut, tut,' said Dr. Fell.

'But since you, Superintendent,' pursued Major Crow, 'are being so infernally superior about this whole affair, perhaps you could help us out. Can you explain why the murderer didn't destroy the film?'

'Yes, sir, I think I can. It was like this. One murderer wasn't in a condition to destroy the film, and the other murderer didn't want it destroyed.'

'What? Two murderers?'

'Yes, sir. Mr. Emmet and Miss Wills.'

Bostwick communed with his pipe, examining it all over. His face wore a heavy, sombre, reflective expression; and he spoke with some difficulty.

'I haven't said much about the business so far. But I've done a lot of thinking, one way or the other. And if you want to know what I think, I don't mind telling you; and I can give you a real bit of evidence too.

'Now, that chap in the picture,' he pointed to the screen, 'that's Mr. Emmet. Not a doubt of it. Look at his height. Look at the way he walks. You ask anybody hereabouts; you show 'em that picture; you ask 'em who's the only man they know that walks just like that; and they'll tell you Mr. Emmet.

'I never did believe all that stuff about somebody hitting Mr. Emmet out and taking his place. I didn't; and that's a fact. Miss Wills, she shoved it down our throats before we knew what she was about. It's too much like a film itself. Lord, now,' he sat up, 'who'd go to all that trouble and fanciness when all he'd got to do was tip a bit of cyanide into the old gentleman's tea any day? Suppose his disguise fell off? Suppose the hat fell off, or the muffler got unwound? It didn't; but it might have. Suppose the old gentleman grabbed him, which might have happened too? No, sir. And it's like Dr. Fell says. Whoever killed the old gentleman wouldn't want a film of it for us to see, so why didn't he get rid of it?

'I didn't get a wink of sleep last night for thinking about it. And all of a sudden I said to myself, "Dash my buttons,"'—he slapped his knee, '"dash my buttons," I said, "where's the other capsule?"'

Elliot looked at him.

'The other capsule?' he inquired, as Bostwick returned the look steadily.

'Ah. The other capsule. We think—Miss Wills makes us think—somebody's hit Mr. Emmet out and put a poisoned capsule in place of an ordinary one. All right, say that's so. If it's so, where's the other capsule? The harmless one? High and low we looked; all over the shop; in the raincoat and the satchel and everywhere else; and did we find another capsule? No, we didn't. Which means there only was one; the one Mr. Emmet had; the one he forced down the old gentleman's throat.'

Major Crow whistled.

'Go on,' he said.

'And there's another thing we didn't find,' argued Bostwick, addressing Elliot. 'That little box. The little pasteboard one he took the capsule out of. Did we find that in the raincoat? No, we didn't. But I thought to myself, "Here!" I said, "where is it?" So I looked this morning where I thought it might be; and it was.'

'Where?'

'In the right-hand pocket of Mr. Emmet's jacket. Hung up on a chair in his bedroom, where they put it when they undressed him.'

'This,' said Major Crow, 'looks—'

'I might as well finish, sir, now I'm on it,' said Bostwick, speaking more rapidly and even more heavily. 'Somebody killed Mr. Emmet last night. That somebody was in cahoots with Mr. Emmet over killing the old gentleman. It's well known Mr. Emmet'd do anything for her. Or else she gave him a capsule with poison in it, without him knowing what was in it, and told him to go on and shove it down the old gentleman's throat. But I wouldn't be sure about this last, because Mr. Emmet hit himself out to get an alibi, so it looks like it was all arranged between them. Anyway, why did she shout out, "*Don't, don't*" when the old gentleman was being murdered—and deny saying it afterwards?

'That's not hardly right or natural, unless she knew what was going on. And she knew, all right. At the last minute she couldn't stop herself. It's happened before, that has. You might not think it, Mr. Elliot, but I read a lot of your London murder cases. And I'll tell you where it happened before. The women can't help themselves, even when they start all the trouble. "Don't, don't" is just what the Edith Thompson woman started to shout out when this fellow Bywaters ran out and stabbed her husband on the way back from the cinema.'

He paused, breathing heavily.

Major Crow made an uneasy movement.

'The evidence against Wilbur Emmet,' admitted Elliot, 'is—well, if you can get people to identify Emmet as the man in this film, it's all up.' He felt disconcerted and half sick, but he faced the facts. 'So far, so good. But where's the evidence against Miss Wills? We can't arrest her just because she says, "Don't, don't." That's not good enough.'

'There's evidence all right,' returned Bostwick. Again his face grew congested. He hesitated, and then he turned round and shouted over his shoulder: 'Hobart Stevenson, if you ever breathe a word of what you've heard in this room, I'll come round here and I'll break your neck. And you know I mean it.'

'I won't say a word, Superintendent,' said Stevenson, who was staring with all his eyes. 'Cross my heart.'

'Mind, I'll hear about it if you do,' warned Bostwick, glowering on him. He turned back to the others. 'I was going to bring this up just as soon as I'd seen the film. I haven't mentioned it yet, even to the Major, because I wanted to be sure. But there's evidence all right. You were saying a minute ago, sir, that not many people bar doctors would know how to use a hypodermic. But *she* would. She learned how to use one during that flu scare six or seven years ago; she helped Dr. Chesney inoculate people.

'And you were saying, my lad,' he looked at Elliot, 'that we didn't seem keen to arrest people for throwing stones at her. Now that's not true, and I didn't like it. Not one bit. If somebody disturbs the peace, I'll do my duty; but I'm betting you the magistrates will go light on whoever it was. I warned you I had evidence. What do you think of this?'

From the inside pocket of his coat he took out an envelope. He held it open so that they could look inside; he walked round the group with it. Inside was a small hypodermic needle. Its plunger was of nickel, and ran through a tiny glass tube inside which they could see a colourless smear. Its odour of bitter almonds was very apparent.

'Yes,' said Elliot. 'Yes.' His throat was very dry and his eyes felt hot. 'Where did you get that?'

'I've got a habit of snooping,' said Bostwick. 'That was why I asked the Major to ask Miss Wills to come over here and get you. I found it in the false bottom of a jewel-case on the dressing-table in Miss Wills's bedroom.'

He handed the envelope to Elliot, and then folded his arms.

'That,' said Major Crow, clearing his throat, 'that, it seems, has definitely done it. What do you say, Inspector? Do you want a warrant?'

'Not until I've had an opportunity to talk to her about it,' Elliot said mildly. He drew a deep breath. 'But, as you say— I'm afraid that's done it. What do you say, doctor?'

Dr. Fell pressed his hands to his big mop of grey-streaked hair. He groaned; he showed a hideous face of indecision.

'If I could only be sure! If I could only,' he argued, 'climb out of what is at present the wreck of my cosmos! I don't know what to say. This business has clattered round my ears in a way I never thought it could. It's quite probable they're right—'

Elliot's own hopes clattered down round his ears.

'—but a little talk with the girl, of course, is indicated before—'

'Talk to her!' roared Superintendent Bostwick, losing control of his restraint at last. 'Talk to her! Ah! That's what we're always doing, that is. The girl's as guilty as hell, sir, and well we know it. God knows she's had every chance, every opportunity. We couldn't have been fairer to her if she'd been royalty. And what does it get us? We know what it gets us. She's Edith Thompson all over again, except much worse. As for the Thompson woman, I've heard she'—he glanced at Elliot—'even tried to vamp the 'tec who went round to question her after the murder; and what I say is, history keeps repeating itself all the time.'

IV

The Spectacles Removed

'He looks so different you can't imagine; so sharp.'

**A JAILER, OF WILLIAM PALMER,
RUGELEY, 1856**

XVI

AT HALF-PAST FOUR IN THE AFTERNOON, DR. FELL AND
Inspector Elliot went with Superintendent Bostwick into
Marjorie Wills's bedroom.

The first two of them had eaten a very silent lunch at 'The
Blue Lion'; silent because Major Crow was with them. And,
though the Major declared that after this particular side of
the matter had been investigated he was having nothing more
to do with the case, Elliot was not at all sure of this. Elliot,
in fact, was inclined to be morose and a trifle queasy about
the stomach when the joint was brought in. He kept telling
himself that there it was, and that was that, and so on. Seen
in retrospect, his interview with Marjorie, and her appeal to
him, seemed to be so theatrically false that it made him gag
like sour-tasting medicine. They were probably going to hang
her; and that was that. But how the devil had she been able
to read his thoughts?

He had twice been present at a hanging. He did not care
to remember the details.

When they arrived at Bellegarde, he found (with a sense of relief which half choked him) that Marjorie was out. She had gone out in the car with Harding, said Pamela, the pretty maid; she had gone to either Bath or Bristol, said Lena, the red-haired maid. Both were in a bad state of nerves, together with Mrs. Grinley the cook, because they were alone in the house. A Mr. McCracken—who appeared to be Emmet's assistant at the greenhouses—would come up to the house from time to time, to give them a hail and make sure all was well. Dr. Chesney, though he had slept at Bellegarde the night before, had now gone. Neither the maids nor the cook had anything to add to the testimony about either death of the night before.

Bellegarde lay pleasant and cheerful-looking in the autumn sunshine. Its yellow and blue bricks, its steep-pitched roof with the trim Dutch gables, seemed to hide no secrets. Wilbur Emmet, too, had died very peacefully. The windows of his bedroom faced west; pale sunlight poured in across the bed between undrawn curtains. His head was bandaged, and there was a slight cyanosis of the face: but this face looked serene and almost attractive in death. He lay straight out, the coverlet drawn to his chest and his right arm, the pyjama-sleeve turned back, outside it. Dr. West was permitted to remove the body for a post-mortem examination; at the moment he could say only that Emmet seemed to have died from a dose of prussic acid administered subcutaneously, probably with a hypodermic needle. Nothing could have been quieter or less suggestive of the terrifying. Yet even Dr. Fell, looking round that sunlit room with its pattern like peaches on the wall-paper, could not keep back a slight shudder.

'Yes,' agreed Bostwick, studying him. 'Now this way, please.'

Marjorie's bedroom was at the front of the house. It also was a spacious, cheerful place, with cream-coloured paper having a panel design. The furniture was of light walnut, the windows had golden-brown draperies over frilled curtains. Beside the bed was a low open-faced book-stand containing twenty or more volumes, and Elliot glanced at the titles. A series of guide-books for France, Italy, Greece, and Egypt. A French dictionary, and a paper-covered *Italian Made Easy. The Sea and the Jungle. Where the Blue Begins. Antic Hay. The Picture of Dorian Gray. The Collected Plays of J. M. Barrie. Fairy Tales of Hans Christian Andersen. La Chronique d'un Amant Vicieux.* And—he wondered if Bostwick had noticed them—several text-books on chemistry.

Bostwick had noticed them. 'Oh, ah. You'll see several things there. In the lower shelf.'

'H'mf. Rather a mixed bag, isn't it?' muttered Dr. Fell, peering over his shoulder. 'The young lady's character begins to seem more interesting than I thought it was.'

'It's already interesting enough for me, sir,' said Bostwick grimly. 'Look here.'

The dressing-table was between the windows. In the middle of it, pushed back against the round mirror, stood an ornate gold box some five inches square. Its sides were rounded, and it stood up on four short legs; the workmanship was Italian, with a coloured design of Madonna and Child on the lid. The false bottom, barely a quarter of an inch high, was well and ingeniously concealed; it worked on a spring mechanism from a tiny rosette in one of the legs. Bostwick illustrated it.

'I suppose,' Elliot said slowly, 'she got this box during the trip abroad?'

'I dare say.' Bostwick was indifferent. 'The point is—'

'And, as a result, other members of the party might know about the false bottom?'

'So?' rumbled Dr. Fell, peering round. 'You suggest it was planted here?'

Elliot was honest. 'I don't know. It's the first thing I did think of, I admit. But if somebody did plant it here, I also admit that I don't see rhyme or reason in it. Let's face this.' He walked up and down the room, brooding. 'We've got to accept the fact that the real murderer is either a member of this household or very intimately associated with the Chesneys. We can't get away from that. If this were fiction, the murderer could conveniently turn out to be a complete outsider—say Stevenson the chemist, for instance.'

Bostwick opened his eyes. 'Here, here, here! You're not saying anything like that?'

'No. That won't work; and we know it. But what person here would have any reason to—'

He checked himself, and both he and Bostwick looked round, for there had been a slight exclamation from Dr. Fell. Dr. Fell was not interested in the jewel-case. Instead he had idly, almost absently, pulled half open the right-hand drawer of the dressing-table. From this he took out the cardboard container for a Photoflood bulb: empty. He weighed it in his hand. He sniffed. After setting his eyeglasses more firmly on his nose, he held the container up against the light as though he were studying a bottle of wine.

'Oh, I say,' muttered Dr. Fell.

'Well, sir?'

'The little more, and oh how much it is,' said Dr. Fell. 'Look here: if nobody has any objection, I should very much like to talk to the maid who does up this room.'

It was Elliot who went in search of her; Dr. Fell's manner had been that of one who begins to pound on a door, and prepares to break it in. Elliot found that Lena, the red-haired maid, was responsible for the room. But Pamela, the pretty one, insisted on accompanying her for moral support; and both of them faced Dr. Fell with a strained and solemn air which (Elliot later learned) covered a wild impulse to giggle.

'Hullo,' said Dr. Fell amiably.

'Hello,' said the red-haired maid, not committing herself. But Pamela, on the other hand, smiled engagingly.

'Heh-heh-heh,' said Dr. Fell. 'Which of you is responsible for tidying up this room in the mornings?'

Lena, after a quick look round, answered defiantly that she was.

'Ever see this before?' inquired Dr. Fell, holding up the cardboard container.

'Yes, I did,' answered Lena. 'She had it yesterday morning.'

'She?'

'Miss Marjorie had it,' said Lena, after receiving a violent nudge from her companion. 'She went up the road and bought it, early, and when she got back I was just tidying the room up, so I know.'

'Is it a clue, sir?' asked Pamela, with innocent eagerness.

'It is. What did she do with it: do you know?'

Lena glowered. 'She put it in that dressing-table drawer

there, that you have open; and you'd better put it back, too, if that's where you got it.'

'Did you see it afterwards?'

'No, I didn't.'

Pure, simple fright was reacting on Lena in this way; but Pamela was made of different stuff.

'*I* saw it afterwards,' she volunteered.

'You did? When?'

'Quarter to twelve last night,' replied Pamela promptly.

'Wow!' said Dr. Fell, with such relief, violence, and tactlessness that even Pamela shied back and Lena's face grew muddy pale. 'I beg your pardon; I am deeply sorry,' he urged, waving his hands and adding to the consternation. Bostwick was staring at him.

'You better be careful,' said Lena passionately. 'You'll go to gaol, that's what'll happen to you.'

'I shan't go to gaol,' said Pamela. 'Shall I?'

'Of course not,' Dr. Fell told her, soothing again. 'Can you tell me about it? Try to tell me about it.'

Pamela stopped long enough to make a secret and triumphant grimace towards her companion. 'I got it for Mr. Chesney,' she explained. 'I sat up last night, listening to the wireless—'

'Where is the wireless?'

'In the kitchen. And when I left it, I came out and started to snoopy up the stairs, but just then Mr. Chesney walked out of the office.'

'Yes?'

'He said, "Hullo, what are you doing up? You're supposed to be in bed." I said please, I'd been listening to the wireless;

I was just going up to bed. He was going to say something, but Professor Ingram came out of the library just then. Mr. Chesney said to me, "Do you know for the Photoflood light bulb that Miss Marjorie bought to-day? Where is it?" I did know for it, because Lena told me—'

'Don't you try to put it on to me,' cried Lena.

'Oh, don't be so daft!' said Pamela, with a sudden touch of impatience. 'There's nothing *in* it, is there? I said it was upstairs. Mr. Chesney said, "Well, run up and get it for me, will you?" And so I did, and brought it down to him while he was talking to the professor, and then I went to bed.'

Whatever line of questioning Dr. Fell had in mind, it was interrupted by Lena.

'I don't care whether there's anything in it or not,' Lena burst out. 'All I know is I'm getting sick and tired of talking here, and talking there, but all the time hush-hush about her.'

'Lena! S-s-t!'

'No, and I won't s-s-t,' said Lena, folding her arms. 'I don't believe for a minute she did the things they say she did, else my Pop wouldn't let me stay here, not for a minute; and he told me so; and I'm not afraid of her anyway. I'm not afraid of ten like her. But she will not do things the way other people do them, and that's why they say what they do about her. Why did she go over to Professor Ingram's yesterday, part of the morning and half the afternoon alone: when her own boy, who's as nice a looking boy as you'll see, sat here? What about those trips she used to take to London, when she was supposed to be going to Mrs. Morrison's at Reading? It was to see a Man, that's what it was.'

For the first time Superintendent Bostwick was interested.

'Trips to London? What trips to London?' he demanded.

'Oh, *I* know,' said Lena darkly.

'I'm asking you, when was all this?'

'Never mind when it was,' said Lena, now thoroughly roused and almost shivering with stateliness. 'It was to see a Man, that's what it was; and that's good enough.'

'Look here, my girl,' said Bostwick, losing his own temper, 'we'll just have no more of that, if you know what's good for you. Why didn't you tell me any of this before?'

'Because my Pop told me he'd beat the behind off me if I ever so much as mentioned it to anybody, that's why. And, anyway, it was five or six months ago, so it's no odds to this. It's nothing that would interest you, Mist-er Bostwick. What *I* say is, if we were all allowed to behave like her—'

'Who was the man she went to London to see?'

'Please, may we go now?' intervened Pamela, jabbing at her companion's ribs with her elbow.

'No, you thumping well can't go now! Who was the man she went to London to see?'

'I'm sure I don't know. I didn't follow her.'

'Who was the man she went to London to see?'

'Oh, ain't we got manners, though?' said the redhead, opening her eyes. 'Well, I don't know; and I still shouldn't know, not if you was to give me all the money in the Bank of England. All I know is that the boy worked in a laboratory or something, because he wrote letters. No, and don't you go thinking things, either, because it was printed on the envelope! That's how I know.'

'A laboratory, eh?' repeated Bostwick, slowly and heavily. His tone changed. 'Out you go, now; and wait outside until I call you.'

This command was all the easier to enforce, since at this moment Lena at last succumbed to a fit of weeping. The events of the night before, working with delayed action, had been a little too much. Pamela, a much cooler card altogether, took her out solicitously; and Bostwick rubbed his forehead.

'A laboratory, eh?' He studied the idea again.

'You think that's interesting?' inquired Elliot.

'Why, I'll tell you. I think we've had a bit of luck at last, and come slap up against the thing that beat us before: where she got the poison,' declared the Superintendent. 'That's my experience. It all comes at once, good luck or bad luck. That's what it does. A laboratory! Well, dash my buttons! I—This young lady has got a mania for chemists, though, hasn't she? First this chap, then Mr. Harding...'

Elliot took his decision.

'Harding *is* this chap,' he said; and explained.

Throughout his explanation, while Bostwick's eyes grew larger and Dr. Fell remained sombrely staring out of the windows, Elliot had an idea that it was no news to the doctor. Memories of the morning returned to him, of Dr. Fell hovering a little too close not to have overheard. But the whistle Bostwick gave was so long and elaborate as to take on the nature of a musical scale.

'How long—when'd you learn this?' he demanded.

'When she was trying, as you say, to vamp a police-officer.'

(He was conscious of Dr. Fell's eye on him.)

'Oh, ah,' said Bostwick, as though enlightened. 'So it was only—never mind.' The Superintendent drew a breath of vague, irritated relief. 'The main thing is, we've got our case now. We're as safe as London. We can tell where she got the poison: she got it from Mr. Harding. She's probably visited his laboratory; she'd have access to everything; she could steal what she wanted, and who's the wiser? Eh? Or else—' He paused, a lowering and heavy expression coming over his face. 'Now, I wonder? I wonder? Mr. Harding's a very pleasant-spoken sort of gentleman; but this is a whole lot deeper, a whole lot, than we thought. What if they've had us from the very start of it? What if she and Mr. Harding planned the whole thing between them? What would you say to that?'

'I'd say you can't have it both ways, sir.'

'As how?'

'Well, sir, you talk about a case.' Elliot was on the verge of a roar. 'But you've got to have a case. What is it? First she committed a murder alone. Then she committed a murder in cahoots with Emmet. Now she kills Emmet and commits a murder in cahoots with Harding. For God's sake, let's be sensible. You can't have her going about the place in a homicidal ring-around-the-rosebush with everybody she meets.'

Bostwick put his hands in his pockets in a leisurely fashion.

'Oh? Now just what do you mean by that, my lad?'

'Don't I make it plain?'

'No, my lad, I'm afraid you don't. At least, you make some things plain, I'm afraid; but other things you don't. You sound as though you still didn't believe this young lady was guilty.'

'As a matter of strict fact,' said Elliot, 'you're quite right. I still don't believe it.'

There was a small, slight crash. Dr. Fell, never what could be called careful in his movements, had just succeeded in knocking a bottle of scent off Marjorie's dressing-table. After blinking down vastly at it, seeing that it was unbroken, and letting it remain, he heaved himself back with an expression of great pleasure. Relief went up from him like steam rising from a furnace.

Dr. Fell said:

'By me alone can the tale be told, The butcher of Rouen, poor Berrold. Lands are swayed by kings on a throne—'

'How's that?'

'Hah!' said Dr. Fell, smiting himself on the chest like Tarzan. Then he dropped his air of lofty quotation, wheezed once or twice, and pointed out of the window. 'We had better,' he continued, 'decide on a plan of campaign. We had better decide whom we are to attack, where we are to attack, and why we are to attack. Miss Wills, Mr. Harding, and Dr. Chesney are at this moment driving up in the car. Therefore a little *causerie* is indicated. But one thing I will say now. Elliot, my lad: I am very glad indeed you said what you have just said.'

'Glad? Why?'

'Because you're quite right,' replied Dr. Fell simply. 'That girl had no more to do with any of these crimes than I had.'

There was a silence.

To cover a blankness of thought, Elliot drew back the curtain of the nearest window and glanced out. Below was the trim front lawn of Bellegarde, with the trim gravel drive and the low stone wall fronting the road. An open car, driven by Harding, was just turning in at the gates. Marjorie sat beside him in the front seat, and Dr. Chesney lounged in the rear. Even at that distance Elliot noticed as a grotesque touch that Dr. Chesney, though he wore a dark suit, had a white flower in his button-hole.

Elliot did not look at the expression on Bostwick's face.

'Now, here was your plan,' pursued Dr. Fell. 'You were going to assume your finest leer, and go at her with a yell. You were going to flourish the hypodermic needle in her face. You were going to bombard her until she confessed. You were going to take the shortest way, in fact to drive her really mad and make her do something foolish. Well, my simple advice to you is: don't. Don't say a word about it. Aside from the fact that she isn't guilty—'

Bostwick looked at him. 'So you're in it too,' he said in a heavy voice.

'I am,' said Dr. Fell. 'By thunder, I am! I am here to see that no harm comes to the lame, the halt, and the blind, or I am not worth a Birmingham groat in this cosmos. Kindly place that in your pipe and light it. I tell you, if you push this thing much further, you'll wind up your case by having a suicide on your hands. Which would be a pity: because that girl's not guilty, and I can prove it. We've been misled by one of the largest and most shimmering red herrings—wow!—I can remember; but you might as well hear the truth now. Oh, and forget your damned laboratories. Marjorie Wills had nothing to do with this. She did not steal, borrow, or obtain any poison from Harding's laboratory, and neither, I am almost sorry to say, did Harding. Is that clear?'

In his excitement or annoyance he was gesturing towards the window. That was how they all came to see what happened below.

The car was idling up the drive, about twenty feet from the front door. Harding was looking down at Marjorie, who seemed rather flushed and uncertain, and saying something to her. Harding did not look into the driving-mirror to see what was going on behind him—as, in fact, there was no reason why he should. Dr. Joseph Chesney sat forward on the rear seat, his fists planted on his knees and a smile on his face. The watchers could note every detail vividly: the lawn still wet from rain, the yellow-leaved chestnut trees along the road, the smile that showed Dr. Chesney was a little drunk.

After a glance at the house, Dr. Chesney took the white flower out of his button-hole and flipped it over the edge of the car into the drive. Joggling on the rear seat, he reached into his coat pocket. What he drew out of his pocket was a .38 calibre revolver. The smile was still on his freckled face. Leaning forward, he steadied his elbow on the back of the seat, pressed the muzzle of the pistol into the back of George Harding's neck, and pulled the trigger. Birds were startled out of the vines at the crash of the shot; and there was a cough and jerk as the engine of the car stalled.

XVII

Superintendent Bostwick was a good twenty years older than Elliot; but he was downstairs only a step or two behind the latter. In the first fraction of a second Elliot wondered if what he had seen was an illusion, a mirage in that quiet front lawn, like one of Marcus Chesney's illusions. But it had been no illusion that Harding tumbled sideways from the driving-seat, and that Harding screamed.

The car, stalled, was drifting gently almost against the front steps when Marjorie had the presence of mind to pull on the hand-brake. When Elliot got there, Dr. Chesney was standing up in the back seat, evidently stricken sober. What Elliot expected to find was Harding lying across the side of the car with a bullet in his brain. What he really found was Harding, who had fumbled at the catch of the door and managed to get it open, scrambling on all fours across the gravel drive to the grass, where he collapsed. His shoulders were hunched up to his ears. Blood was coming out of the back of his neck round his collar, where he could feel it, and scaring him into a frenzy. The words he spoke sounded grotesque; they might have been ludicrous on any other occasion.

'I'm shot,' he was saying in a voice little above a whisper. 'I'm shot. Oh, my God, I'm *shot.*'

Then he kicked out with his heels, and writhed on the grass; so that Elliot knew they were dealing with no corpse or even near-corpse.

'Lie still!' he said. 'Lie still!'

Harding's plaint rose to a note of horror. Nor was Dr. Chesney, in a different way, more coherent. 'It went off,' he insisted, holding out the revolver; 'it went off.' What he seemed to wish to impress on his hearers' minds, over and over, was the startling news that it went off.

'We noticed that, sir,' said Elliot. 'Yes, you're shot,' he told Harding. 'But you're not dead, are you? You don't feel dead, do you? Hoy!'

'I'm—'

'Let me have a look. Listen!' urged Elliot, taking him by the shoulders as Harding gave him a glazed, uncomprehending glance. 'You're not hurt, d'ye hear? His arm must have joggled or something. The bullet went sideways and grazed the skin at the back of your neck. It's burnt, but all you've got is a crease not a tenth of an inch deep. You're not hurt, d'ye hear?'

'Never mind,' muttered Harding. 'No good complaining; let's face it. Chin up, eh? Ha, ha, ha.' Though he seemed not to have heard, and muttered the words with an absent, almost jocular calm, he gave Elliot a new impression. Elliot thought that a very keen brain had heard the diagnosis; had translated it instantly, even in a daze of fear; had realised that it was on the edge of making a fool of itself; and in a flash was up and putting on a remarkable show of acting.

Elliot dropped his shoulders.

'Will you attend to this?' he asked Dr. Chesney.

'Bag,' said Doctor Joe, gulping once or twice and waggling his wrist in the direction of the front door. 'Black bag. My bag. Under stairs in hall.'

'What ho,' said Harding amiably.

And Elliot was compelled to admire him. For Harding was now sitting up on the grass and laughing.

All very well to talk. But that wound was a very painful one from the powder-burning alone; if the crease had gone half an inch deeper it would have meant death; and he was now losing a good deal of blood. Yet Harding, though he was still pale, seemed transfigured. He looked as though he honestly enjoyed it.

'You're a rotten shot, Doctor Joe,' he pointed out. 'If you can miss such a sitter as that, you'll never succeed. Eh, Marjorie?'

Marjorie climbed out of the car and ran to him.

Dr. Chesney—who bumped into her when they both moved—stopped shakily with his foot on the running-board, and stared.

'My God, you don't think I did it deliberately, do you?'

'Why not?' grinned Harding. 'Steady, Marjorie. 'ware claret.' His eyes were large, fixed, and of a dark luminousness, but he almost chirped as he patted her shoulder. 'No, no, sorry; I know you didn't mean it. But it's no great fun having guns loosed off into the back of your neck.'

This was all Elliot heard, for he went into the house after the doctor's bag. When he returned, Dr. Chesney, aghast, was demanding the same thing of Bostwick.

'You don't think I did it deliberately, Superintendent?'

Bostwick, more heavy-faced than ever, spoke grimly.

'I don't know what you meant, sir. I know what I saw.' He pointed. 'I was standing up at that there window. And I saw you deliberately take that revolver out of your pocket, point it at Mr. Harding's neck, and—'

'But it was a joke. The gun wasn't loaded!'

'No, sir?'

Bostwick turned round. On either side of the front door was a small ornamental pillar, painted dull yellow, supporting a flattish triangular hood over the doorway. The bullet had lodged in the left-hand pillar. By a freak turn of the hand it had passed between Harding and Marjorie: missing the windscreen of the car, and, miraculously, missing Marjorie herself.

'But it wasn't loaded,' insisted Dr. Chesney. 'I could swear to it! I know it. I clicked it several times before. It was all right when we were at—' He stopped.

'At where?'

'Never mind. Man, you don't think I'd do a thing like that, do you? Why, that'd make me a,' he hesitated, 'a murderer.'

The hollow incredulity with which Dr. Chesney spoke, the hint of a bursting laugh as he pointed to himself, carried conviction. There was something almost childlike in the way he said it. He was a good fellow surrounded by accusers. He had, metaphorically, offered to stand drinks all round; and they had refused him. Even his short ginger beard and moustache bristled with hurt surprise.

'I clicked it several times,' he repeated. 'It wasn't loaded.'

'If you did that,' said Bostwick, 'and there was a live cartridge in the magazine, you only brought it into position.

But that's not it, sir. What were you doing carrying a loaded pistol about with you?'

'It wasn't loaded.'

'Loaded or unloaded, why were you carrying a pistol?'

Dr. Chesney opened his mouth, and shut it again. 'It was a joke,' he said.

'A joke?'

'A kind of joke.'

'Have you a licence to carry that revolver, sir?'

'Well, not exactly. But I could get one easily enough,' snorted the other, suddenly becoming truculent. He thrust out his beard. 'What's all this fiddle-faddle? If I wanted to shoot somebody, do you think I'd wait till I was smack-bang outside this house to draw a gun and do it? Oh, bosh. Rubbish. What's more, do you want my patient to die on me? Look at him, bleeding like a pig! Let me go. Gimme that bag. Into the house with you, George my lad. That is, if you still think you can trust me.'

'Right you are,' said Harding. 'I'll take a chance.'

Though Bostwick was furious, he could hardly interfere. Elliot noticed that Dr. Fell had now lumbered out of the house; both Harding and Dr. Chesney gave him a surprised glance as they went in.

Bostwick turned to Marjorie.

'Now, miss.'

'Yes?' said Marjorie coolly.

'Do you know why your uncle was carrying a revolver?'

'He told you it was a joke. You know Uncle Joe.'

Again Elliot could not fathom her attitude. She was leaning against the side of the car, and seemed occupied in trying to detach on the gravel several tiny white spots which clung to the damp sole of her shoe. Her glance at him was brief.

Elliot moved in front of an angry Superintendent.

'Have you been with your uncle all afternoon, Miss Wills?'

'Yes.'

'Where did you go?'

'For a drive.'

'Where?'

'Just—for a drive.'

'Did you stop anywhere?'

'At one or two pubs. And at Professor Ingram's cottage.'

'Had you seen that revolver of your uncle's before he took it out here and fired it?'

'You'll have to ask him about that,' answered Marjorie, in the same toneless way. 'I wouldn't know anything about it.'

Superintendent Bostwick's face said, 'Wouldn't you, by George?' Bostwick braced himself. 'Whether you would or you wouldn't, miss,' he said aloud, 'it might interest you to know that we've got a question or two—about yourself— that you *can* answer.'

'Oh?'

Behind the Superintendent, Dr. Fell's expression grew murderous. He was puffing out his cheeks for a blast of speech, but an interruption was not necessary. The interruption came from another source. The staunch maid Pamela opened the front door, put her head out, made a gesture that indicated all the investigators, moved her lips rapidly without uttering a sound, and closed the door again. Except for Marjorie, only Elliot saw it. Two voices spoke almost at once.

'So you've been pulling my room about?' said Marjorie.

'So that's how you did it!' said Elliot.

If he had designed the words to startle her, he could not have succeeded better. She twitched her head round; he noticed the extraordinary shining of the eyes. She spoke quickly:

'How I did what?'

'How you seemed to be reading thoughts. As a matter of fact, you were reading lips.'

Marjorie was clearly taken aback. 'Oh. You mean,' she added rather maliciously, 'when you called poor George a clever swine? Yes, yes, yes. I'm quite a proficient lip-reader. It's probably the only thing I *am* good at. An old man who used to work for us taught me; he lives in Bath; he—'

'Is his name Tolerance?' demanded Dr. Fell.

By this time, Bostwick later admitted, the Superintendent was coming to the conclusion that Dr. Fell was insane. Up to half an hour ago the doctor had seemed sane enough; and Bostwick had always remembered with respect his work in the case of the Eight of Swords and the case of Waterfall Manor. But during that conversation in Marjorie Wills's bedroom something seemed to have slipped in Dr. Fell's brain. Nothing could have exceeded the joy, the almost evil joy, with which he now pronounced the name of Tolerance.

'Is his name Henry S. Tolerance? Does he live in Avon Street? Is he a waiter at the Beau Nash Hotel?'

'Yes; but—'

'What a devilish small world it is, you know,' said Dr. Fell through his teeth. 'Never has that noble cliché fallen more soothingly on the ear. I was mentioning my fine, deaf waiter to my friend Elliot this morning. I heard my first report of your uncle's murder from him. Thank Tolerance, ma'am. Cherish Tolerance. Send Tolerance five bob at Christmas. He'll deserve it.'

'What on earth are you talking about?'

'Because he's going to prove who killed your uncle,' said Dr. Fell, changing his tone and speaking seriously. 'Or, at least, he will be responsible for proving it.'

'You don't think I did it?'

'I know you didn't do it.'

'But you know who did?'

'I know who did,' said Dr. Fell, inclining his head.

For what seemed a long time she looked at him, with no more expression in her eyes than you will find in a cat's. Then, groping vaguely, she reached into the front of the car and drew out her handbag as though she were preparing to make a dash for the house.

'Do they believe it?' she asked, suddenly nodding towards Bostwick and Elliot.

'What we believe, miss,' snapped Bostwick, 'is neither here nor there. But the Inspector,' he looked at Elliot, 'came over here (came over here, mind) expressly to ask you some questions.'

'About a hypodermic needle?' said Marjorie.

The trembling in her fingers now seemed to have spread to her whole body. She stared at the catch of her handbag, opening and shutting it in a series of nervous clicks; her head was lowered, so that the brim of the soft grey hat hid her face.

'I imagine you found it,' she went on, clearing her throat. 'I found it myself, this morning. In the bottom of the jewel-casket. I wanted to hide it, but I couldn't think of a better place in the house, and I was afraid to take it out of the house. How *can* you dispose of a thing? How *can* you put it down somewhere and make sure nobody's seen you do it? There aren't any fingerprints of mine on it, if there ever were any, because I wiped it off. But I didn't put it in the jewel-casket. I didn't.'

Elliot took the envelope out of his pocket and held it so that she could see inside.

She did not look at him. There was now no more sense of communication between them than though it had never existed. It was a snapped cord, a dead line, a new wall.

'Is this the hypodermic needle, Miss Wills?'

'Yes. That's it. I think.'

'Is it yours?'

'No. It's Uncle Joe's. At least, it's like the ones he uses; and it's got "Cartwright & Co.", and a grade and trade number on it.'

'Would it be possible,' requested Dr. Fell wearily, 'to forget that hypodermic needle for just one moment? Would it be possible, even, to expunge the hypodermic needle from our minds? Confound the hypodermic needle! What difference does it make what's on it, whose it is, or how it could have come into the jewel-box, provided you know who put it there? No, I say. But if Miss Wills really believes what I told her a minute ago'—he contemplated her steadily—'she could tell us, instead, about the revolver.'

'The revolver?'

'I mean,' said Dr. Fell, 'you might tell us where you and Harding and Dr. Chesney really went this afternoon.'

'You don't know that too?'

'Oh, Lord, I don't know!' roared Dr. Fell, making a hideous face. 'Maybe I'm wrong. It's all a question of atmospheres.

Dr. Chesney had the atmosphere, in his own way. Harding had it in his way. You have it: in your way too. Look at you. Please tell me if I'm a blundering ass, but there are other outward signs.'

Lifting his stick, he pointed to the white carnation lying in the drive; the carnation which Dr. Chesney had taken out of his button-hole and thrown overboard as the car approached the house. Then Dr. Fell moved his stick down and touched Marjorie's shoe. Instinctively she jerked away, drawing her foot back and up, but one of the minute whitish spots adhering to the sole of the shoe now adhered to the ferrule of the stick.

'They wouldn't have thrown confetti at you, of course,' said the doctor. 'But I seem to remember that the pavement outside the registry office in Castle Street is usually thick with it. And this is a damp day.—Have I *got* to do this sort of thing?' he added, fiercely.

Marjorie nodded.

'Yes,' she said coolly. 'George and I were married at the registry office in Bristol this afternoon.'

As still nobody spoke, during a pause in which they could hear noises inside the house, she tried again.

'It was a special licence. We got it the day before yesterday.' Her voice rose a little. 'We—we intended to keep it a dead secret. For a year.' Her voice rose still higher. 'But since you're such clever detectives, and we're such rotten criminals that you guessed straightaway, all right. There you are.'

Superintendent Bostwick stared at her.

Then he was shocked into honest speech.

'My girl,' he said in an incredulous tone, 'God alive! I don't believe it. I can't believe it. Even when I thought there was something wrong with you; but we won't discuss that, look; even then I never thought you'd go and do a thing like this. Or that the doctor would let you. That's what beats me.'

'Don't you approve of marriage, Mr. Bostwick?'

'Approve of marriage?' repeated Bostwick, as though the words meant nothing to him. 'When did you decide to go and do this?'

'We were going to do it to-day. That's what we'd planned. We were going to be married quietly at a registry office any-way, because George hates church-services and fuss. Then Uncle Marcus died; and I felt so—so—well, anyway, we decided this morning we'd go and do it anyway. And I had my reasons. I had my reasons, I tell you!'

She was almost screaming at him.

'God alive,' said Bostwick. 'That's what beats me. I've known your family for sixteen years. I have: I tell you straight. And that the doctor would go and let you do this, with Mr. Chesney not even in his grave!'

She had backed away.

'Well,' said Marjorie, with the tears starting into her eyes, 'isn't anybody at least going to congratulate me, or at least tell me they hope I'll be happy?'

'I do hope it,' said Elliot. 'You know that.'

'Mrs. Harding,' began Dr. Fell gravely; and she flinched with surprise at the name, 'I beg your pardon. My lack of tact is so notorious that it would have been surprising had I been anything but blundering. I do offer you my congratulations. And I not only hope you will be happy. I promise you that you shall be happy.'

Whereupon Marjorie's mood changed in a flash.

'And aren't we being sentimental, though?' she cried, with a satiric kind of grimace. 'And here's a great booby of a police-man,' she looked at Bostwick, 'suddenly remembering how he knew my family; or at least the Chesney family; and how he'd like to put a rope around my neck! I got married. All right. I got married. I had my reasons. You may not understand that, but I had my reasons.'

'I only said—' began Elliot.

'Forget it,' interrupted Marjorie, with deadly coolness. 'You've all had your say. So now you can stand round as smug and solemn-faced as owls. Like Professor Ingram. You should have seen *his* face, when we drove by his house and asked him to be the second witness. No, no. Oh, no. Horrible. He couldn't countenance it.

'But I forgot. All you want to know is about the revolver, isn't it? I can easily tell you that, and it really was a joke. Perhaps Uncle Joe's sense of humour isn't as refined as it might be, though at least he rallies round when others don't. Uncle Joe thought it would be a great j-joke to pretend that this was what he called a "shotgun" wedding; and he would hold that revolver in such a way that the registrar couldn't see it but we could, and he could pretend he was there to see George made an honest woman of me.'

Bostwick clucked his tongue.

'Oh, ah!' he muttered, with a gleam of something like relief in his face. 'Why didn't you say so before? You mean—'

'No, I do not mean,' said Marjorie almost tenderly. 'What a master of anti-climax you are! I get married to avoid being hanged for murder, and you're filled with understanding when you think I got married to be made an honest woman of. This is beautiful.' Her mirth grew. 'No, Superintendent. After all the things you think I've done, it may startle you terribly; but (as you would say) my purity remains unsmirched. What a world! Anyway, never mind that. You wanted to know about the revolver, and I've told you. I don't know how a bullet managed to get into it; it was probably Uncle Joe's carelessness; but it was a pure accident, and nobody meant anybody to be killed at all.'

Dr. Fell said politely:

'That is your impression?'

With all her quickness of understanding, she did not at first understand this. 'You don't mean George's being shot wasn't an—' she began; and broke off. 'You don't mean the murderer's been at it again?'

Dr. Fell inclined his head.

Evening was drawing in over Bellegarde. Towards the east the low hills were turning grey, but the sky to the west was still fiery: the sky on which faced the windows of the Music Room, the office, and the windows of Wilbur Emmet's bedroom above. Out of one of these windows, Elliot remembered in an idle sort of way, Dr. Chesney had put his head last night.

'Do you want me for anything more?' said Marjorie in a low voice. 'If you don't, please let me go.'

'Of course,' said Dr. Fell. 'But we shall want you to-night.'

She was gone, and the other three stood by the bullet-hole in the yellow pillar. Elliot hardly even noticed her. It was, he afterwards remembered, a vision of those windows facing the sunset light which made a window open in his own mind. Or it may have been the shock of a combination of circumstances, of what Marjorie Wills said and thought and did, which shook him out of a mental paralysis. His judgment was released, as a blind is released, with a snap. And, in the pouring clearness of that revelation, he cursed himself and all the works about him. A. plus B. plus C. plus D. raced into a pattern, clearly forming. He had not been a police-officer: he had been a blasted fool. Wherever it had been possible to take a wrong turning, he had taken it. Wherever it had been possible to read a wrong meaning, he had read it. If one clear piece of folly be allowed once to every man, then by the Lord Harry, he had had his! But now—

Dr. Fell had turned round. Elliot felt the doctor's sharp small eyes on him.

'Oho?' said the doctor suddenly. 'Got it, have you?'

'Yes, sir. I think I've got it.'

And he made the gesture of one who strikes with his fist at nothing.

'In that case,' said Dr. Fell mildly, 'we had better go back to the hotel and talk about it. Ready, Superintendent?'

Elliot was again cursing himself, rearranging bits of evidence, sunk so deep that he only vaguely heard Dr. Fell whistling a tune when they went towards their car. It was a tune to which you could keep step. It was, in fact, the wedding march of Mendelssohn; but never before had it sounded evil or ominous.

XVIII

AT EIGHT O'CLOCK THAT NIGHT, WHEN FOUR MEN SAT before the fire in Elliot's room at The Blue Lion, Dr. Fell spoke.

'We now know,' he said, holding up his fingers and checking off the points, 'who the murderer is; how he worked; and why he worked. We know that the whole series of crimes were the work of this one man, acting without a confederate. We know the astonishing weight of the evidence against him. The guilt, we see, will prove itself.'

Superintendent Bostwick uttered a decisive grunt.

Major Crow nodded with great satisfaction.

'Even granting everything, which I'm only too happy to grant,' he said, 'the idea of this fellow living among us—!'

'And disturbing the atmosphere,' supplied Dr. Fell. 'Exactly. That's what upsets the Superintendent so. The influence touches everything it comes into contact with, however harmless. You cannot pick up a tea-cup, go for a motor drive, or buy a film for a camera, without this influence somehow touching the action and somehow twisting it wrong. A quiet corner of the world, like this, is turned upside-down because of it. Guns are fired in front gardens, where people would have stared even to see a gun before. Stones are flung in the street. A bee buzzes in the Chief Constable's bonnet, and another under the Superintendent's cap. And all because of an influence or emanation which a certain person chooses to give out at last.'

Dr. Fell took out his watch, looked at it, and laid it on the table beside him. He filled and lighted his pipe with massive deliberation, sniffed, and went on.

'Therefore,' he said, 'while you think over the evidence, I should like to lect—ahem!—I should like to discuss the art of poisoning, and give you a few tips.

'In particular, since it applies to this case, we might classify a certain group of murders under one head. Oddly enough, I have never seen them set down into a class: though their characters are as a rule so startlingly alike that they might be cruder or subtler copies of each other. They are the eternal arch-hypocrites and the eternal warning to wives: I mean the male poisoners.

'Women poisoners are (Lord knows) dangerous enough. But the men are a more uneasy menace to society, since to the slyness of poisoning they add a kind of devilish generalship, an application of business principles, a will to make good by the use of arsenic or strychnine. They are a small band, but they are evilly famous; and their faces are all alike. I grant you certain exceptions who will not fit into any category:

Seddon, for instance.[2] But I think that if we take a dozen well-known examples from real life, we shall find the same mask on the face and the same false stuff in the brain. Note how our murderer here at Sodbury Cross fits into the group.

'First of all, they are usually men of some imagination, education, and even culture. Their professions indicate as much. Palmer, Pritchard, Lamson, Buchanan, and Cream were doctors. Richeson was a clergyman, Wainewright an artist, Armstrong a solicitor, Hoch a chemist, Waite a dental surgeon, Vaquier an inventor, Carlyle Harris a medical student.

'And immediately our interest springs up.

'We do not care about the illiterate blockhead who bashes somebody in a pub. We are interested in the criminal who should know better. Of course, that most (if not all) of the above men were blockheads, I should be the last to deny. But they were blockheads of a sort whose manners fascinated, whose imaginations really moved, whose acting ability was of the first order; and some of them startle us with the ingenuity of their devices to kill or avert suspicion.

'Dr. George Harvey Lamson, Dr. Robert Buchanan, and Arthur Warren Waite committed murder, each one for financial gain, in 1881, in 1882, and in 1915. At this time the form of fiction we know as the detective-story was in its infancy. But consider the way in which each of them went about it.

---

2   And it will be noted that there is missing from this list the name of Crippen. The omission is deliberate. To many of us there will always remain a strong suspicion that Crippen never meant to kill Belle Elmore, and that the overdose of hyoscine was accidental. This was the view of no less an authority than Sir Edward Marshall Hall (see Mr. Edward Marjoribank's admirable *Life*, p. 277 *et seq*). Crippen refused to plead accidental death because it would have involved Ethel Le Neve.

'Dr. Lamson killed his victim, a crippled nephew of eighteen, by means of raisins poisoned with aconitine and baked into a Dundee cake. He went so far as to cut the cake in the presence of the boy and the headmaster of the boy's school; all three ate a piece of it at the tea-table, so that Lamson might protest his innocence when only the boy was affected. Somewhere, you know, I seem to have heard of that device in fiction.

'Dr. Buchanan poisoned his wife with morphine. Now morphine is a drug which (he knew) would easily be spotted by any physician, due to the contraction of the victim's eye-pupils. So Dr. Buchanan added to the morphine a little belladonna, which prevented contraction of the eye-pupils, made the victim's appearance normal, and obtained from the attending physician a certificate of natural death. It was a brilliant device; and it would have succeeded if Dr. Buchanan had not himself let the trick slip in incautious talk with a friend.

'Arthur Warren Waite, the boyish happy criminal, attempted the murder of his wealthy mother- and father-in-law by means of pneumonia, diphtheria, and influenza germs. This proved too slow, and he at last fell back on less subtle poisons; but his first attempt was the death of the father-in-law by tubercular bacilli administered in a nasal spray.'

Dr. Fell paused.

He had plunged into his subject, steaming with earnestness. Had Superintendent Hadley been present, Hadley would have shouted for an arrest of the bus and an end of the lecture. But Elliot, Major Crow, and Superintendent Bostwick only nodded. They saw its application to the murderer of Sodbury Cross.

'Now,' pursued Dr. Fell, 'what is the first most outstanding characteristic of the poisoner? It is this. Among his friends he usually has the reputation of being a thoroughly good fellow. He is a jovial soul. An open-handed companion. A real sport. Sometimes he may display slight Puritanical scruples, about strict religious observance or even good form socially; but his boon-companions can easily forgive him for this because he is such a decent sort.

'Thomas Griffiths Wainewright, that stickler for the social rules who poisoned people wholesale to get their insurance money, was the most hospitable of hosts a hundred years ago. William Palmer of Rugeley was himself a total abstainer, but nothing pleased him more than to stand the drinks genially to his friends. The Rev. Clarence V. T. Richeson of Boston charmed the devout wherever he went. Dr. Edward William Pritchard, he of the great bald skull and the great brown beard, was the idol of the Glasgow fraternal societies. You see how it applies to the man we want?'

Major Crow nodded.

'Yes,' said Elliot, grimly satisfied; and there was an image in the firelit room at The Blue Lion.

'Whereas actually there is in their characters, as a reverse side to the same picture and perhaps an essential part of it, such a blind indifference to pain in others—such a cool doling-out of death in its most horrible forms—that our ordinary imaginations cannot grasp it. Perhaps the thing that strikes us most is not alone their indifference to death, but to the pain of death. Everybody has heard of Wainewright's famous reply. "Why did you poison Miss Abercromby?" "Upon my soul, I don't know, unless it was because she had such thick ankles."

'That, of course, was swank; but it really does express the attitude of the poisoner towards human life. Wainewright had to have money, so (obviously) someone had to die. William Palmer needed money to bet on horses, and so it became clear that his wife, his brother, and his friends must be given strychnine. It was a self-evident proposition. And it is also true in the case of those who blandly or even plaintively "have to have" something. The Rev. Clarence Richeson, of the magnetic eyes, would have denied with tears that he was marrying Miss Edmands for her money or her position. But he poisoned a former mistress with potassium cyanide so that she should not interfere. The sentimental Dr. Edward Pritchard gained little by killing his wife with slow doses of tartar emetic over a period of four months; and he gained only a few thousands by killing his wife's mother. But he wished to be free. He "had to have" it.

'Which brings us to the poisoner's next characteristic: his inordinate vanity.

'All murderers have it. But the poisoner possesses it to a bloated degree. He is vain of his intelligence, vain of his looks, vain of his manners, vain of his power to deceive. He is touched with the brush of the actor, even the exhibitionist; and as a rule he is a very good actor indeed. Pritchard opening the coffin so that he might kiss for the last time the lips of his dead wife: Carlyle Harris debating science and theology with the chaplain on his way to the electric chair: Palmer's shocked indignation in the presence of the investigators: these footlight scenes are endless, and their root is vanity.

'This vanity need not appear on the surface. Your poisoner may be a mild, blue-eyed, professorial little man, like Herbert

Armstrong, the Hay solicitor, who disposed of his wife and then attempted to dispose of a business rival by means of arsenic spread on a scone at tea. Which makes it all the worse when the conceit at last comes bubbling up, under examination or in a dock. And nowhere does the male poisoner's vanity more clearly express itself than in his power—or what he thinks is his power—over women.

'Nearly all of them have, or think they have, this power over women. Armstrong had it, concealed though it was. Wainewright, Palmer, and Pritchard made use of it to commit their murders. Harris, Buchanan, and Richeson got into their difficulties because they had it. Even squint-eyed Neill Cream thought he had it. It goes with a huge preen and swagger behind everything they did. Hoch, the Bluebeard murderer, disposed of a dozen wives, with arsenic neatly hidden in a fountain-pen. Few spectacles seem more ludicrous than that of Jean Pierre Vaquier, the Byfleet poisoner, smirking over his oiled whiskers in the dock. Vaquier had doctored the publican's bromo-salts with strychnine, trusting in his power over women to get both his victim's wife and his victim's public-house. He was dragged away from his appeal screaming, "*Je demande la justice*," and it is quite possible he thought he had not got it.

'For, whittling the thing down, we can see that all these fine fellows committed murder for financial gain.

'Cream, I grant you as an exception; for Cream was mad, and those frenzied demands for blackmail cannot be taken too seriously. But at the root of the others' crimes is a wish for money, a wish for a softer position in the world. Even when a wife or a mistress is eliminated, she is eliminated so that the poisoner may get a richer one. She stands in the way of his talents. But for her, he might be comfortable. But for her, he might be eminent. In his own mind he is already eminent; the world owes him its good things. Therefore the unwanted wife or mistress becomes only a symbol, who might be an aunt or a next-door neighbour or Barnacle Bill the Sailor. It is the rotted fabric of the brain we have to consider; and that, I think we can agree, is the murderer of Sodbury Cross.'

Major Crow, who had been brooding and staring into the fire, made a fierce gesture.

'I know it's true,' he said. He looked at Elliot. *'You've proved that.'*

'Yes, sir. I think I have.'

'But everything he does is enough to make you want to hang the blighter,' snapped Major Crow. 'Even the reason why he failed to get away with this, if I understand you properly. The whole show failed because—'

'It failed because he tried to alter the whole history of crime,' replied Dr. Fell. 'That never works, believe me.'

'Stop a bit, sir!' said Bostwick. 'I don't follow you there.'

'If you are ever tempted to commit a murder by poison,' said Dr. Fell with complete seriousness, 'remember this. Of all forms of murder, poisoning is the most difficult to get away with.'

Major Crow stared at him.

'Hold on,' he protested. 'You mean the easiest, don't you? I'm not what you'd call an imaginative man, as you'll agree. But I've sometimes wondered—well, look here, I'll admit it! There are people dying every day around us; supposed to be natural deaths; doctor's certificate and everything;

but who's to know how many of them may be murders? We don't know.'

'Ah!' said Dr. Fell, drawing a huge breath.

'What do you mean, "ah"?'

'I mean that I have heard the remark before,' replied Dr. Fell. 'You may be quite right. We don't know. All I wish to emphasise is that we don't know. And therefore your argument is so extraordinary that it makes my brain reel. A hundred persons, let us say, die in Wigan in the course of a year. You darkly suspect that a number of them may have been poisoned. And, because of this, you turn round to me and quote it as a reason why poisoning is so very easy. What you say may be very true; for all I know, the graveyards may be filled with murdered corpses clamouring for vengeance from here to John o' Groats; but, hang it all! Let us have some evidence before we assume a thing to be true.'

'Well, what's your position, then?'

'Arguing,' said Dr. Fell more mildly, 'arguing on the only cases we can possibly use as a test—the cases where poison has been discovered in a body—it is clear that poisoning is the most difficult crime to get away with because so very few people ever do get away with it.

'I mean that the poisoner, by the very nature of his character, is doomed from the start. He cannot, he never does, let well enough alone. When he does happen to get away with it the first time, he keeps right on poisoning until he is inevitably caught. See the list above. He is betrayed by his own character. You or I might shoot or stab or bludgeon or strangle. But we should not become so passionately fond of a bright revolver or a shiny new dagger or a life-preserver or a silk handkerchief that we insisted on playing with it all the time. The poisoner does just that.

'Even his first risks are bad enough. The ordinary murderer runs a single risk. The poisoner runs a triple risk. Unlike a shooting or a stabbing, his work is not over, even when he has done it. He must make sure the victim does not live long enough to denounce him, a bad risk; he must show he had neither opportunity to administer the poison nor reason for administering it, a very deadly risk; and he must obtain the poison without detection, perhaps the worst risk of all.

'Over and over again it is the same dismal story. X dies under circumstances which arouse suspicion. It is known that Y had good reason to wish X out of the way, and every opportunity to tamper with X's food or drink. The body is exhumed. Poison is found. From there it is as a rule only a question of tracing a purchase of poison to Y; and we have, in inevitable procession like a series of pictures in a moral album, the arrest, the trial, the sentence, and the eight-o'clock walk.

'Now, our friend here at Sodbury Cross knew this. He did not have to be a deep student of crime to know it; he only had to read his daily newspaper. But, knowing it, he set out to construct a design for murder which should cover all these three risks with a kind of triple alibi. He tried to do a thing which no criminal has ever succeeded in doing. And he failed because it is possible for an intelligent person (such as you are) to see through each detail of the triple plot. Now let me show you something else.'

Fumbling in his inside pocket, Dr. Fell produced a note-case stuffed with odd papers: the sweepings that he always gathered about him, pushed into his pockets, and refused to part with. Among these he succeeded in finding a letter.

'I told you,' he pursued, 'that Marcus Chesney wrote to me only a few days ago. I have jealously guarded this letter, because I did not want you to be misled. There is too much real evidence. And this would have misled you badly. But read it now, in the light of what we have determined to be the truth, and see what interpretation you put on it.'

He spread the letter out on the table beside his watch. It was headed, 'Bellegarde, October 1st,' and dealt with much the same theories they had already heard. But Dr. Fell's finger indicated a passage towards the end:

All witnesses, metaphorically, wear black spectacles. They can neither see clearly, nor interpret what they see in the proper colours. They do not know what goes on on the stage, still less what goes on in the audience. Show them a black-and-white record of it afterwards, and they will believe you; but even then they will be unable to interpret what they see.

I expect to give my little entertainment before a group of friends soon. If this goes well, may I ask whether you would be kind enough to come and see it, at some later date? I understand you are now at Bath, and I can send a car for you whenever you like. I promise to hoodwink you in every possible way. But, since you are new to the terrain, since you are only very slightly acquainted with any of the persons, I will be fair and give you a straight tip: keep a close eye on my niece Marjorie.

Major Crow whistled.

'Exactly,' grunted Dr. Fell, folding up the letter. 'And that, together with what we are going to see and hear to-night, should complete our case.'

There was a discreet knock at the door. Dr. Fell, drawing a deep breath, looked at his watch. He glanced round the circle, and all of them nodded that they were ready. Dr. Fell put away his watch as the door opened; a familiar figure, looking rather unfamiliar in ordinary clothes instead of the usual white jacket, poked its head into the room.

'Come in, Mr. Stevenson,' said Dr. Fell.

XIX

WHEN ELLIOT'S CAR DREW UP AT BELLEGARDE, IT WAS crowded even though Bostwick and Major Crow were following in another one. Dr. Fell occupied most of the back seat, the rest of which was filled with the large case Stevenson had been instructed to bring along. Stevenson himself, seeming fascinated but uneasy, sat beside Elliot.

Well, it was nearly over. Elliot yanked on the hand-brake, and looked up at the lighted façade of the house. But he waited until all the others joined him before he rang the bell. It was a chilly evening, with a slight mist.

Marjorie herself opened the door. When she saw their official countenances she looked round quickly.

'Yes, I got your message,' Marjorie said. 'We're all in to-night. Not that we should have gone out anyway. What is it?'

'We're very sorry, miss,' Bostwick told her, 'to interrupt your wedding night.' He could not seem to leave off harping on the subject: it had become a kind of obsession. 'But we won't trouble you long, and then we'll leave you to—'

He broke off, muttering, at the cold and angry look Major Crow gave him.

'Superintendent.'

'Sir?'

'This lady's private affairs need not be discussed. Is that quite clear? Thank you.' Though Major Crow was not at ease, he tried to speak cheerfully to Marjorie. 'However, Bostwick is right about one thing. We'll clear out as soon as we can. Ha, ha, ha. Yes. Definitely. Where was I? Ah, yes. Will you take us to the others?'

Whatever else the Major was, he was no actor. Marjorie glanced at him, glanced at the large box Stevenson was carrying by a handle, and said nothing. Her colour was high; she had clearly taken brandy with dinner.

The same atmosphere met them in the library to which she took them. It was at the back of the house, a pleasant conventional room with open book-shelves and a big rough-stone fireplace. A log fire was burning pleasantly there. On the hearth-rug had been set up a card-table, at which Dr. Chesney and Professor Ingram were playing backgammon. Harding lounged in a chair with a newspaper, his head carried unnaturally stiff by the wadding of bandages across the back of his neck.

Both Dr. Chesney and Harding were a little drunk. Professor Ingram was coldly and easily sober. Only bridge-lamps illuminated the room, which was very hot and full of the scent of coffee, of cigars, and of brandy in fat-bowled glasses. All pretence of a backgammon game had been given up, though Professor Ingram held the dice and continued to roll them idly on the board.

Putting his hands flat on the table, Dr. Chesney peered round with a red and freckled face.

'All right,' he growled. 'What is it? Get on with it.'

At a nod from Major Crow, Elliot took over.

'Good evening to you, sir. And you. And you. I think you've all met Dr. Fell at one time or another. And you all know Mr. Stevenson, of course.'

'We know him,' said Dr. Chesney, still peering round and conquering the brandy-induced huskiness in his speech. 'What's that you've got there, Hobart?'

'His cinema-projector,' answered Elliot.

'This afternoon, sir,' Elliot went on to Professor Ingram, 'you were very keen to see the film that was taken of Mr. Chesney's show. I'd like to suggest that, if it's convenient for you, you all have a look at it. Mr. Stevenson has very kindly consented to bring his projector and the other materials along; and I'm sure you won't have any objection if we set them up here.' He spoke in that manner which Superintendent Hadley had drilled into him. 'I'm afraid it won't be very pleasant for you to look at, and I apologise. But I can assure all of you that it will help us, and you as well, if you do see it.'

There was a slight, sharp rattle as Professor Ingram rolled the dice across the board. He glanced at them briefly to see the score, picked them up, and looked at Elliot.

'Well, well, well,' he murmured.

'Sir?'

'Come, now,' said Professor Ingram. 'Be fair. Is this'—he rolled the dice again—'is this a kind of French-police reconstruction of the crime, at which the guilty wretch is supposed to scream out and confess? Don't talk such nonsense,

Inspector. It will get you nowhere, and it's bad psychology: in this case, at least.'

His tone was light, but his underlying meaning was serious. Elliot smiled, and was relieved when Professor Ingram also smiled. He hastened to reassure them.

'No, sir, word of honour, it's nothing like that. We don't want to scare anybody. We only want you all to *see* the film. We want you to see it so that you can convince yourselves—'

'Of what?'

'—convince yourselves who Dr. Nemo really was. We've made rather a careful study of that film. And if you look closely, and in the proper place, and in the right way, you can tell who killed Mr. Chesney.'

Professor Ingram dropped the dice into their cup, shook it, and rolled again.

'So it gives him away, does it?'

'Yes. We think so. That's why we want you all to see the film, and to see if you agree with us: as we're certain you will agree with us. It's plain in the film itself. We saw it ourselves the first time we showed the film, even if we didn't notice what we saw; but we think you'll notice first off. And in that case, of course, everything will be simple. We're prepared to make an arrest to-night.'

'Good God,' said Joe Chesney. 'You don't mean you're going to take somebody and hang him for this?'

He spoke with a kind of simple surprise, as though he had heard some startling fact whose possibility had not yet occurred to him. And his face grew more fiery.

'That's for the jury to decide, Dr. Chesney. But do you have any objection? To seeing the film, that is?'

'Eh? No, no, not a bit. Tell you the truth, I want to see it.'

'Have you any objection, Mr. Harding?'

Harding ran his fingers round nervously inside his collar, touching the bandage. He cleared his throat. He reached for the brandy at his elbow and drained the glass.

'No,' he decided. 'Er—is it a good film?'

'A good film?'

'Clear, I mean.'

'Clear enough. Have you any objection, Miss Wills?'

'No, of course not.'

'Has *she* got to see it?' demanded Dr. Chesney.

'Miss Wills,' said Elliot slowly, 'is the one person of all who must see it, even if nobody else does.'

Again Professor Ingram rolled the dice and contemplated their spots idly. 'Speaking for myself, I am more than half inclined to sulk about this. I was extremely keen (as you say) to see the film. I got a fine snub for my pains to-day. I am therefore inclined,' his bald forehead shone in the heat of the room, 'to tell you to go to the devil. But I can't. That infernal blow-pipe dart haunted me all night. The real height of Dr. Nemo haunted me all night.' He banged the dice-cup on the table. 'Tell me. Does the film show how tall Dr. Nemo was? Can you tell his height from it.'

'Yes, sir. About six feet.'

Professor Ingram put down the dice-cup and looked up. Dr. Chesney first looked puzzled, then curious, then jovial.

'That's established?' asked the professor sharply.

'You'll see for yourself. That isn't what we want to direct your attention to, chiefly; but you can take it as established, yes. Now: do you mind if we use the Music Room to show the film?'

'No, no, anywhere you like,' thundered Joe Chesney. He had evidently been shaken like medicine in a bottle; and, like certain medicines, he frothed and changed colour. He was all hospitality. 'Shall I show you the way? Let me. Get some drinks in there too. See it through to the end, but we ought to have a drink.'

'I can find my way, thanks.' Elliot grinned at Professor Ingram. 'No, sir, you needn't look like that. Holding it in the Music Room isn't a form of French third-degree. It's because you will see certain things better there, I think. Mr. Stevenson and I will go along, and Major Crow will bring the rest of you in about five minutes.'

He never realised, until he got out of the room, how hot his forehead had been. But he realised, too, that he had not been thinking about the murderer at all; he knew the murderer; the murderer had no more defences now than a pared onion. He was thinking about other considerations that made him feel half sick.

The hall was chilly, and so was the Music Room. Elliot found the light-switch behind the Boule cabinet. He drew the grey curtains; mist was rising outside the windows. He went to the radiator and turned on the steam heat.

'Your screen,' he said, 'can go in the space between the double-doors. Get the projector fairly close, if you can; I'd like as large a picture as possible. We can roll out that radio-gramophone and use it as a table to support the projector.'

Stevenson nodded, and they went to work in silence. The sheet was tacked up on the frame of the doors; the projector connected with the same electric socket that had been used for the gramophone. But it seemed a long time before a big square of light flashed out on the screen. Beyond it was the dark office, the office where Marcus Chesney had sat, and in which the clock was still ticking loudly. Elliot arranged the brocade arm-chairs so that two were on either side of the screen.

'Ready,' he said.

And he had hardly said it before a queer little procession came into the Music Room. Dr. Fell, he saw, was now in charge of the ceremonies. Marjorie and Harding were taken to the two chairs at one side of the screen, Professor Ingram and Dr. Chesney to the two chairs at the opposite side. Major Crow (as last night) leaned against the grand piano. Bostwick took up a position at one side of the door, Elliot at the other side. Dr. Fell stood behind Stevenson at the projector.

'I acknowledge,' said Dr. Fell, wheezing heavily, 'that this is not going to be easy for you—particularly Miss Wills. But will you, Miss Wills, please pull your chair just a little closer to the screen?'

Marjorie stared at him, but she obeyed without a word. Her hands were trembling so much that Elliot went over and moved the chair for her. Though well to the side, she was within a foot of the sheet between the open doors.

'Thank you,' grunted Dr. Fell, whose face was not quite so ruddy as usual. His voice roared out. 'And amen! Let her go.'

Bostwick switched out the lights. Again Elliot noted the intense darkness, broken when Stevenson switched on the light of the projector. It dimly touched the faces of those just outside it. Since the projector was within five feet of the screen, the image on the sheet, while not quite life-size, would be enormous.

The rhythmic humming began, and the screen flashed to darkness. It was easy to hear people breathe now. Elliot was conscious of Dr. Fell's huge bandit shape towering over those who sat down, but conscious of it only as a background: he was concentrated on the images they were to see again, the meanings that were so plain if you once stopped to think of them.

Down the blackness of the screen crept the vertical blur of light, flickering at its edges. Again phantom doors were being pushed open. Out of that blur gradually emerged a sharp picture of the actual room behind the double-doors at which they were staring. And, as they saw the glimmering mantelpiece, the white light on the table, the white-faced clock, Elliot had an uncanny feeling that they were looking into the real room rather than at a picture of it. It was as though they saw the real room through a transparent veil, a veil which washed all colours to grey and black. The illusion was aided by the ticking of the real clock. Its ticking fitted into the switch and swing of the pendulum on the spectral clock. Before them was a hollow room, a looking-glass room, with a real clock recording last night's time and windows open to last night's air.

Then Marcus Chesney looked out at them from the office.

It was not surprising that Marjorie cried out, for the figure was nearly life-size. Nor was the effect caused by Chesney's ghoulish appearance under the effect of lights; it came from the mere illusion of reality among them. In the looking-glass room Chesney went gravely about his business. He sat down to face them, pushed the grey-patterned chocolate-box to one side, and began his pantomime with the two small articles on the desk...

'O blind as a bat,' whispered Professor Ingram, straining forward so that his skull touched the beam of the projector. 'I see. Blow-pipe dart, eh? I see now! I see—'

'Never mind that!' snapped Dr. Fell. 'Don't bother with that. Keep your mind off it. Watch the left side of the screen. Dr. Nemo is coming on.'

As though summoned, the tall lean figure in the top-hat appeared, turning round to face them as soon as it appeared; and they looked at close range into the blind black spectacles. Details were sharpened and enlarged. You noted the worn nap of the top-hat, the fuzzy scarf with a crack opening across the nose, and Nemo's curious stride as he moved in the hollow room. Striding to the desk with his back now partly turned to them, he went through his swift substitution of the chocolate-boxes...

'Who is it?' demanded Dr. Fell, as the figure first moved. 'Take a good look. Who is it?'

'It's Wilbur,' said Marjorie.

'It's Wilbur,' she repeated, getting up from her chair. 'Don't you see? Can't you tell that walk? Look at it! It's Wilbur.'

Dr. Chesney's voice was powerful but dazed. 'The girl's right,' he insisted. 'My God, it's as sure as you're born. But it can't be Wilbur. The boy's dead.'

'It certainly looks like Wilbur,' admitted Professor Ingram. Out of the gloom his whole personality seemed to sharpen; he shifted and grew intent; they felt it. 'Wait! There's something wrong here. This is a trick. I'm willing to swear—'

Dr. Fell cut him off. The steady humming of the projector dinned in their ears.

'Now we're coming to it,' Dr. Fell interrupted, as Dr. Nemo moved to the other side of the table. 'Miss Wills! In about two seconds your uncle is going to say something. He's looking at Nemo. He's going to say something to Nemo. Watch his lips. Read his lips for us, and tell us what he says. Steady!'

The girl was standing by the screen, bent forward so that her shadow almost touched it. Now it was as though they could not even hear the hum of the projector. It was a silence, an unnatural silence. As Marcus Chesney's grey lips moved in the looking-glass room, Marjorie spoke with them. Her voice was of an unnatural pitch, as though her thoughts were not there at all. It was a soft, ghostly voice, following a sort of rhythm in itself.

Marjorie said:

> 'I do not like you, Doctor Fell;
> The reason why I cannot tell,
> But—'

A sort of uprising had taken place in the group.

'What the devil's all this?' snapped Professor Ingram. 'What are you saying?'

'I'm saying what he's saying, or said,' cried Marjorie. 'I do not like you, Doctor Fell—'

'I tell you this is a trick,' said Professor Ingram. 'I'm not mad enough to believe that. I was here, watching and listening to him. And I know he damned well never said anything like that.'

It was Dr. Fell who answered.

'Of course he didn't,' Dr. Fell said in a heavy, tired, bitter voice. 'And therefore you're not looking at a film of what you saw last night. And therefore a wrong film was palmed off on us. And therefore the murderer is the person who gave us the wrong film with the assurance that it was the one, true original. And therefore the murderer is—'

He did not need to finish.

Elliot was across the beam of light in three strides as George Harding got to his feet. Harding saw him coming and lashed out, clumsily and right-handedly, for his face. Elliot had been hoping for a fight. He had been dreaming of and almost praying for a fight. All the dislike boiling into hatred, all the things he had been compelled to suppress, all the knowledge he had of what George Harding had done and the reasons why he had done it, all came into Elliot's mind with a kind of inner shout; and he plunged for his adversary in a mood of pure pleasure. But the opposition did not last. That one spasm had broken the last of Harding's nerve. His eyes wavered; his face grew contorted with self-pity; and he tumbled over across Marjorie, catching at her skirts, in a dead faint. They had to revive him with brandy before they could administer the usual caution in the formula of arrest.

XX

IT WAS AN HOUR LATER WHEN DR. FELL SAT WITH THEM in the library before the log-fire. But Marjorie was not there; and neither, for obvious reasons, were Bostwick or Harding. The others sat round the fire in attitudes which Elliot, his mind deadly tired but still satirically working, compared to a Dutch still-life.

Dr. Chesney spoke first. He had been sitting with his elbows on the bridge-table and his head in his hands; but now he looked up.

'So it was an outsider all the time,' he muttered. 'Gaa! I think I knew it in my bones all the time.'

Professor Ingram spoke politely. 'So? I think you were the one who kept assuring us what a fine young fellow Harding was. At least, when you managed that fine and tasteful wedding this afternoon—'

The other's face flamed.

'Don't you see I had to do it, curse it all? Or I thought I had to do it. Harding convinced me. He said—'

'He said a lot of things,' observed Major Crow, with measured grimness.

'—but when I think of what this night is for her—'

'Do you?' asked Professor Ingram, picking up the dice and dropping them into the cup. 'You always were a bad psychologist, my lad. Do you think she loves him? Do you think she ever loved him? Why do you think I entered such strong protests against the whole devilish, sickening performance this afternoon?' He picked up the dice-cup and shook it. He looked from Dr. Fell to Elliot to Major Crow. 'But I think, gentlemen, you owe us an explanation. We want to hear (as people usually do at the end of a story) how you dropped to Harding as the murderer, and how you hope to convict him. It may be clear to you; but it isn't clear to us.'

Elliot looked at Dr. Fell.

'You do it, sir,' he suggested glumly, and Major Crow nodded. 'My wits aren't quite up to the mark.'

Dr. Fell, his pipe lighted and a tankard of beer at his elbow, stared meditatively at the fire.

'I also have many regrets in this business,' he began, in what was for him a quiet voice. 'I have those regrets because, nearly four months ago, what I regarded as a scatterbrained idea of mine was really the beginning of a solution. Perhaps it would be as well to start even before the beginning; to show you events in consecutive order as I saw them, and to follow them as they passed under our eyes to-day.

'On June 17th, then, the children were poisoned by chocolates from Mrs. Terry. I outlined to-day to Inspector Elliot my reasons for thinking (even at that time) that the poisoner had used no such clumsy device as dropping a handful of poisoned creams into an opened box. I thought it much more probable that the trick had been managed by some such means as a spring-grip bag, which would have made easy the somewhat difficult exchange of open boxes. I thought it would be better to look for someone who (say at some time in the previous week or so) had gone into the shop carrying a bag. Now that immediately postulated somebody who could carry in a bag without its being noticed or remembered afterwards as an unusual thing: say Dr. Chesney or Mr. Emmet.

'*But,*' said Dr. Fell, pointing with his pipe, 'as I indicated to the Inspector, there was still another possibility. Even Dr. Chesney or Mr. Emmet carrying a bag would have been noticed, in the sense that every habitual thing is noticed. But there is still another type of person who could have carried a bag in there without Mrs. Terry ever thinking twice about it then or afterwards.'

'Another type of person?' inquired Professor Ingram.

'A tourist,' said Dr. Fell.

'As we know,' he went on, 'Sodbury Cross carries the main tourist traffic. There is a great volume of it at most times, and at certain times it grows dense. X or Y or Z, a tourist and a stranger, travelling through in a car, could have gone in with a bag, asked for a packet of cigarettes, and vanished again, without the shop-owner thinking of his bag or thinking of him afterwards. Dr. Chesney or Mr. Emmet, natives, would have been in the eye of the shopkeeper; X or Y or Z, strangers, would be sponged out of her mind before they even appeared.

'But this seemed mere lunatic nonsense. Why should a stranger wish to do anything like that? A stranger, a criminal lunatic, could have done it; but I could hardly say to Major

Crow, "Look for (in all England) a stranger to Sodbury Cross, a stranger of whom I can give you no description travelling in a car about which I have no hint and carrying a trick bag which I have no reason to suppose exists." I thought I was being too fantastic; I shelved the idea; and I remember this now with curses.

'For what happened this morning?

'Elliot came to me and stirred bad memories with his story. I already had Marcus Chesney's letter; I had got the gist of the business from my deaf waiter; and Elliot's outline rather startled me. I learned from him (heaven knows I learned) that in Italy Miss Wills had met and become engaged to her sloe-eyed charmer, George Harding. There was no reason to suspect Harding just because he was a stranger. But there was thundering good reason to suspect *somebody*, somebody in that right little, tight little group grappled round Marcus Chesney, somebody who had thrown the extra sleight-of-hand of murder into a carefully designed sleight-of-hand performance. So let us begin by an examination of this performance.

'We knew it was planned far in advance. We knew (in fact, it was crammed down our throats) that this was a sleight-of-hand in which you couldn't believe your eyes any of the time. We could suspect that the fun and games might be not alone on the stage, but extend to the audience as well. Hear Chesney's letter on this point. He is speaking of witnesses:

'*They do not know what goes on on the stage, still less what goes on in the audience. Show them a black-and-white record of it afterwards, and they will believe you; but even then they will be unable to interpret correctly what they see.*

'Now, in attempting to read the riddles of the performance, we have three points or contradictions which clamour for an explanation. They are these:

'(A) Why did Chesney, in the list of questions he was going to ask you, insert a totally unnecessary question? Why did he tell you that Dr. Nemo was Wilbur Emmet, if immediately afterwards he was going to ask you the height of the figure in the top-hat?

'(B) Why had he insisted that everybody should wear dinner-jackets that night? It was not your usual custom to wear them; but on this particular night of all nights he demanded it.

'(C) Why had he included the tenth question in that list of his? The tenth question has been rather overlooked, but it bothered me. He meant to ask, you recall, *"What person or persons spoke? What was said?"* And immediately afterwards he added a note that he wanted the literal answer to the above. But where was the trap in that? It seemed generally agreed by the witnesses that only Chesney himself had spoken on the stage, though it is true that a few other words were whispered or spoken by members of the audience. But where is the trap?

'Gents, the answer to points (A) and (B) seemed almost certainly clear. He told you Dr. Nemo was Wilbur Emmet for the far-from-complicated reason that Dr. Nemo was *not* Wilbur Emmet. Dr. Nemo was not Emmet, but somebody wearing the same dress trousers and evening shoes as Emmet. But this person could not have been the same height as Emmet, obviously. Otherwise the question, "What was the height of the person who entered by the French window?"

would again have lost its point. If the person had been the same height as Emmet, six feet, and you had said six feet, you would still have been right after all. So he had to trick you with someone who was several inches off Emmet's height, but was still wearing dress trousers and evening shoes.

'Harrumph. Well, where do we look for a person like that? It might, of course, have been an outsider. It might have been any acquaintance of his in Sodbury Cross. But in that case the joke would completely have lost its point. It would not have been a good trick at all: it would only have been a lie: and it will not square with those words, *"They do not know what goes on on the stage, still less what goes on in the audience."* If that means anything at all, it means the figure in the top-hat was a member of the audience.

'And straightaway the false-bottom drops out of the trick. We see that Marcus Chesney had another accomplice besides Emmet. An innocent-looking accomplice. An accomplice, as is usual in conjuring entertainments, sitting in the audience. In the twenty seconds of complete dead blackness after the lights were turned out, Emmet and this other accomplice changed places.

'The accomplice in the audience slipped out through the open French window in those twenty seconds of dead blackness, while Emmet slipped in and took his place. It was the other accomplice, not Emmet, who played the part of Dr. Nemo. It was Emmet himself who was sitting or standing in the audience throughout the performance. That, gents, was how Marcus Chesney *planned* the trick to take place.

'But which member of the audience?

'Whom did Emmet impersonate?

'Here we are on pleasantly easy ground. Miss Wills would be out, for obvious reasons. Professor Ingram would be out, for at least three reasons: he was sitting furthest away from the Music Room windows, in the chair Chesney assigned to him; he has a conspicuous and shining bald head; and it is highly unlikely that Chesney would take as an accomplice the very man he wanted most to deceive.

'But Harding?

'Harding is five feet nine inches tall. Both he and Emmet are lean, and of much the same weight: Harding 11 st. and Emmet 11 st. 8. Both of them have smooth-brushed dark hair. Harding was placed at the extreme left—the very worst possible position for anyone wishing to photograph the stage, in fact a ridiculous position; but in the position Chesney assigned him, and within two strides of the windows. Finally, Harding was standing with a ciné-camera pressed to his eyes in such a way that his right hand could naturally hide the side of his face. Admitted?'

'Admitted,' said Professor Ingram gloomily.

'Nothing could be easier—psychologically speaking—than such an exchange. The difference in height would not be noticed, because he was standing up and the other two witnesses were sitting down. Also, Harding says he was "crouching," meaning that Emmet was crouching. If you were deceived at all, it was because the superficial differences in their appearance were so easily hidden by the darkness. Harding is good-looking; Emmet was sensationally ugly, but this would not be observed in the dark and with the figure's hand hiding its face. You obviously did not concentrate on that figure. You hardly glanced at it at all; otherwise you could not have seen what went on on the stage. To state that you saw both Harding *and* the stage is a contradiction in terms. You say you saw Harding "at the corner of your eye"; and that is true: what you vaguely noticed was a shape and nothing more. You saw Harding because you expected to see Harding.

'The darkness, too, concealed another psychological trick which I think was played on you. You say that the figure holding the ciné-camera spoke out loud. I will offer the meek suggestion that it did nothing of the kind. The psychological effect of darkness at an entertainment is to make people speak, automatically, in whispers. These whispers sound like ordinary voices; sometimes they even sound like roaringly loud voices, as you will agree (with profanity) if you go to a theatre and hear some idiot jawing away behind you. Actually it is a whisper, though you would not believe it unless you heard the whisper under conditions of ordinary speech. I will therefore offer the suggestion that when the figure said, "Sh-h-h! The Invisible Man," it whispered. Therefore you were deceived because all voices sound alike when they whisper. And you heard Harding's voice because it never occurred to you that it could be anybody else's.

'In fact, for the role of the other accomplice, Harding is the only reasonable choice. Chesney would not have chosen you, Professor Ingram, with whom he had been arguing for years. He would not have chosen you, Dr. Chesney, with whom he had been arguing all his life: even if the fact that you are the same height as Emmet had not automatically excluded you to begin with. No. He would choose the deferential, sycophantic Harding, who hung on his every word, who flattered his vanity, who believed in his theories; and who, above all, had a ciné-camera which could be useful in more ways than one.

'Whereupon we are led back to another pointer straight at Harding. If there is anything we have heard constantly in this case, it is the attitude of extreme deference Harding never failed to show towards Marcus Chesney. It never faltered, never abated, never jarred. It never jarred, that is, except at the one point where it should not have jarred. This performance was the pride of Chesney's heart. He took it with deadly seriousness, and expected everybody else to do the same. But at one of the high points of the show—the dramatic entrance of Dr. Nemo through the French window—this (alleged) Harding, after being expressly warned to keep silent, jeered out with the whispered words, "Sh-h-h! The Invisible Man." Such sudden facetiousness at Chesney's expense seemed odd. It might have provoked laughter. It might have spoiled the whole show. But this (alleged) Harding said it.

'Now, in just a moment I want to point out to you why that one remark in itself proves the case against Harding. But for the time being, here is all I thought about it: "That's wrong. That's Wilbur Emmet posing as Harding in the audience. And, since Emmet would no more think of being funny at Chesney's expense than Harding would—by the temple of Eleusis, *that* remark is prearranged too." Even those words were a part of the show; and back we went to the old question, "What person or persons spoke? What was said?"

'I'm not going ahead of myself, gents. I'm telling you the thing just as it unfolded. This was how my trend of ideas went when Elliot first told me the story. I didn't dare, at first, give him too much hope that Harding was guilty—'

Dr. Chesney stared at them.

'Hope?' he demanded, with a suspicious blink. 'What hope? Why should he hope Harding was guilty?'

Dr. Fell cleared his throat with a long rumbling noise.

'Ahem,' he said. 'A slip of the tongue. Shall I go on?

'But even at this point, shutting our minds firmly against motive, against any other consideration except the mere mechanics of the crime, it was obvious that Harding could have played Dr. Nemo's part.

'Look at our time-schedule. In the twenty seconds' complete darkness between the time the lights were switched out and the time Chesney opened the double-doors, Emmet could have slipped through the window into the Music Room. He could then take the camera from Harding, who slipped out through the same window to put on Dr. Nemo's disguise. The substitution of places would take no more than two or three seconds. Even so, forty seconds more elapsed before Dr. Nemo entered the office. That gives Harding nearly a full minute to put on his disguise; and Professor Ingram will tell you the remarkable list of things that can be done in one minute.

'After thirty seconds in the office, Nemo goes out. Next consider the switch back again, when Harding returns; how will this fit our time-schedule?

'Now, at this point I had not yet seen the film. But Elliot quoted Harding's testimony to me. Harding said: "Just after this top-hatted bloke stepped out of the picture, I looked up, and stepped back, and shut off the camera." In other words, that's what Wilbur Emmet (posing as Harding) really did. He stopped filming just as soon as Dr. Nemo left the office. But why? The performance was not yet over, you know. Marcus

Chesney still had to flop forward, in his dramatic pretence of death, and then get up and close the double-doors. Chesney was giving them plenty of time for the change back.

'It seemed clear that Emmet, after the departure of Nemo, immediately "stepped back"—past the line of the others' vision—and slipped out of the Music Room to meet Harding. That would be their plan, Marcus Chesney's plan. But Harding (if my theory were correct) had an interesting variation of it. He would just have finished giving Chesney a poisoned capsule. (Of course there never was more than one capsule at any time. This debate about a second capsule is unnecessary. If it had been arranged that Harding should play the part of Dr. Nemo, why should there have been a second capsule? There was only one: the one with which Harding had previously been entrusted, and which he had loaded with prussic acid.) After this, then, Harding would be ready for his next variation of the plan.

'At Nemo's exit, Wilbur Emmet stops filming and slips out through the Music Room window. Harding, needing only a few seconds to strip off his disguise as opposed to putting it on, is waiting. Propped in the shadow behind a tree, and just beyond that narrow grass border, is a poker which has been waiting there for hours. Harding—his Nemo disguise flung in a heap by the office window—is now waiting by that tree. He beckons Emmet there. He takes the camera. He points in pantomime towards the house. As Emmet turns, Harding, with his hand wrapped in a handkerchief, strikes with the poker. He then slips back through the Music Room window before the lights go on. Time (as Professor Ingram has estimated it), fifty seconds.'

Professor Ingram was rattling the dice in their cup. He frowned, shaking his head.

'Fair, I grant you. He would have had enough time. But didn't the man run an insane risk?'

'No,' said Dr. Fell. 'He ran no risk at all.'

'But suppose somebody—I or anybody else—had put the lights on too soon? Suppose the lights had been put on before he got back to the Music Room?'

'You are forgetting Chesney himself,' said Dr. Fell sadly. 'You are forgetting that the man practically planned his own murder. He above all people wanted Harding to get safely back to home base before the lights went on. It would have ruined *his* scheme, it would have made him a laughing-stock, had Harding been caught. That must be prevented. You recall, as I said a moment ago, that Chesney treated you to more of the show—sitting there quietly at his table for a while, and then falling forwards on his face: obviously an impromptu bit of business, since no questions are asked about it in the list—he treated you to more of the show after Nemo's exit. That was to give Harding time. It seems clear that Harding gave some prearranged signal, like a cough, to let Chesney know he was back in the Music Room. Then Chesney wound up the show by closing the doors. It might have taken Harding as short or as long a time as he liked to break Emmet's skull. It might have taken him twenty seconds or a hundred and twenty. But Chesney would not end the show until he was back.'

'Damn his soul!' suddenly roared Joe Chesney, bringing his fist down on the card-table so that the backgammon board jumped. 'Then he was simply playing a sure thing the whole time?'

'Yes.'

'Go on,' said Professor Ingram quietly.

Dr. Fell sniffed. 'That, then, was the position this morning. And, as you can understand, I was very eager to get a look at that film—the film I thought Emmet had taken. Harding, just before I got my first great setback, was beginning to appear in curious if not definitely sinister colours. He was a research chemist. He could have manufactured prussic acid at any time. He, alone of those in the case, would have known the trick of putting on and taking off rubber gloves in an instant. I do not know whether you have ever tried this experiment. To get the gloves on is comparatively easy, provided they are powdered inside. But to get them off in a hurry is almost impossible unless you know the trick. You cannot get them off by pulling at the fingers in the ordinary way; you will only split the glove to blazes or stand yanking away at the fingers while you swear. You must roll them from the wrist, as these were found neatly rolled; and I exhibited about them an interest which seemed to surprise Inspector Elliot.

'But the image of Harding as the murderer came out with a clear, hard stamp before we had even seen the film. It became plain from a conversation Elliot had with Miss Wills in the room over Stevenson's chemist-shop. I overheard that conversation, gentlemen. I listened without dignity and without shame. There was a sheet hung between double-doors, between the sitting-room and the bedroom; and behind that sheet in the bedroom I (if you imagine the manoeuvre possible) lurked.

'Up to this time, I knew nothing of Harding except what I had been told by Elliot. But now, by thunder, I was beginning to know something! Elliot had assured me that Harding had never even heard of Sodbury Cross until he met Miss Wills on the Mediterranean trip. I found, on the contrary, that he had known her long before that; that he had known her before the poisonings at Mrs. Terry's; and that she used to go up to London to meet him. Kindly do not look so startled, gentlemen,' said Dr. Fell testily; 'and restrain any impulse you may have, Dr. Chesney, to whang those fire-irons at my head. Even the maids in this house know it. Ask them.

'But the real information was the insight it gave into two sides of Mr. George Harding's character. You could not blame him, of course, for wanting to go a crooked way in hiding his previous acquaintance with her from her family, though it seemed rather an elaborate, florid manner of going about it. I could not blame him for that. But I could blame him, and Inspector Elliot could have murdered him, for suggesting meltingly that he needed a holiday anyway; that he could do with a trip abroad; and that she had better pay the expenses of his trip while he was meeting her family. But that was not all. Gentlemen, I stood in the chemist's bedroom and I was (if this can be credited) struck dumb. I saw visions, and I heard voices. I thought I sniffed Wainewright's scented locks. I thought the ghost of Warren Waite sat in the rocking-chair. I thought I saw, outside the window like banshees, the magnetic eyes of Richeson and the great bald skull of Pritchard.

'But there was another side to this. Whatever else George Harding was, he was a magnificent actor. Now, I had heard about that little scene at Pompeii. One moment: never mind how I heard about it. But, if what I had just learned by eavesdropping at the chemist's were true, just think for a moment what that Pompeian scene meant! Think of Harding, innocent, staunch, heroic, standing among you and letting you tell *him* about Sodbury Cross. Think of the way he introduced the subject of poisoners and prodded your wits until you told him: "I suppose it was easy to get away with wholesale poisoning in those days." Think of his start of surprise, the hasty way in which he put away the guide-book with a confused apology, when he realised he had blundered up against a sore subject with you. Think of—

'Well, it need not be stressed. But let the scene remain in your mind as a kind of symbol of everything that followed. It forms a neat, small painting of Harding's mind. For at the complete and minute hypocrisy of everything he said and did there, the way he pushed, pulled, dragged, and posed, I saw him (in my ghostly company) received with welcome beside Holy Willie Palmer.

'I will grow less metaphysical. We next saw the cinema film: and that tore it. The slip was so bad that I thought Harding had done for himself then and there.

'Now, you have all seen that film. But one thing, when we first saw it, some of us tended to overlook. It is this. If we accepted Harding's story, if we agreed that he had taken the film, if we allowed his alibi and suspected no jiggery-pokery of any kind: allowing all this, then *that film constituted Harding's eyesight.*

'You follow that?' inquired Dr. Fell with great earnestness. 'That film constituted what he saw, and all he saw. It was his own version of what had happened in the office. It was as though we had a record, from a kind of picture in his own mind. We could see, therefore, only what Harding himself saw.

'Now, by the testimony of the other witnesses and by Harding's own testimony, what had happened? Go back to the beginning of Chesney's show. The grotesque figure in the tall hat steps in at the window. As it walks forward, Harding whispers, "Sh-h-h! The Invisible Man!" And the figure turns round and looks at the audience.

'But what do we get in the film? We see that, the instant the figure appears in the film, it is *in the act* of turning round to look at us. It appears; it turns, and this is our first view of Dr. Nemo. This turn to look at us undoubtedly occurs just after Harding has said, "Sh-h-h! The Invisible Man," for that is the only time Dr. Nemo looked out at the audience. But how in blazes did Harding come to use those remarkable words, or any words at all? For up to that time we couldn't see the Invisible Man; and neither could he.

'He couldn't see the French window at all. He was too far to the left. So we couldn't see it. We couldn't see the figure come in; we couldn't see it until it turned round to look at us. Then how (ask yourselves) did Harding know what Dr. Nemo looked like? How could he give a very apt description of Dr. Nemo before Dr. Nemo had even come within his line of eyesight?

'And the answer is not complicated. Whoever was crouching there with that ciné-camera, that person was an accomplice in the show; he knew already what Dr. Nemo looked like; he had been given that line to whisper; he had seen Chesney's head turn, knew it was time, and whispered it a few seconds too soon, when the others could see Dr. Nemo but he couldn't. Since Harding later swore up-hill-down-dale that he had said the words, he was therefore an accomplice whether he had taken the film or whether Emmet had taken it. It confirmed my former belief that Emmet had taken the film and Harding had taken the part of Dr. Nemo.

'At the pre-view early this afternoon, I was just about to sing out and announce this. I had already made definite noises when Major Crow stumbled slap over the truth by saying that Marcus Chesney actually planned the way in which the murderer could kill him. It was true, though Crow applied it to something else. But at that very point, my case fell down with a crash.

'We got a clear view of Dr. Nemo in the film.

'And he was six feet tall.

'Not only was he six feet tall, but he was positively identified by his walk as Wilbur Emmet.

'And I received a blow in the solar-plexus from which it took several hours to recover.

'I commend to you the virtue of humility. It is a refreshing virtue. I had been so confoundedly sure I was right: not only building my tower but putting mortar on the bricks to stick them together. It was not until we found the Photoflood-bulb container in Miss Wills's drawer later in the afternoon that I realised: again, once more, and for the umpty-umph time, we had been hocussed by still another of Chesney's ingenious tricks. It was the final one, but it had made Harding's scheme triple secure.

'Of course, one point had been putting us on brambles for some time. Never mind who the murderer is: whoever he was, why hadn't he destroyed the film? He had every opportunity to destroy it unobserved. It was lying there openly in an empty room. Anybody could have wrecked it in five seconds by exposing it to the light. No murderer, not even a lunatic, could possibly want the police to pore over a real film of him committing his murder. But it wasn't touched. If I had had the sense to interpret this plain indication from the first, I should have seen that it was shoved into our hands, pressed on us tenderly, because it wasn't a film of the real murder at all.

'It was, in fact, the film of a rehearsal which Chesney, Emmet, and Harding had staged that afternoon—the afternoon before the show—with Emmet in the role of Dr. Nemo.

'The Photoflood bulb gave it away. Already, in a musing, curious, but entirely perplexed way, I had been asking questions about those bulbs. What intrigued me was the report I had heard of Miss Wills's obvious astonishment when she was told that the bulb had burned out. Why should she have been astonished? The question, possibly, was of no importance; but it is just that sort of wrongness which presses the button when a door is obstinately stuck. Now, she bought the bulb that morning. It was not called into use until that night. How long had it been in use that night?

'That was easy enough to determine. Chesney's show started (roughly) about five minutes past twelve. The bulb was turned on. It was left burning until the police arrived at twenty-five minutes past twelve: at which time (do you recall?) it was turned out. That's twenty minutes to start with. It was turned on again, very briefly, when the police had a short look at the room before they were interrupted by you, Professor Ingram. Out it went again, after a period of a very few minutes: less than five, anyhow. The third and final time it was turned on was when the police-surgeon and the photographer arrived. There again the period was brief, just long enough for Elliot to explain to Major Crow about a spring-grip bag, and for them to make an examination of the clock on the mantelpiece; then it burned out. Say five minutes more.

'Even agreeing that all these times are approximate, still there's too great a discrepancy. That bulb has burned out after a total of only half an hour's use altogether. For Stevenson the chemist assured me that the bulbs would burn for well over the full hour.

'It burned out after half an hour's use because somebody had been using it before, earlier in that same day.

'That simple fact stared me in the face when I found the cardboard container in the drawer. Miss Wills had bought the bulb that morning, and put it into the drawer. *She* hadn't used it afterwards, because we heard from the maids that she went over to Professor Ingram's house in the morning and stayed there until late afternoon; and, in any case, we have had impressed on us over and over that she never dabbles with photography.

'We were supposed to believe, in fact, that nobody had used it up to the time Pamela was sent upstairs to fetch the bulb at a quarter to twelve that night. But, as I have just indicated, this couldn't be so. And it was emphasised by another reason. We found the cardboard container. Now, if Pamela had been told to go upstairs and get the bulb, and the bulb was still sealed into its box, she would have brought it down box and all. But she didn't: she brought the bulb alone. Which meant that the container had been already opened, which meant either that the bulb was lying loose in the drawer or stuck back into an open box.

'It had already been plain, I grant you, that Chesney, Emmet, and Harding must have had long, careful rehearsing for this little show. The thing had to go without a hitch. And the question was, when did they do the rehearsing? Clearly that afternoon. Chesney had got the bulb bought that morning. Miss Wills was absent in the afternoon; and since you, Dr. Chesney, do not live here anyway, there was no reason why you should be here. But Harding was here right enough: we heard that from the maid.

'You now perceive the nature of Chesney's final trick and joke, his last hoax for the witnesses. He was going to deceive you even after all possible deception had ended. By having Harding take a film of the show in advance—*a show which in several subtle points should be completely different from the real one*—he would keep an ace up his sleeve. He would say, "Well, you have made your replies. Now see what really happened. The camera cannot lie." But the camera could lie; for it was Emmet who played Dr. Nemo's part, and the words Chesney spoke were totally different, though the number of syllables was approximately the same. I darkly believe that this fraud was intended for my benefit. In a few days, you know, he was going to invite me over to see his show. Then he would say to me as well, "Now look at a film we took of it the other night." And (presumably) I should have been gulled as well, while all the time he, uproariously amused, should be saying from the screen, "I do not like you, Doctor Fell." He almost admits as much in his letter. "Show them a black-and-white record of it afterwards, and they will believe you; but even then they will be unable to interpret correctly what they see."

'Changing those films on us was George Harding's one great, smashing mistake. There were, of course, duplicate cameras. He let Emmet take the film with one camera; he gently handed us the other camera with the other record. It will probably soothe you to learn that Bostwick has found the other camera hidden in his room, with the film miraculously undestroyed; and that little bit of pure conceit is going to hang him.

'But the solution of the two films provided our last answer and drove in the last nail. For a long time I had been wondering dimly: was the fact that George Harding took the picture from so far to the left *only* an indication that he wanted to be close to the windows? And here was still another reason. He wasn't placed so that he could film the window of the office, through which Nemo appeared, because he didn't dare film it. It would have shown the afternoon sunlight—when he took the rehearsal-film—blazing in at the windows as Nemo entered. The windows of the office face west, and yesterday was a day of brilliant sunshine. So he had to stand at one side; and, in the same way, Emmet had to stand at one side for the evening performance. When Inspector Elliot suddenly realised what was happening from my questions about the Photoflood bulb, he also hit on the meaning of what we may call the Left-handed Photographic Stance; and a picture of the truth appeared plain and clear on the wall.' Elliot grunted. Dr. Fell, whose pipe had gone out, drained his tankard of beer.

'Now let us sum up the rather painful business of George Harding and Marjorie Wills.

'Harding planned a series of clever and savagely cold-blooded crimes some months ago for just one motive:

financial gain. He meant to show first off that, whoever the poisoner at Sodbury Cross might be, it could not possibly be George Harding. His method of attack was not new. It has been tried before. All along you have been quoting the case of Christiana Edmunds in 1871. I told Elliot there was a moral in that story; but some of you have discussed the case and persistently refused to see the moral. The moral is not: beware of women who run after doctors. The moral is: beware of the person who may poison innocent people at random merely to show he could not have been the poisoner. That is what Christiana Edmunds did; and it is what George Harding did.

'In his fat-witted vanity, a vanity comparable to Palmer's or Pritchard's, he believed he could do exactly as he pleased with Marjorie Wills. I grant you he had reason to think so. A woman who pays your expenses for a several months' holiday may fairly be described as indulgent or even doting; and, if it is any consolation to him, he will be the legal husband of a rich woman until the hangman turns him loose into other pastures.

'Marcus Chesney was a very rich man, and Miss Wills was his heiress. But until Chesney (a tough-fibred man in every sense of the word) until Chesney died, Harding could hardly hope for a penny. He knew that all along, and I understand Chesney made it very clear to him. Harding really did want to launch his new electro-plating process along large lines, and for all I know it may be a very fine process, though it is a different sort of electrical treatment I should like to see applied to him. He thought himself a great man who had to have it, so Marcus Chesney must be eliminated.

'He was thinking along these lines, I suspect, from the very time he met Marjorie. He therefore "planted" a poisoner at

Sodbury Cross along the lines you know. One visit to Mrs. Terry's shop, in any sort of disguise, would give him the lay-out and the position of the chocolate-boxes; a visit a few days later would enable him to switch the boxes. He used strychnine for a deliberate reason—because it is one of the few poisons a research chemist does *not* deal with. Where he bought it we don't yet know, but it is hardly a wonder the police failed to trace it: they had never heard of George Harding.'

'Thanks,' said Major Crow.

'Nor do we know what his original scheme was for eliminating Chesney. But bang into his lap, a gift from heaven, dropped this opportunity to poison Chesney with his victim's actual encouragement and co-operation. Also, Chesney had tumbled to the trick with the chocolate-boxes; and Harding had to make haste. Ironically, Chesney never for an instant suspected Harding's guilt. But he must not go on too far with his investigations, or he might uncover too much. Now, one thing rather worried Harding. If he were to carry out the murder in that way, he had to use a poison which struck and killed almost instantly, paralysing the vocal cords so that the victim could not speak. That meant that it had to be one of the cyanides; he was working with potassium cyanide; and suspicion would instantly be directed at him.

'He got round it with a great dexterity of acting. I said this afternoon that I was sorry to tell you Harding had obtained no poison from his laboratory. He hadn't. He manufactured it here. This house, as you have noticed, and particularly the grounds roundabout, are both haunted by a faint odour of bitter-almonds. The one difficulty about concealing prussic acid anywhere is its faint smell even when corked down;

but this smell would never be noticed at Bellegarde unless somebody got a deep whiff from the opened bottle. So he manufactured his prussic acid, and he deliberately left some of it in the bathroom cabinet. He did this so that he could point out to you how easy it was for anybody with a small knowledge of chemistry to make prussic acid, and that some-one was trying to throw suspicion on him. I have no doubt he made a good story of it.'

'He did,' said Major Crow.

'I do not think he had any idea, at the beginning, of try-ing to throw suspicion on Marjorie. That would have been foolish and dangerous. He might want the girl's money, but he certainly didn't want the girl arrested. Chance, however, threw heavy suspicion on her, and Harding saw a way of using it to his own advantage. For he was getting a bit alarmed over something else: the girl was cooling off.

'You all noticed that. For some weeks her ardour had been definitely on the wane. She no longer looked with be-dazed eyes at her charmer; she had got, perhaps, a glimpse or two into his soul; she had a tendency to snap at him, she even considered suicide. Harding, even in the fulness of his van-ity, could not help dimly suspecting something like this. He couldn't lose her now, or he would have run several horrible risks for nothing, and that was bad business. The sooner he could stampede her into marriage, the better for him.

'He did it by a combination of tenderness and terrorisa-tion. The murder of Wilbur Emmet, a necessary part of his plan, he committed with a hypodermic stolen from you, Dr. Chesney. And the next day he planted it in the false bottom of the jewel-casket. The girl was already half mad with fear;

and Harding, missing no opportunity, had got her into such a state that she was willing to cling to him for the pure and insane relief of letting someone carry her troubles. That last effort, with the hypodermic, did the trick. She told us herself she got married to avoid being arrested for murder. I have no doubt Harding pointed out many things to her: among them, that the police might uncover her visits to the laboratory and find she had access to poison; but if she were arrested, and they were married, he would not have to testify against her in the witness-box. Gentlemen, when you stop to consider the smooth, the calm, the complete eye-dazzling cheek of an approach like that—'

Dr. Fell paused, with a guilty kind of start; Major Crow hissed at him; and then they all stared steadily, and with a furious embarrassment, at the fire.

Marjorie had come in.

Elliot would not have imagined that she could look so pale, or that her eyes could acquire such a glitter. But her hands were steady.

'It's all right,' Marjorie said. 'Please go on. You see, I've been listening at the door for five minutes. I want to hear.'

'Hrr!' said Major Crow. He bounced out of his chair, and began to fuss. 'Would you like a window open? Or a cigarette? Or a brandy? Or something?'

'Have this pillow,' urged Dr. Chesney earnestly.

'I think, my dear, that if you were to lie down—' began Professor Ingram.

She smiled at them.

'I'm quite all right,' she said. 'I'm not nearly as brittle as you think. And Dr. Fell is quite right. He *did* do all that. He even took the books on chemistry I've got upstairs in my room, and used them against me. I got them, you know, so that I could read up and try to take an intelligent interest in the work he was doing; but he said what would the police think when they found them there? What's more, he—he knew what Inspector Elliot knew: about my trying to buy potassium cyanide in London—'

'*What?*' roared Major Crow.

'Didn't you know?' She stared at him. 'B-but the Inspector said—at least, he hinted—'

This time Elliot's face was so hot that there was no mistaking it in anyone's eyes.

'I see,' Major Crow remarked politely. 'Let it pass.'

'A-and he even said they might suspect me of having something to do with the show where Uncle Marcus was killed. He said he knew Uncle Marcus had written a letter to Dr. Fell, and the letter said to keep an eye on my actions...'

'It did,' said Dr. Fell. '"I will be fair and give you a straight tip: keep a close eye on my niece Marjorie." That is why I so carefully kept the letter away from the impressionable Superintendent Bostwick until I could show who was really guilty; it would only have led him in the wrong direction. Your uncle was trying to gull me in the same way he tried to gull you by saying Dr. Nemo was Wilbur Emmet. But the effect on Bostwick—'

'Please wait,' the girl urged, clenching her hands. 'You don't need to think you can make me faint by telling me the truth. When I saw George this afternoon, I mean when he thought he'd been shot, I was so utterly disgusted that I felt sick. But that's what I wanted to know. Was it an accident that he got shot?'

'I wish it hadn't been,' said Dr. Chesney from deep in his throat. 'Lord, I wish it hadn't been! I wish I'd put a bullet in the swine's skull then and there. Still, it was an accident just the same. I swear to you I didn't know there was a live cartridge in it.'

'But Dr. Fell said—'

'I am sorry,' returned Dr. Fell, making an uncomfortable movement. 'Not once in this entire case, I maintain, have I misled you by word, deed, or suggestion; but I had to mislead you then. There were too many Ears close at hand. I refer particularly to the sharp Pamela and the even sharper Lena, whose ears were open just inside the door; and an extraordinary amount of shouting was going on in a public place. Lena's obvious fondness for Harding would probably have led her to report anything I said; and, if Harding heard my version of an attempted murder, he would think he was safe beyond all his dreams of bliss.'

'Thank God,' said the girl. 'I was afraid it might be you.'

'Me?' demanded Dr. Chesney.

'The murderer, I mean. Of course, at first I thought it might be Professor Ingram—'

Professor Ingram's mild eyes opened wide. 'This is rather astonishing,' he declared. 'I am flattered, but why?'

'Oh, it was your talk about committing the perfect psychological murder. And then, when I went over to your house and stayed there all afternoon, and asked you whether I ought to marry George, and you psychoanalysed me and said I didn't love him and he wasn't the type for me—oh, I didn't know what to think. But you were right. You were right. You were right.'

Dr. Fell blinked round. 'Psychoanalysed her?' he demanded. 'And what type should she marry?'

Marjorie's face flamed.

'I never,' she said through her teeth, 'I never even want to *see* another man as long as I live.'

'Present company excluded, I hope,' said Professor Ingram comfortably. 'We can't let you acquire any neurosis, you know. I have often thought that in a well-ordered community such a neurosis would be cured by the same principle that is used when airmen crash without being hurt. In order to get back their nerve permanently, they are immediately sent up again in another plane. Your type? I should say, after consideration, that it is one in which the inhibitions correspond to—'

'Oh, rubbish,' said Major Crow. 'The type she wants is a policeman. Now, when this is settled, I promise you, I give you my word of honour, that I'm not having anything more to do with this case. That's definite. But what *I* say is—'

THE END

If you've enjoyed *The Black Spectacles*,
you won't want to miss

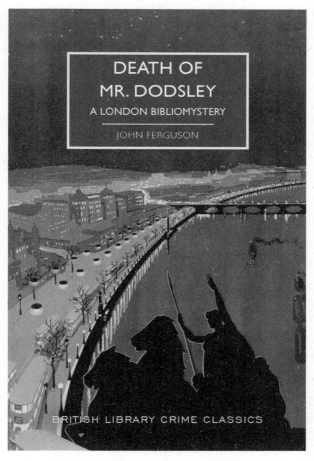

the most recent British Library Crime Classic
published by Poisoned Pen Press,
an imprint of Sourcebooks.

Praise for the
British Library Crime Classics

"Carr is at the top of his game in this taut whodunit... The British Library Crime Classics series has unearthed another worthy golden age puzzle."

—Publishers Weekly, STARRED Review,
for *The Lost Gallows*

"A wonderful rediscovery."
—Booklist, STARRED Review, for *The Sussex Downs Murder*

"First-rate mystery and an engrossing view into a vanished world."
—Booklist, STARRED Review, for *Death of an Airman*

"A cunningly concocted locked-room mystery, a staple of Golden Age detective fiction."

—Booklist, STARRED Review, for *Murder of a Lady*

"The book is both utterly of its time and utterly ahead of it."
—New York Times Book Review for *The Notting Hill Mystery*

"As with the best of such compilations, readers of classic mysteries will relish discovering unfamiliar authors, along with old favorites such as Arthur Conan Doyle and G.K. Chesterton."

—Publishers Weekly, STARRED Review, for *Continental Crimes*

"In this imaginative anthology, Edwards—president of Britain's Detection Club—has gathered together overlooked criminous gems."

—Washington Post for *Crimson Snow*

poisonedpenpress.com